You Shouldn't Have Come Here

BOOKS BY JENEVA ROSE

Standalone Novels

The ~~Perfect~~ Marriage

The Girl I Was

One of Us Is Dead

You Shouldn't Have Come Here

The Detective Kimberley King Books

Dead Woman Crossing

Last Day Alive

You Shouldn't Have Come Here

JENEVA ROSE

BLACK
STONE
PUBLISHING

Printed in the United States of America

First edition: 2023
ISBN 979-8-212-18280-5
Fiction / Thrillers / General

Version 1

Blackstone Publishing
31 Mistletoe Rd.
Ashland, OR 97520

www.BlackstonePublishing.com

To Dad,
Sorry, this one's not a zombie book.
Love, your fourth favorite child
(Well, actually, I might be in first place with this dedication.
Let me know.)

Day One

1.

Grace

I didn't want to stop, but when the low fuel light lit up on the dashboard of my car, I knew I had no choice. Gunslinger 66 was the only gas station I had seen in forty miles, right off highway 26. If it weren't for the neon sign that read Open—well, actually, Ope because every few seconds the letter *N* flickered out—I would have thought it was permanently closed. The station was run-down, with clouded windows and wooden beams barely holding up the structure. The old Mazda2 Hatchback sputtered as I pulled up next to a pump. I let out a sigh of relief and shook out my hands. They ached from gripping the steering wheel so tightly. I had barely made it here, running on fumes and hope for the last mile or so.

Closing the door behind me, I secured my bag over my shoulder and held it tight. There was nothing in both directions except the black snaking highway, open fields, and the sun that was turning its back on me. In the distance I could see the mountains. They looked like anthills, but I knew up close they'd be bigger than the skyscrapers I was used to. A tumbleweed floated across the road. Honestly, if it weren't for the movies, I'd have no idea what it was.

A small worn sticker on the pump read "Cash Only. Please See Attendant." *Of course.* I groaned. I tied my hair back in a low ponytail and made my way across the gravel lot. High heels weren't the best choice, my ankles wobbling side to side over the treacherous terrain. The door squeaked as I pulled it open. A fan buzzed in the corner, oscillating the smell of beef jerky and gasoline throughout the station. Most of the shelves weren't fully stocked. I assumed they didn't get regular deliveries way out here. Behind the counter stood a mammoth of a man dressed in dirty overalls. The skin on his face was a mix of deep-set wrinkles, cavernous pores, and thick scars like a topographic map. His neck craned in my direction, but one of his eyes didn't follow suit. He let out a low whistle.

"You ain't from around here, sweetheart." The man's voice was thick like honey, but the way he looked at me was anything but sweet.

I raised my chin and took a couple of large steps toward him. My heels clicked against the wooden floor.

"What gave it away?" I asked, cocking my head.

His one eye scanned from my head to my toes while the other was fixed on the front door. He brought his hand to his wiry beard and ran it down the sides of his face to the few scraggly hairs that extended past his Adam's apple.

"Just the way you look gave it away." He twisted the strands of his beard.

"Good," I said. "I need sixty in gas." Reaching into my wallet, I pulled out three twenty-dollar bills and slid them across the counter.

He stood there for a moment, staring at me like he was trying to pinpoint where a woman like me would come from.

"Chicago?" He grabbed the money and hit a few buttons on an old metal register.

"New York."

The drawer popped open with a chime.

"You're far from home, miss."

"I'm well aware," I said, watching his every movement.

He placed the money inside and slammed the drawer closed. "You're all set."

I gave him a small nod and walked out of the gas station, careful to keep an eye on him until I was outside. My pace quickened when I reached the gravel parking lot. I could feel his eyes on me as I pushed the nozzle into the gas tank. The numbers clicked slowly on the display, too slowly. I slid on a pair of sunglasses from my bag and glanced back at the gas station. It took me no more than a second to spot him. The man's face was pressed against the window. His worn skin now resembled raw hamburger meat. Pulling out my cell phone, I found the words No Service in the top right corner. *Useless.*

The panel next to gallons flicked to six. It was as though time had slowed down. I busied myself by clicking my long red nails against the car. *Tap. Tap. Tap. Squeak.* The door of the gas station opened. The man leaned a little left as though one of his legs was longer than the other. He started toward me, his steps short and crooked. Sixty dollars would fill my tank, but I didn't need a full tank. I had about a hundred and fifty miles left. I only needed half. The man didn't say a word as he traveled across the lot. I didn't say anything either. Beads of sweat gathered at his forehead and followed the path of his deepest wrinkles. His fat tongue slithered across his upper lip, licking the sweat away. My eyes bounced back and forth from him to the gas pump. *Come on. Come on.*

Click, click, click from the gas pump.

Thump, thump, thump from my chest.

And then there was a new sound. A jingle. It came from his pocket. Coins rustling around, tapping into each other. The muscles in my legs and arms trembled, instinctively priming themselves for action.

When the number of gallons hit seven, I ripped the nozzle from the tank and tossed it aside. Gasoline soaked my heels and the ground below me. I darted around the front of the car and slipped into the driver's seat, slamming the door closed behind me.

The Mazda spit up gravel as I smashed my foot against the gas pedal, aiming my car at the mountains. In the rearview mirror, I watched him cough on my dust. He smacked his hand against his leg and stomped his foot. He yelled something or another, but I couldn't make out what he was saying nor did I care to. A few miles down the highway, I cranked the window down and inhaled the fresh air. Four counts in through the nose. Hold for seven. Exhale through the mouth for eight. The air smelled different, tasted different. Probably because it *was* different. After three rounds I was calm again. My heart rate returned to normal and the muscles in my arms and legs relaxed—no longer on alert and ready to explode for a fight-or-flight response.

The road ahead was like a black snake twisting its way across flat fields as far as the eye could see. I slid my gasoline-soaked heel from one foot and tossed it on the floor beneath the glove box. While my bare foot kept the pressure on the gas pedal, I quickly pulled off the other and tossed it aside. I turned on the radio hoping for a pop song, something that would elevate my mood. It was just static. Every station was static like the twisting black snake whose back I had been coasting on, hissing and letting me know that it knew I was there. It was oddly comforting. The trip up until Gunslinger 66 had been uneventful. At times it felt like I was the only person in the world, rarely encountering another vehicle. There was something both beautiful and terrifying about isolation. It made you feel important and insignificant at the same time.

Wyoming wasn't a state I had ever thought about, which was a shame now that I was seeing it in all its beauty. As I made my way closer to my destination, the landscape began to change. And the farther west I went, the more drastic it became. Soon the plain, drab fields turned into rolling hills of great pines, changing colors of moss, and grass cut through by rushing rivers; a mosaic of colors on a canvas still wet, still forming. The majestic Rocky Mountains loomed over the land, casting a permanent cover to all who neared. Buffalo and elk roamed the plains, a piece of land that forever will be and always was theirs, one of the few places that still was true. Everything was on a scale so grand that it was difficult to take in just how big it all was. It was like nothing I had ever seen, a different planet within my own country—its own microuniverse—and I was happy to have picked it.

It was after seven, and the sun was cascading its final stretch of light for the day.

"In one thousand feet, your destination will be on the right," Siri announced.

I clicked End Route on the car's GPS as just over the hill I could start to see the ranch. Tucked in the woods, right on the Wind River, the property was something out of a storybook. The ranch was large and rustic with a wraparound porch and big bay windows. There was a shed and a barn. Ducks, chickens, sheep, cows, and horses roamed freely in a fenced-in pasture with a large pond in the center of it. The gravel driveway was long, and I took it slow.

Just as I was about to step out of the car, I spotted him. He threw open the front screen door and placed his hand just above his eyes to cover them from the little bit of sun that was left. He was dressed in blue jeans, cowboy boots, and a white T-shirt, exactly what I had expected. Crossing the porch with a few large steps, he casually jogged toward me. He was tall, at least six feet, tan, and had a muscular build that was clearly from working with his hands and not in a gym like so many of the meatheads in the city.

Before stepping out of the car, I quickly slid my heels back on. They reeked of gasoline, but I hoped he wouldn't notice or ask. Tossing my purse over my shoulder, I stood tall and pushed my sunglasses on top of my head. As he got closer, I noticed smaller details about him like the pink scar above his left eyebrow. It was an inch in length, and the color revealed it was new. We all had scars and each one had a story. I wondered what story his would tell. His facial hair was short and scruffy—not intentionally, but more like he hadn't found the time to shave in recent days. His jawline was sharp and defined, and his eyes were green like the pasture the cows and sheep were grazing from. I closed my mouth, pressing my lips firmly together to ensure it wasn't hanging open like some dog salivating over a nice piece of meat.

"You must be Grace Evans," he said, extending his hand out for mine. His voice was deep, and his handshake was strong.

"I am. Nice to meet you." My voice came out a little meeker than usual, not commanding and authoritative like my peers were used to hearing in the office. My handshake was a bit weaker, coming only from the daintiness of my wrist rather than the strength of my full arm. Was I flirting? Or was I still shaken up from the creepy gas station attendant? I wasn't sure but instinctively, I pulled my hand back toward me.

"I'm Calvin Wells, and the pleasure is all mine." His smile revealed white teeth that lined up perfectly and a dimple on only the right side.

"How was your trip in?" Calvin asked, slipping his thumbs in the loops of his jeans. Several thin, long scratches marred the inside of his right forearm.

"It was good up until Gunslinger 66." I let out a sigh as I looked him up and down. He was like a piece of artwork, fitting for the landscape around him. He begged to be examined, observed closely. I knew then he would be a distraction.

The pink scar bounced as Calvin raised his eyebrow.

"This creepy old gas station attendant a ways back . . . kind of chased after me. I didn't even get to finish filling my tank because of him." I twisted up my lips.

"Well, shit. I'm sorry about that. You okay?"

I nodded. "Yeah, I'm fine now. Just caught me by surprise."

"You don't have to worry about any of that here. I'll keep you safe, Grace," Calvin said with a smile.

I let out a small laugh and shook my head.

"What's so funny?" he asked, never letting his smile falter.

"Oh, nothing. I just realized how I sounded, like some damsel in distress."

"I didn't think that at all." Calvin chuckled. "But let me help you with your bags and get you settled in." He walked toward the back of the vehicle.

"Oh, you don't have to do that." I didn't really like people touching my stuff.

"Nonsense." He pressed the button below the license plate, popping the trunk.

"Is this because of the whole damsel thing?" I teased.

"No, Grace. I specialize in hospitality."

Hoisting both bags out of the car, he threw one over his shoulder and carried the other. "I'll treat you so good, you won't want to leave. That's my motto," Calvin said, widening his smile.

"Follow me," he added in a cheerful voice as he walked across the driveway toward the ranch.

I glanced at the old beat-up car I drove here in and then back at him, hesitating for a moment. A sinking feeling hit me in my gut, and it felt like I was free-falling for a moment. It passed quickly, before I even had a chance to react to it, to consider it, to wonder what it was. I swallowed hard and pushed myself to follow him. One foot in front of the other.

2.
Calvin

I set Grace's bags down beside the queen bed. "This is your room," I said, gesturing with my hand.

Grace walked in behind me carrying a tote and her purse. She looked around the room, her face expressionless as she studied every corner and square foot. I couldn't tell if she was disappointed or not. I thought about redecorating when I started renting rooms out on Airbnb, but I couldn't bring myself to do it. My mother had put it together, a mix of things she made and things she found. It was last decorated in the seventies but was back on trend again, or so my neighbor lady had told me.

Grace put her items on the bed and hesitated for a moment before turning back toward me. Her eyes started at my waist and moved up to my face. She smelled like a mix of daisies and gasoline, which was odd, but I didn't say anything. That would be rude. Her hair was golden blond and went right to the middle of her back. Her eyes were the bluest blue I had ever seen, so blue, they almost didn't look real. She was wearing a tight black skirt, heels, and a blouse with some sort of bunched-up fabric. I'm sure where she was from, it was fashionable, but girls 'round here didn't wear stuff like that. Her soft face was in direct contrast to her all-black attire, and I couldn't help but stare at her pouty lips, waiting for her to say something.

"It's perfect." She smiled, but I caught a hint of apprehension in her voice.

I let out a deep breath, and she laughed.

Grace raised an eyebrow. "Were you nervous I wouldn't like it?"

"Well." I shifted my stance from one leg to the other. "I don't really get any female guests, and I wasn't sure a city girl like yourself would be comfortable in a place like this."

"If I can find comfort in New York City amongst the rats and cockroaches, I can find it anywhere." Grace swung her suitcase onto the bed in one fell swoop. She most certainly was strong because that thing had to have weighed at least fifty pounds.

"Need any help?" I offered.

This was the awkward part of hosting guests. I never knew if they wanted me to stay and chat or leave them alone. I was sure Grace was the latter but I was already drawn to her like a moth to a flame or them damn coyotes to my chickens, so anything I could do to buy some more time with her, I would.

She shook her head. "No, I got it," Grace said matter-of-factly. She grabbed her black leather bag, bent down beside the bed, and slid it all the way under.

"Top secret stuff?" I joked, scratching at the back of my neck.

She stood and looked at me, her brows drawn together. "Just work stuff for emergencies only. If I don't put it out of sight, I'll find myself replying to emails and taking calls, and I am here to relax, not work." It seemed she was trying to convince herself of that more than me. We had more in common than she knew. I too had to keep busy. Idle hands, as they say, are the devil's workshop.

"I can lock it away in the basement if ya want."

"I like the idea but that won't be necessary." Grace unzipped her large suitcase and flung it open, revealing a stack of books and a perfectly organized bag. I knew she liked to read. It was on her Airbnb profile, and I figured she'd spend a lot of her time here with her nose in a book. Everything was contained in individual packing cubes. Grace opened one up and dumped a pile of lacy bras and silky panties onto the floral bedspread. She glanced at me briefly and then directed her attention back at her task. I took that as my cue that Grace wanted to be left alone.

"I'll leave you to it." I tipped an imaginary hat and took a couple of steps back toward the hall.

Her head snapped in my direction, and her mouth slowly parted. "Actually, why don't you show me around first. I can unpack later."

"I'd love to. Let's start with the fridge, cuz I could use a beer right about now." I chuckled.

Grace cracked a smile. "Same," she said.

I didn't take her for a beer girl, and I couldn't help but smile either.

Before she stepped toward me, Grace pulled off her heels and let out a sigh of relief while she wiggled her toes. Her toenails were painted a deep scarlet red like her fingernails.

Out in the kitchen, I pulled two Bud Lights from the fridge and popped the tops off against the heavy wood countertop. Grace took one from me. The lip of the bottle rested in between her full lips, and she made a refreshing sound when she was done. I stared in awe.

Grace held the bottle in her hand, rotating it a couple of times as if she were actually reading the label. I took a long swig. The beer fizzled against my tongue and warmed my insides almost immediately.

"This right here is the kitchen," I said, gesturing to the room.

"I figured that much," she teased.

The corners of my lips stretched in opposite directions. I tried to hide my enthusiasm but my body wasn't listening to my brain. I'm sure my cheeks were red too.

Grace glanced around the room.

The kitchen matched the available resources of our surroundings. Wood cabinets and counters with the raw material exposed made it look like the inside of a tree. Since I was the only one here, everything in the kitchen was for function, not form. No excess decorations or unnecessary show pieces like copper pots hanging from a rack. Just a simple wooden kitchen with a knife block, coffee pot, sink, and some appliances. I thought it was perfect but maybe that's just for me.

"It's simple, minimalist. I love it," Grace complimented.

"Thanks. It doesn't really match the rest of the house because, well . . ." I trailed off. It wasn't something I liked talking about, and I hoped she wouldn't ask. I led her into the living room.

"This was decorated by my mother. So it matches the style of your room."

Old copies of unread magazines from publishers long out of print stood in a magazine rack. Afghans were piled next to the fireplace, and random portraits of old friends and moments from her past hung on the walls. Some of them I couldn't even tell you who or what they were, but rather preferred to make up the story on my own.

Grace walked to a large bookshelf and ran her fingers along the spines of several books.

"You like to read?" she asked, glancing in my direction.

"Yes, ma'am," I said with a nod.

"Me too." She smiled.

I almost said I know, but I stopped myself. Her eyes went to the taxidermy mounts hung haphazardly around the living room. No rhyme or reason to their placement. My father's touch. The head of a deer, elk, wolf, bighorn sheep, and mountain lion. No matter where you were standing in the room their black marble eyes followed you. I could tell Grace wasn't fond of them. She crumpled up her face, carefully staring at each animal. Perhaps she thought one might leap right off the wall.

"They won't bite," I said with a laugh.

"I know that." She bit at her lower lip. "It's just a bit un . . . usual."

"Around here, they're not. But you're not from around here." I looked over at her, my gaze sliding from her feet up to her eyes. What was a girl like her doing in a place like this? "Want me to take them down?" I offered.

Grace looked like an alien who'd just landed on a new planet. She shook her head. "Oh no. Of course not."

"You sure?"

"Yeah."

"You'll get used to them," I said. It was true though. You get used to most anything.

She gave a slight nod but didn't say another word.

We moved down the hall, and I pointed out the bathroom, the third bedroom, and the door to my bedroom. I showed her the linen closet where the towels and extra blankets and pillows were. She was quiet, just observing and taking it all in. We headed back down the hall, and she stopped.

"What's this?" she said, gesturing to a door with a padlock on it.

"Oh, that goes down to the basement. It's off-limits. You don't want to go down there anyway. It's unfinished so it's just a bunch of spiders and old stuff and a heavy odor of mildew." I quickly beckoned her with my hand, "Right this way."

When I didn't hear her move, I turned back. She was stopped in front of the door, staring at it. I knew then she wanted to see what was on the other side. When you told someone they couldn't do something, it always made them want to do it. Curiosity always got the best of us, hence why I added the padlock. Grace must have felt my eyes on her because she snapped her head in my direction and gave a smile that seemed to quiver.

"Shall we?" she said in a high-pitched voice. I found her change in tone a bit odd but then again I was just getting to know her—so everything was odd.

Back in the kitchen, I pulled open the sliding door to a large wooden deck I had installed last summer. It was a nice sitting area with several outdoor couches, chairs, and end tables. Two grills stood next to each other near the railing, a gas and a charcoal.

"It's beautiful," she said, taking in the view.

It was the perfect backdrop of what Wyoming had to offer. A pasture with sheep and cows, the river cutting across the back forming the edge of the property line, thick pine woods jutting up just beyond the banks of the river, and the mountains in the distance, towering over the entire scene. It was about the only thing I liked about being back in Wyoming. There ain't much to do. There ain't many people my age. But it is beautiful. I'll give it that.

"It really is," I said, looking over at Grace. She glanced at me, smiled again, and drank the rest of her beer in one swig. I was about to ask her why she picked Dubois, Wyoming, but she spoke first.

"I'm going to finish unpacking." She turned on her foot and headed toward the sliding door.

"Let me know if you need any help."

"I'm a big girl. I can take care of myself." Her voice was flirty, or at least I thought it was. She disappeared inside without another word. I felt my cheeks flush. There was just something about Grace, something different. But I wasn't ready to chase after another girl. It was too soon.

3.

Grace

A set of mismatched wire hangers clanged against one another as I hung up my clothes in the closet. I lined up an array of shoes on the floor in front of the window. Pulling open the top drawer of the dresser, I found several pairs of women's underwear and a sports bra. They were nice brands: Lululemon and SKIMS. *Odd.* I held up a pair of thong underwear, size small. A previous guest must have left these behind, or perhaps Calvin had a girlfriend. I dropped them back in the drawer and closed it. The next one down was empty, so I filled it with my undergarments, swimsuits, and shorts.

Bringing my stack of books to the desk, I lined them up all on end in the order I planned on reading them. I'm a speed-reader and expected I could finish all five of them before my time was up here.

I planned to start with a light beach read that would be quick and easy to devour. I liked those because they were mindless. After that, I wanted something sad, and this one was guaranteed to make me cry—or so a blurb on the cover said. I figured I should have something that I could learn from as well, so I brought along a self-help book about habits. I had several bad habits that I knew I needed to break and plenty of good ones that I should instill further. Habits ensured one wouldn't make mistakes. The horror novel I brought promised I'd be frightened, but I'd be the judge of that. It took a lot to scare me. Finally, a thriller.

This one promised a twisty ending I wouldn't see coming. It seemed every thriller promised that these days, but few actually delivered.

After unpacking my makeup, hairstyling tools, and toiletries, I glanced out the bay window above the long dresser. A large crack ran from the lower left corner all the way to the center. I traced it with my finger. The lip of the fractured glass sliced through my skin. *Ouch.* I brought the wound to my mouth and sucked on it. The pain dissipated quickly. A streak of blood was left behind, stretching a few inches across the glass, causing the landscape beyond it to appear cracked and tinted red. It reminded me of how I saw the city. I had traveled so far to see the world in a different light, but it somehow always looked the same. The sun fell behind the mountains, leaving darkness behind. I had forgotten about the dark. You don't really have that in the city—too many lights.

Remembering I had promised to text when I arrived, I slid my phone from my pocket. In the upper right-hand corner were the words No Service. I felt a twinge in the pit of my stomach and swallowed hard. It wasn't something I was used to seeing.

I found Calvin at the stove in the kitchen, cooking up something that wasn't exactly pleasing to smell—an earthy, meaty, sweet scent. He stirred the pot with a wooden spoon while casually drinking a Bud Light.

"Hey," I said.

Calvin turned around quickly, startled. A smile crept across his face when he saw me. "Hay is for horses."

I forced a smile back. "Do you have a Band-Aid?"

He set the spoon down on a folded-up paper towel. "Of course. What happened?"

I held up my finger, and a drop of blood slithered out of the cut. It hadn't stopped bleeding. "Battle wound from your cracked window."

"Oh shoot. Sorry about that." He disappeared down the hall and reappeared moments later with a small first aid kit. "I meant to fix that. Some of my guests aren't good guests."

Calvin pulled out a chair and gestured for me to take a seat. He sat kitty-corner and unpacked his kit, pulling out ointment, cotton balls, rubbing alcohol, and a Band-Aid. This was clearly not his first time tending to an injury.

"That's a shame about your window," I said.

"Don't worry. They paid for it." He ripped the corner of the packaging with his teeth and pulled out a tiny folded wipe.

"Do your guests usually get rowdy?" I held out my finger. Droplets of blood oozed from the cut and dripped onto the kitchen table. They immediately seeped into the unfinished wood, leaving behind a stain. Calvin didn't seem to notice, or he didn't care. He wiped it up and continued tending to my wound.

"Only the bad ones," he said, glancing up at me for a brief moment.

I winced when he pressed a soaked cotton ball of rubbing alcohol on the wound. The stinging lasted only a few seconds.

"Is it uncomfortable having strangers stay in your house?" I asked.

Calvin paused, and his eyes met mine. "They're only strangers at first," he said with a serious face before finishing up with a Band-Aid wrapped snuggly around my finger.

"There you are. Good as new." He let on a smile while he collected his things.

"Thanks."

Calvin retook his place at the stove, slowly stirring the pot.

"By the way, there's some women's clothes in the top drawer of my dresser. I just left them there. Thought you should know."

He froze for a second. It seemed as though his shoulders tensed up, but I couldn't be sure. Calvin turned back. "That would be my ex, Lisa." He folded in his lips and went back to stirring the pot.

I chewed on my words, unsure of what to say, but then they all tumbled out. "You know they say an ex will purposefully leave something behind after a breakup just so they have a reason to come back."

"Well, I hope that's not the case."

"Why's that?" I asked.

"Because she's dead," he said.

I swallowed and broke into a coughing fit. Calvin quickly pulled a glass from the cupboard and filled it with water. I understood why he said it in such a matter-of-fact way. That's what death was. You're either alive or you're dead. There is no in-between. He handed the glass to me, and I drank nearly all of it.

"You all right?" he asked, giving me a small pat on the back.

"Yeah." I cleared my throat. "Just swallowed wrong."

He nodded and returned to the stove.

"I'm sorry about your ex."

Calvin turned off the burner and took a swig of his beer.

"May I ask how she died?" I added.

"Car accident . . . about a year ago." He rotated the bottle in his hands a couple of times like he was deciding whether or not to say more. "We had actually broken up the night she died, but I'm sure we would have gotten back together. We always did." He wasn't looking at me when he spoke. He was staring at the white wall as if there were something important for him to gaze at.

"I'm sorry, Calvin." I didn't know what more to say because I wasn't good with these sorts of conversations. I had encountered death many times throughout my life but seeing it and talking about it were two very different things.

His eyes swung back to me.

"That's life, I suppose." He shrugged and shook his head like his thoughts and feelings were an Etch A Sketch that he could just shake away. "Ya wanna beer?"

The subject was changed.

I nodded. He pulled one from the fridge and popped the top off.

"Do you not have service here?" I held up my phone as he handed me the opened beer.

"No, ma'am. Gotta go into town for that, but I do have a landline if you need to make a phone call." Calvin pointed to a pale green phone hanging on the wall. A long, coiled cord connected to the phone and the base, practically stretching down to the floor like it had been pulled too tight at one point.

"Oh, I just wanted to send a quick text to a friend to let them know I arrived safely. What about Wi-Fi?"

"I did. But the router needs replacing." He leaned against the counter and took another swig.

The breath got stuck in my airway as I tried to release it, and I nearly choked. I took a quick swig. There was no mention in the listing about a lack of cell service. You'd think that would be something to note but perhaps that was the norm around here. No Wi-Fi was frustrating as well, but then again, maybe I was just too attached to being attached.

"You all right?" he asked. His eyes were full of concern.

I nodded. "Yeah."

It wasn't the time to make a fuss over cell phone service or the internet. I had just gotten here, and I was here to relax. Besides, it was probably for the best that no one would be able to get ahold of me.

4.

Calvin

"What's on the stove?" Grace asked.

She looked at me a little different now that she knew about my ex. Death always changed how we viewed the world and one another. I hoped I hadn't made a mistake by mentioning it.

"My specialty. Baked beans, bacon, and hot dogs," I said with a smile.

Her face remained in neutral. Grace was clearly not impressed with my cooking skills. If I had known how pretty my guest was, I would have picked up something a bit more civilized, but her profile picture on the site was grainy at best.

"Do you want some?" I offered. Food was included in her stay if she wanted it. Most of my guests only used the ranch as a place to rest their heads at night, leaving early in the morning and returning late in the evening. It was nice to have someone here for dinner.

Her nose crinkled up but she quickly relaxed it. She shook her head. "I planned on grabbing something in town, and I wouldn't want to be an inconvenience."

"Nonsense. You're not an inconvenience. Besides, it's getting a bit late to be driving on these roads. Lots of wild animals come out at night." I grabbed two bowls from the cupboard and filled them up.

"You're not one of them vegetarians, are you?" I asked, placing the dish and a spoon in front of her.

Grace looked at the food and then up at me. "No, not at all. I just . . .
I don't really eat this type of thing."

Taking a seat beside her with my food and beer, I immediately
shoveled a spoonful of it into my mouth. The sweetness of the beans,
the meatiness of the hot dogs, and the saltiness of the bacon melded
together with each bite.

Her eyes were wide, and she hovered the beer right in front of her
mouth as if she were trying to hide her reaction from me.

"Just try it." I smiled. "I promise you'll love it, and if you don't, I'll
eat yours too."

Grace set the beer down and hesitated for a moment before picking
up the spoon. She scooped up a single bean.

"You've gotta get the bacon and the hot dog too."

She glanced in my direction and then dove her spoon into the bowl.
Holding it in front of her, she stared. "Here goes nothing."

Grace closed her eyes and pinched her nose shut with her other hand
and stuck the spoon straight into her mouth. It was rather dramatic,
but I'd expect that from a woman like her. While she chewed, she kept
her nose plugged and her eyes closed. When the flavors hit just right,
just like I knew they would, her eyes burst open and her fingers let go
of the sides of her nose.

"That's actually really good." She happily scooped up another spoonful.

"I told ya so. You've gotta trust me." I chuckled.

We ate quietly for a few minutes. The only sound was our spoons
clanking against the bowls.

"So, you said you don't eat stuff like this. What do ya eat?" I asked,
breaking the silence.

"Normal stuff."

"Oh, so I'm not normal?" I teased.

She laughed and told me that wasn't what she meant.

"I'm just joshing ya." I smiled.

There was another silent period for a few minutes. It was like neither of us knew what to say, or perhaps we were both being cautious
with our words.

"Tell me about yourself, Grace," I said, leaning back in my chair.

She took a swig of her beer and looked at me, her blue, blue eyes fixated on mine. It was the only way I knew how to describe those eyes of hers. Blue, blue.

"What do you want to know?"

"Everything, but let's start with, what do you do for a living?" I folded my arms in front of my chest.

"I work in banking," she said matter-of-factly.

"Impressive." I took another drink, and she nodded.

"Your turn. What about you, Calvin Wells? What do you do for a living?" She cocked her head.

I liked the way she said my full name. "I do a lot of things. Farming, Airbnb, gardening, odd jobs here and there. Anything to keep me busy and to keep this ranch afloat."

She leaned back, matching my posture, and took another drink of her beer. "Admirable."

"Why Wyoming?" I asked.

"Why not?" She shrugged.

I raised an eyebrow, letting her know I wasn't satisfied with her answer. The corner of her lip perked up.

"It's silly, really," she said.

"I like silly. Hit me with it."

Grace took a swig of her beer. When her gaze met mine again, she spoke. "Every year, I close my eyes and throw a dart at a map of the United States. Wherever it lands, that's where I go for vacation." Her cheeks flushed like she was embarrassed or something.

"That's not silly at all. It's like fate." I let on a small smile. "But why do it that way though? Why not pick a place you really want to go? Heck, you could be in California or Hawaii right now, lying up on a beach with a piña colada in your hand. Not here in Dubois, Wyoming, eating beans and hot dogs with me." I chuckled.

She laughed too but then got a little serious. Her blue, blue eyes flickered, and she let out a sigh.

"My life is very routine. Everything is planned and planned again.

Every minute of my day is scheduled. This gives me freedom in a way." Grace tilted her head.

I drank my beer and nodded. "I can relate to that. I had that freedom prior to taking over this ranch. Now everything that lives on it depends on me."

"Why'd you give up the freedom?" she asked.

It wasn't a question I wanted to answer. I didn't like talking about what brought me back, but I figured Grace was the type of woman that would get the answer one way or another.

"Had to. My parents passed away so I moved back about a year and a half ago to take over the ranch."

Grace swigged her beer. What thoughts were running through her head? In under an hour, she had learned three people close to me had died, and they all had lived on this ranch. Almost seemed as though it was cursed. At least that's what the folks around town said. If I were her, I'd run for the hills before this land swallowed her up too.

"That must have been tough," she said, folding in her lips.

"Yeah, it was."

We sat in silence for a few minutes again. It seemed both Grace and I were comfortable with silence. Most people weren't. They had to fill it with words. What they didn't realize is a person could say so much more by not saying anything at all. She took another drink, and when she set the bottle down, it echoed, signaling it was empty. I considered offering her another but it was getting late, and I figured I should wrap this up before she asked me any more about my family or my past.

"I must ask: Was picking my ranch random too, or did you throw a dart at the Airbnb website?" I teased but I was serious. I wanted to know if this was fate too, or maybe not fate, maybe a part of the curse.

"No," she said with a half smile. "I picked this place, Calvin."

I smiled back and grabbed both our empty bowls, bringing them to the sink. I was happy to hear it was Grace's decision to come here. There are so many things that are decided for us. We don't choose where we're born, who we're born to, how our parents raise us, what values they instill in us, or even how long they're a part of our lives. I hate that part of life, not having any control over it. It smacks you right in the face whenever it wants, and you're just expected to take the hit and carry on.

I glanced over at Grace while I washed up the rest of the dishes. She look tired and was staring off at the patio door, almost as though she were in a trance or something.

I shut off the sink and dried my hands.

"Well, I gotta get up early. Cows aren't going to milk themselves."

Grace stood and tossed her empty bottle into the trash can.

"I'll have coffee in the pot for ya in the morning. And I'll leave the bread and peanut butter out in case you want a little something to eat."

"Thanks, Calvin."

"Need anything else before I turn in?" I started walking toward the hall. She leaned a little and lost her balance, stepping right into me. My arm brushed up against her, sending a small static shock. It was a spark like when you jump-start a car. The two cables. They're electric. My heart rate sped up, and I took a deep breath to calm it down. I wasn't ready for anything like that, I reminded myself. No matter how drawn I was to this peculiar woman, it was too soon.

I looked to her waiting for an answer. I couldn't go off to bed without making sure she had everything she needed.

Grace shook her head. "I'm good. Thanks for dinner."

"Anytime, Miss Grace. You sleep tight." I nodded and continued down the hall toward my bedroom. It took everything in me not to turn back.

Day Two

5.

Grace

I had the best sleep of my life. Most people didn't sleep well in strange places, but I'm not most people. I take comfort in the unusual. And there was something about the isolation the ranch offered that made me feel secure and at ease. The clicking sounds from the cicadas, howls of some animal or another, and hoot of an owl outside my window last night lulled me into a deep sleep. Quite the opposite effect of the blaring sirens and car horns in the city. Knowing there was nothing I had to be awake for was also a relief.

Dressed in a pair of black silk pajamas, I slipped out of bed and popped my head out the bedroom door. It was silent. A creaking sound somewhere deep in the home interrupted the stillness. It was impossible to tell where it came from, but the house had old bones and old bones cracked and groaned. I quickly padded to the kitchen, following the scent of the freshly brewed coffee Calvin had promised me. It was such a rare luxury for me to wake up after the sun did, and I relished in it. He must have been out somewhere on the ranch, tending to the animals or doing whatever it was country boys did. I picked up the mug Calvin had left out for me. It had a cow on it and the words, *Wyoming, a place that will mooo-ve you.* I laughed at the cheesiness of it and poured myself a cup of coffee. A door squeaked open just as I was about to head back to my room.

Calvin's presence was punctuated by the slam of the screen door. His shirt was off, and my God, he looked better shirtless than I had imagined he would. It was like an artist had chiseled each ridge in his abs and perfectly sculpted his pecs. Beads of sweat covered his chest, neck, and forehead. I nearly dropped my mug. Calvin looked me up and down and blew out his red cheeks while taking me all in.

"Sorry," he said, averting his eyes. He shuffled his feet in place as though he had forgotten how to stand up.

I crossed one leg in front of the other and brought an arm across my chest. "Don't be," I said, realizing how ridiculous it was that I hadn't gone out and bought something like plaid pj's. I'm sure girls around here didn't wear silk and lace to bed.

"You just . . . uh . . . caught me by surprise. That's all." Calvin smiled. He forced his eyes to look at my face, and I did the same. "I see you found the coffee." He gestured to my cup.

"I got a nose like a bloodhound for it." I brought the mug to my lips and took a sip. Steam rose off the top of the liquid.

"Good. You make yourself at home at here," Calvin said, reaching into the pocket of his jeans. "By the way, I forgot to give you this last night." He handed over a silver key on a single loop.

"What's this?"

"Key for the house. I usually leave it unlocked with it being the country and all, but with a lady in the house, figured I'd better lock up. Wanna make sure you feel safe . . ."

I slid the key ring onto my pointer finger and clasped the coffee mug with two hands, taking another slow sip. "Thanks . . ."

Safe? I had felt safe. Even slept like a baby last night. But what was out there that he needed to lock out? I considered asking but I didn't want to come off as skittish. I wasn't that type of person, so I brushed the thought aside. It was just my crazy brain, seeing the worst in everyone and every situation. When you've seen the worst in people, it's hard to unsee it. It's in all of us. However, I liked the idea of Calvin wanting to protect me, and I knew where it came from. When you lost someone, you ended up holding on to everything tighter. And Calvin had lost a lot.

"Got any plans for today?" he asked, shuffling his feet again.

"No plans, just relaxing. That's the name of the game," I said with a cool, laid-back tone.

"And how do you relax, Miss Grace?"

"Reading, yoga, running."

"Some of that sounds like work," he teased. "I don't want to intrude on any of your relaxing time, but if you'd like me to, I can show you the grounds."

I brought the mug to my mouth and took a slow sip. I could see in his eyes he wanted me to say yes. I took my time, making him squirm a little bit.

"I'd like that," I finally landed on. "I'll change quick."

Turning on my foot, I started down the hallway. I glanced back at Calvin before disappearing into my bedroom and caught him staring at me. There was this intensity beneath his eyes. I had seen that look before. I couldn't place it but I knew I liked it.

6.

Calvin

After seeing Grace in her—for lack of better words—night attire, I went outside to wait. I took a seat in a rocking chair on the porch and rocked back and forth slowly, replaying the image of her sipping coffee in my very own kitchen. She was a sight to be seen, dressed in silk and lace in a country kitchen—truly out of place. And I knew I saw the same look in her eyes that she had to have seen in mine—attraction, infatuation, lust, or maybe it was something else. I rubbed my hand over my cheeks and chin, trying to scrub the thoughts from my mind. She was here for nothing more than time to relax and get away from whatever it was she disliked about her current life. She wasn't here to fall in love with a country boy, and I knew I couldn't get involved without complicating things.

The screen door swung open, and Grace emerged. She was dressed in a tank top and them tight leggings that some girls think are pants. Her tennis shoes were a pristine white, like what the porch looks like after I give it a good pressure wash.

"Don't you have anything you can get dirty?" I teased.

She looked down at her outfit and then back at me. "No, I don't really get dirty in New York City—except with my clients," she said with a laugh.

I chuckled and stood from my chair. I wasn't sure exactly what she did in banking or what she did with her clients, but I got the feeling she was ruthless, or at least she could be.

"Maybe I'll have to take you into town to get you some proper Wyoming wear." I walked down the porch stairs while delivering a half smirk.

"Maybe you will," she said, following behind.

As we walked, I kept turning back to look at Grace. I couldn't help myself and nearly tripped over a rock while staring at her. When I got to the edge of my garden, I stopped.

"This here is my garden. I sell ninety percent of it to the local grocery store. The rest I eat."

Grace stood beside me, taking it all in. It was just a large plot of land with an array of plants and vegetables lined up in neat rows with fencing all around it to stop the rabbits and other animals from getting in. Nothing too special, but it was special to me.

"What do you grow or plant or whatever the right terminology is?"

A small smile crept up on my face before I spoke. I was happy to hear she was actually interested in this—in what country folks did. I had assumed a city girl would think this stuff was beneath her. But Grace was different.

"Spinach, cabbage, brussels sprouts, onions, tomatoes, cauliflower, carrots, peppers, lettuce, kales, peas, and the list goes on and on."

She rocked back and forth on her heels. "I have a great recipe for brussels sprouts." There was enthusiasm in her voice.

Grace was definitely different, and in only the fourteen hours I had known her, she was surprising me in more ways than one. Around here not many people surprised me, not anything really surprised me. Every day was the same mundane thing. Wake up, take care of the animals, take care of the garden, take care of the house, and if there was still time in there, take care of myself. I had become an afterthought in my own life. But in the little bit of time I had known Grace, I thought of her before me but thinking about her made me feel like I was thinking about me—like we were one and the same, a cracked walnut. Sure, the inside is nice but that's just because the two ugly halves made it.

"I should be able to harvest them this week," I said with the most amount of fervor I think I had ever had in my voice, but I quickly tapered it down. "And I'd love to try it," I added in my typical deep, country tone. I left out the fact that I hated brussels sprouts. I only grew them because they didn't take up much space in the garden, and they sold well at the grocery store.

"Great," she said. "They're my favorite vegetable."

"Mine too," I lied. It was just a little white lie. Grace was clearly excited about cooking them for me, so I didn't want to ruin that.

We continued walking toward the pond where the ducks and chickens roamed practically free. I had always been a big believer in free range, and I really tried to follow that. But not everything was meant to be free. Some things had to be kept in cages.

As we edged toward the pond, a mallard with a dark green head and a bright yellow bill walked right across Grace's shoe. She giggled, and the rays from the sun highlighted her perfect smile and her cute crinkled nose. My Pekin ducks followed closely behind us, about a dozen of them. They acted more like dogs than ducks due to their friendly and docile nature. The chickens on the other hand kept to themselves and only approached when I had feed in hand. I always thought they were more like cats. They purred when you pet them, but you had to earn their attention.

"They're real friendly." I bent down to pet a Pekin duck that took its place beside me, letting out a couple of squeaky sounds.

"You must treat them well."

"I do my best." I nodded. After a few minutes, we continued walking toward the stable where my horses were. I only had two horses. One was my father's and the other my mother's, and aside from riding them around the property, they were quite the money pit. I didn't show or breed them, and I'd never sell them. But sometimes, I'd talk to them like they were my mom and pop, and that right there, I couldn't put a price on.

I slid a hand down the side of Gretchen, a buckskin Thoroughbred with light tan coloring and a dark mane. She was calm and still, just like my momma. Grace ran her hand along the face of George, a black Quarter Horse. He was stoic and moody, just like my pops.

"They're beautiful," she said, stroking George's head.

"They are." I glanced over at Grace. "And highly intelligent. They say horses can read human emotions. They know what we're feeling before we even know."

"Fascinating." She ran her hand up and down George's muzzle.

"Have you ever ridden one before?" I raised an eyebrow.

Grace shook her head.

"Well, a horseback ride is included in your stay if you're up for the challenge."

She took a step back and put her hands on her hips. "I'm always up for a challenge."

"That's what I like to hear." I smiled. "Shall we?"

I headed in the direction of the field, and we walked side by side through the pasture. I pointed out the couple dozen cows and sheep that took care of most of the lawn mowing. I told her how I milked the cows most mornings and shaved the sheep in the spring, selling the wool to a local yarn shop. She listened attentively, and I liked that about her. It was like she really heard me. I hadn't felt understood or heard in a long time.

"Does anyone help you with the ranch? It sounds like a lot of work for one person."

"A bit. My brother does when he can, and I have a girlfriend that helps with harvesting the vegetables and collecting the duck and chicken eggs."

"A girlfriend?" Grace asked, raising an eyebrow.

She seemed a little jealous, but I think I liked that.

I let out a laugh. "A girl that's a friend, I mean."

She smiled, and I couldn't help staring at the curve of her lips.

"What's that over there?" Grace pointed at several rows of covered boxes just in front of the woods.

"That's my honeybee farm."

Her face lit up. "You farm them?"

"Actually, no. A family friend of mine does. Betty—she's almost like a second mom. They're hers, but she keeps them on my property and takes care of them. I get a small cut of the sales and about half a dozen bottles of honey every year."

Grace's eyes were wide. "Can I see them?"

"Probably not too safe without wearing a beekeeping suit." I craned my neck toward her. "You like bees or something?"

"Yeah. They're fascinating." She looked up at me, our eyes meeting. "When a honeybee stings, their stinger gets lodged in skin, so they have to self-amputate their digestive tract, muscles, and nerves. They literally die protecting themselves."

"Sounds like a gruesome death."

"It is. Sorry, I watch a lot of Discovery channel," Grace said with a laugh.

"Nothing wrong with knowing interesting facts. Did you know honey never goes bad?"

Her plump lips curved into a grin. I could have kissed them right then and there, but I broke eye contact, looking at my feet instead. Grace made me nervous, real nervous. I think she probably had that effect on a lot of people. I had forgotten what nerves felt like—them little tingles on the skin and that whoosh of butterflies in my belly. I couldn't remember the last time I had that feeling. Well, actually, I could and it didn't end well.

Grace walked in step beside me. "I think I read that somewhere. But my brussels sprouts recipe calls for honey, so I can use up a little bit of your collection."

"Kismet."

"Indeed," she said with a nod.

I pointed up ahead at Wind River. "I get some good fishing out of there and some good swimming too."

We stood at the edge of the water. It babbled in some parts where it brushed over large rocks. In other parts it sounded like a *whoosh*, like water coming too quick out of a faucet. Beyond it was the woods— thick, twisting, and dark. My father always used to say: Anything goes in the woods. It's like Vegas for wildlife. Has its own boundaries, its own cover, and the plants and animals do whatever it takes to survive in there.

Past that were the mountains. They served as a reminder of how small and insignificant we all were. I liked looking at them when I felt frustrated with my own life. The tops were white from snow that wouldn't touch the ground we stood on for another few months.

"What do you catch?" Grace looked at me and then back at the water.

I slid my hands into my pockets. "Most everything. Walleye, perch, largemouth bass, but my favorite is golden trout."

We stood in silence for a few moments, taking it all in.

"I'm going to assume you ain't ever fished." I glanced over at her.

She cocked her head. "You know what they say about assuming."

"So, you have?"

"No, I haven't." Grace laughed.

"Now you're just yanking my chain, Grace Evans, aren't you?" I smirked, tipping my head toward her.

She playfully bumped her shoulder into me. "I could have fished. I just don't know how to."

The sun reflected off of her eyes. I could get real used to looking at them blue, blue eyes.

"I can teach ya if ya want." I smiled.

She nodded. "I'd love that, Calvin Wells."

There she went again, using my full name, making my stomach get all turned upside down. I missed that feeling, but I wasn't ready for a girl like her. She was going to make resisting her the hardest thing I've ever done. But deep down, I already knew I'd fail at that.

7.

Grace

I put the car in park right in front of Betty's Boutique, a local clothing shop that offered western-style women's clothing. From what I had seen, downtown Dubois was the whole town, one street full of local businesses and angled parking on both sides. It felt like I had walked into the 1950s. There wasn't a chain store or restaurant in sight, and everyone seemed to know one another—well, except me. I got out of the car and flung my purse over my shoulder. This is where Calvin had said I could get myself some proper "Wyoming wear," as he put it. He had more work to tend to on the ranch, so I figured if I was going to fish and ride horses, I may as well look the part. A woman walked by, delivering a friendly smile and a hello. I nodded back. She gave me an odd look, and I couldn't tell if it was from my curt acknowledgment or because I was a stranger, both oddities around here.

I went inside the store and before I even got the chance to look around, I was greeted by a plump woman with short graying hair, a round face, and rosy cheeks. She walked right up to me from behind the counter, wearing a floral dress that had no shape to it.

"Welcome to Betty's Boutique," she said. "What brings you in today?" I could have fit a pencil sideways in her mouth, that's how wide her smile was.

The shop was a hodgepodge of used and new clothing. Everything was either jean or leather or covered in prints like floral, plaid, and flannel. It was very, very country, like nothing I had ever seen before. I only started doing the throw-a-dart-at-a-map vacation six years ago. It had led me to Florida, California, Maine, Pennsylvania, Wisconsin, and California again, but thank God it was on the opposite end of the state the second time around. So, this style of the country was very foreign to me. Personally, my wardrobe stuck to neutral colors, mostly black. If I wanted to bring attention to myself, I'd dress otherwise.

"I'm just looking for some proper Wyoming wear." There was apprehension in my voice as I picked up the sleeve of a brown leather jacket complete with tassels.

"You've come to the right place. My name's Betty. You're not familiar to me. You new here?" She looked me up and down—not in a judgmental way, more like I was brought in on consignment, and she was determining my worth.

"Yes . . . no. I'm just vacationing here through next week." I gave her a tight smile, hoping I could get on with it. I wasn't one for small talk, and I'd much rather shop in silence.

She raised an eyebrow. "You here with your husband?"

It was a 1950s question, like women couldn't travel alone.

"No." I eyed up a mannequin dressed in a floral print summer dress. It had way more shape than the one Betty was wearing.

"That's very *Eat, Pray, Love* of you," she said with a smile.

"Yeah, something like that." I shrugged.

Pushing some clothing around on a nearly stuffed rack, I pulled out a pair of Daisy Dukes and a black tank. Also not my style, but sometimes you have to look the part.

"You're sure to get the boys' attention 'round here with an outfit like that." She raised both her brows this time. I couldn't tell if she was judging me or making conversation.

"I'm just looking for something I can get dirty."

"That'll work. Perhaps a pair of cowboy boots right over there too." Betty pointed to a neat row of boots.

I nodded and moseyed around the store, picking up another pair of jean shorts and a white tank. Betty watched me carefully. Her mouth kept opening and closing as if she was torn between chatting with me or making a sale. She seemed like one of those people who knew everything about everyone. Like the neighbor who watches out their window, two fingers separating a set of blinds to peek at the outside world. If there was a neighborhood watch around here, she was surely the president of it.

"Where ya staying?" she finally settled on, just as I was slipping on a pair of cowboy boots. I walked back and forth in front of the mirror with them on. They were comfortable, but I wasn't used to them.

"On a ranch about twenty minutes down the road. Airbnb . . ." I said as I wiggled my toes in the boots and rocked back on my heels. I sat down, slid them off, and put my tennis shoes back on.

"Oh, you must be staying with Calvin Wells. He's the only one who does that rental property stuff around here. Aside from the local motel, we don't get too many visitors." Her brows slightly drew together.

I stood, grabbing the boots, two pairs of shorts, a couple of tops, and snagged the floral dress as well. Betty took her place behind the register as I walked over to the counter.

"I'll take these," I said, plopping them next to the old register.

"Good choice." The price tags on the clothes were all handwritten, so she entered them in manually.

"Calvin's a good man, ya know," Betty said as she bagged up the clothes. It was an odd thing to say, and I wasn't sure how to respond.

"Yeah. He seems nice." I glanced around while she switched between focusing on her task at hand and trying to get a read on me. The wall behind her was covered in framed photos of all different sizes. She was smiling in all of them, standing shoulder to shoulder with another random person. The real Betty looked up and smiled at me while forty pictures of Betty smiled at me behind her. It was rather unnerving.

"He's like a son to me. I take care of them honeybees up on his farm."

"Oh yes. He showed me them earlier today. You're Honeybee Betty."

"That's right." She nodded. "That'll be $41.09."

I handed her a fifty-dollar bill. The register drawer flung open, and she slowly counted out my change while placing the money in my hand.

"You enjoy the rest of your stay, Grace. I'll be seeing you around." Betty smiled wide as she handed over my bag.

I told her goodbye and returned a tight, forced smile. Something didn't feel right. Something about that exchange was off. I felt it in the pit of my stomach. I looked back at the store and saw her in the window, watching (like I knew she would). I nodded and quickly got into my car. Just as I started to reverse out of my parking spot, the Mazda beeped several times and the check engine light flickered on. I smacked my hand against the steering wheel in frustration and glanced up through the windshield. Betty was still staring at me through the window of her boutique, almost smiling like she knew I was in deep shit. And that's when it hit me. I had never told her my name.

8.

Calvin

It was just after nine when I finished with the evening chores: feeding and watering all the animals, bringing the sheep in from the pasture, putting Gretchen and George back in their stalls, and dealing with an animal that refused to listen. I was done much later than usual because I had to prep for shearing. My sheep were sheared once a year, and it was a grueling task that I never looked forward to. Pulling my shirt up to my face, I wiped the sweat from my brow and made my way up the porch steps. I hadn't seen Grace since this morning and wondered what she had done all day. My mind kept going back to her, no matter what chore I was doing. Cutting the grass, Grace. Cleaning the horse stalls, Grace. Fixing and fortifying a shed, Grace. She was staying in my home and living in my mind. I was consumed by her.

I slid off my work boots before going inside. An unfamiliar smell invaded my nose as I pushed open the door. Earthy and sweet and acidic and meaty. It definitely wasn't anything I had ever cooked. I strolled into the kitchen and found Grace at the stove, dressed in those leggings she was wearing earlier today. She was swaying her hips while stirring a wooden spoon in a frying pan. A country song played softly on the radio, and a glass of wine and an open bottle sat on the counter beside her. She clearly hadn't heard me come in, and I was appreciating the time I got to watch her, to examine her. Goddamn, she looked good in those leggings.

Leaning against the wall, I dusted my shirt off so I was somewhat presentable.

"Whatcha doing, Grace?"

She jumped a little, turning around quickly. Her mouth was partially open but she forced it into a smile. Grace set the wooden spoon down and grabbed her glass of wine, bringing it to her lips for a slow sip.

"I'm cooking you a proper meal." She raised one eyebrow just over the rim of her glass.

"Is that so?" I slipped a hand in my front jeans pocket. I was never sure what to do with my hands when I was around Grace because I wanted to put them on her.

"Oh, it is," she said, setting the glass down.

"I thought the meal I prepared for you last night was pretty proper. But I'm intrigued, Miss Grace. What's a proper meal to you?" I smirked.

"Come here, and I'll show you." She beckoned me with her hand and returned to stirring one of the pots.

Just as I started walking over to Grace, I heard it. Clucking that grew louder, faster, and more persistent. Immediately, I realized the grave mistake I had made.

"Shit," I yelled, running into the living room. I grabbed the 12-gauge shotgun from the fireplace mantel and slipped on my work boots.

"What's wrong?" Grace called out. I heard her footsteps padding behind me as I burst through the screen door onto the porch. There was no time to explain, so I didn't answer.

The chickens and ducks were huddled in a group off to one side of the pond, moving in sync. The ducks practically screamed and the chickens clucked nonstop. I took off running toward them, spotting a couple of chickens on the other side of the pond, lying still. Heads were completely ripped off and blood pooled around their open necks. A light shined behind me, and I turned quickly to find Grace just a few yards back with a flashlight in hand. *Smart girl*, I thought. She moved it in all directions as I got closer to the pond.

I held the shotgun up, ready to shoot, as I looked for the creature that did this. Technically, I had a hand in this too. Grace was only a couple of steps behind me now, and she gasped when she spotted the dead chickens. Death was something you just got used to way out here. Too many predators. Finally, there it was, chomping on the head of a chicken. Three feet long from nose to tail and weighing at least thirty-five pounds. The creature's eyes lit up like yellow orbs. The body of the chicken laid a couple of feet away. I held the gun steady and fired off a round, missing by a few inches. *Lucky bastard.* The raccoon quickly scampered off. The second shot missed too. *Shit.* There was no time to reload. The animal was gone, and four of my chickens were dead. I had gotten lucky too though. A raccoon could kill a flock in minutes.

I let out a deep breath and lowered the shotgun, wiping the sweat from my brow.

"Are you okay?" Grace asked. She was standing beside me, looking up at me with those blue, blue eyes.

"Yeah," I said, shaking my head.

Grace was clearly confused by my answer and my body language. I was fine, but I was pissed at myself for making such a careless mistake. What if this had happened to one of my more valuable animals? It could have cost me everything.

"I forgot to put the chickens and the ducks in their coop, which is the equivalent of ringing a dinner bell out here for predators." The birds were much quieter now that the animal was gone.

"I can't believe a raccoon did this," she said as her eyes scanned over the bloody carcasses.

I looked over at Grace, drawing my brows together.

"They may look cute and cuddly but don't let them fool you. They're vicious killers."

Her eyes met mine. "What do you do now?"

"I've gotta get rid of the dead chickens. They'll just draw in more predators, and there's no shortage of those around here. Then, I gotta get the rest of them secured in the coop."

"I can help." She didn't even hesitate to offer.

"I've got it. You go in and eat." I waved a hand dismissively.

"No, I want to help, and then we can have that proper dinn gether," she said. Grace didn't smile, but it was like her eyes did.

I nodded and returned the smile she hadn't given me. Most women couldn't stomach the harsh reality of ranch life. But Grace clearly wasn't most women.

I showered after we took care of everything outside. Grace got the chickens and ducks back in the coop while I disposed of the dead ones. She had surprised me again by staying out and helping me with the worst part of ranching. Walking down the hallway dressed in a clean tee and sweatpants, I could smell that sweet, acidic, earthy scent again. It was late, and I had told her she didn't have to wait up for me while I showered, but she insisted on sitting down for dinner.

In the kitchen I found Grace taking her seat at the table. She set two glasses of red wine beside two plates that were already served.

"It smells amazing," I said.

She looked up and smiled. "It tastes even better. Take a seat." Grace gestured to the chair across from her.

"What do we have here?" I asked while I sat down.

Grace pointed to the plate. "These are balsamic-and-honey-glazed brussels sprouts with bacon. I picked them myself."

"You know how to pick brussels sprouts?" I raised an eyebrow in a teasing way.

"Of course. They sell them by the stalk at the farmers markets in the city."

I let on a grin and nodded.

"This right here," she pointed, "is honey-glazed salmon with a spicy soy sauce."

I laid a napkin in my lap, never taking my eyes off of her. "You are an impressive woman."

"Thanks."

"Cheers." I held out my glass.

She picked hers up and tilted her head. "What are we cheers-ing to?"

"To proper meals and good company." I wanted to add *that lasts forever* but I left it out. Coming on too strong was a quick way to get shot down. I knew from experience.

Grace smiled and clinked hers against mine. "Cheers."

I watched her bottom lip press against the glass as she swallowed the liquid, and then I took my drink. I wanted that bottom lip. It was plump and begged to be bitten or sucked on. I ran my tongue against my teeth and imagined sinking them into her.

"Almost forgot. Shall we say grace first, Grace," I said, extending my hand out to hers.

She shook her head and looked awkwardly at me and then at her plate. "I'm not religious."

I retracted my hand. "Yeah, me neither. I just like tradition. My mistake." I grabbed my fork and dove into the brussels sprouts first, just to get them out of the way. If I still had my dog, I'd have "accidentally" tossed these things on the ground for him to eat. But he passed last spring. Most things didn't survive this ranch. I was the exception.

Grace watched me, waiting for my reaction.

"These are fantastic," I lied through a mouth full of food. "Hands down, best sprouts I've ever had." The second part wasn't a lie. I had eaten a single one when I was a child and immediately spit it out. I gulped red wine, forcing those fart-smelling, poor excuse of a vegetable down my throat.

She smiled wide. I'd lie to Grace every day to keep her happy. "Okay, now the salmon . . ." she pointed at my plate.

I sliced through the corner of it and scooped it onto my fork. The refreshing taste of the fish mixed with the sweetness of the honey, the saltiness of the soy, and the spiciness of the hot sauce melded together perfectly. "Incredible," I said in between bites, and I meant it.

Grace beamed and then proceeded to finally start eating. She was pleased that I was pleased. I liked that about her.

"You feeling all right after the chicken incident?" I asked. I hoped that hadn't scared her away but she seemed to have already put it behind her.

"Yeah," she said, tilting her head. "I'll admit, it was quite jarring, but I understand things like that happen out here."

"I lost the whole flock when I first took over the ranch. Coop wasn't secured enough and a weasel got in there." I shook my head and sipped my wine.

"A weasel? Aren't those tiny little things?"

"Yep. They don't weigh more than a pound, but they're killers. They can slink through something as small as the diameter of a wedding ring." I shoveled a forkful of salmon into my mouth.

Grace took small bites and chewed many times before she swallowed. "How'd you know it was a weasel?"

"From how they kill. They bite the base of an animal's skull. Two bites and it's dead. They stack the carcasses up neatly too like some sort of ritual. And they'll only eat part of one or two chickens but will slaughter the rest of them for fun."

"That's awful." Grace brought her glass of wine to her lips and took a slow sip.

"It is, but that's ranch living."

"Well, I don't deal with any of that in the city. The only predators that live there are other humans," she said with a forced laugh.

"I'll take a weasel and a raccoon over *that* any day." I smirked.

We ate in silence for a few minutes, stealing glances from one another. I was drawn to Grace. We were from very different worlds, but deep down, I felt like we were alike in some way—not sure which, but I knew we were. And I think she liked my world.

"I didn't see ya until late, what did ya do all day?" I asked.

The corner of her lip perked up. "I went out and got myself some 'proper Wyoming wear,' as you put it."

"I'd love to see you in that." I let out an awkward cough, realizing how forward that was. Grace dabbed her mouth with a napkin, and I quickly moved the conversation along.

"Did you meet Betty?"

She nodded and stirred the food around on her plate like she wanted to say something but wasn't sure how to say it. "Did you mention her to me?"

I thought back to my conversations with Betty. I couldn't recall if I did or not. "I'm sure I did. I talk to Betty about everything. She's like a second mom to me." I took another bite of salmon.

Grace nodded slightly and gave a tight smile. I'm not sure what that was about, but I assumed there was something about Betty she didn't like. Betty meant well. She was a woman that spoke her mind and sometimes it didn't come off all that great. But she didn't have a mean bone in her body . . . at least that I knew of. Or perhaps Grace looked down on us country folks, and she was just being polite toward me. Maybe I was reading her all wrong. I held my head a little higher and took another bite of her nasty brussels sprouts.

Grace paused her eating and furrowed her brow. "Do you know anything about cars?"

"Not really my specialty. What's up?"

"The check engine light came on when I was leaving Betty's store, and it started shaking when I drove back. Like when I accelerated." She let out a sigh.

That must be what's got her acting tense. I suppose I'd feel the same way if I was staying in a strange place so far from home with a shoddy car.

"Well, my brother Joe is real good with cars. He'll be over here this week, and I can have him take a look at it."

Grace took a long sip of her wine. "That'd be great."

I wondered why she hesitated. Maybe she didn't like accepting help—typical city girl type of thing.

"You said you moved back to take over the ranch. Your brother, why didn't he do it?" Grace asked.

I shoveled a forkful of salmon into my mouth and chewed slowly. "Mom and Dad wanted me to. It was in their will, and I respected their wishes."

She tilted her head and looked at me like she was looking into my soul. "You must have really loved them to do that, to give up your life and come back to live theirs."

I sipped my wine while deciding how to respond. I didn't like talking about them. Even though they were gone, their presence was here, heavy and dark.

I set the empty glass down and looked to Grace. "Yeah, I guess you could say that."

Standing, I grabbed my plate. "You done?" I asked.

Grace nodded, pushing her dish toward me. Over at the sink, I turned on the faucet.

"Let me help you clean up," Grace said, half standing.

I flicked my hand at her. "Nonsense. You cooked. I'll clean," I said, closing the drain and squirting Dawn dish soap into the basin.

Grace smiled and took her seat. She refilled both our glasses and brought hers to her lips. "I could get used to this," she said, taking a sip. Her eyes peered over the glass, running up and down my body.

"I could too, Grace." I gave her a coy smile and slid the pans into the dishwater. If I'm being honest, I was already used to it. Grace would be a hard habit to break. Nearly impossible.

9.

Grace

I stepped out of the bathroom dressed in a white silk nightgown that stopped a few inches above my knees. I forgot to pick up plain plaid or cotton pajamas earlier today, but at this point, I had decided I'd wear my pj's in this house. Calvin's reaction to me was enjoyable. His cheeks would instantly turn red and his voice would get deeper. I'd catch him forcing his eyes to look away, but they'd always find their way back. Calvin looked at me like I was the only girl he had ever seen, and I liked it. It was that dance at the beginning of a relationship—intoxicating, addicting. You just couldn't get enough, until you could. It was probably why I had had so many of them. Every relationship eventually loses its luster. You get bored. It becomes routine, mundane. And then you find yourself seeking that excitement and spark elsewhere.

Tousling my damp hair with a towel, I moseyed out into the living room, hoping he hadn't gone off to bed. He wasn't there, and I was about to turn in for the night when the porch door squeaked. Calvin's eyes were wide and his mouth hung open. A blue knit cardigan wrapped tightly around his shoulders and biceps. He quickly snapped his mouth shut, but his eyes remained wide, wandering up and down my body as though they were lost.

"I was just heading to bed," I said with a soft smile.

Dinner had gone well enough, a little on the depressing side with the chicken slaughter beforehand and death as the major topic of conversation. But I learned a lot about Calvin.

"Oh." He shuffled his feet. "Want to join me for a nightcap?" He held up a bottle of whiskey and two glasses.

I ran my hand through my damp hair, hesitating for a moment. I didn't want to be too eager. "Sure," I finally landed on.

His lips curved into a grin as he held open the door. Out on the porch, I took a seat on the steps. Calvin poured a double into both glasses and handed one to me. His fingers grazed across mine, sending a shiver down my spine. I wasn't sure if it was from his touch, the cool night air, or how the middle of Wyoming made me feel. I brought the glass to my lips and sipped. It didn't burn because I didn't let it. Mind over matter as they say.

"You must be cold." He removed his cardigan and draped it over my shoulders.

I thanked him and pulled it a little tighter around me. It smelled like Calvin: woodsy.

I looked up at the night sky full of millions of stars, like tiny little lights watching us, reminding us that there was a bigger world out there—that no matter what we think we knew, we didn't really know anything at all. The blanket of lights is just a trick though, an illusion to make us feel like we're a part of something magical, but really, it's all random. All of it—atoms just mashed together, particles, subatomic particles . . . creating everything we've ever known and felt. Even this, this right here—this moment between Calvin and me.

"It's beautiful," I said.

"Yeah, it's a real slice of heaven." He sipped his whiskey.

See? Magic. It's easy to be fooled by pretty things. We look at them and think something special went into creating them, like extra time was spent, like they are good because of their beauty. I rarely trust beautiful things.

"I never see the stars in the city. I think I actually forgot they existed."

Calvin looked over at me and then back at the night sky. "That's a shame."

"It really is. Sometimes I think about leaving and moving someplace quiet, someplace simple, where people live for the moment and not for the next," I said, taking another sip.

"Someplace like this?" Calvin gave a half smile paired with a quick glance.

I looked at him and smiled back. "Yeah, maybe."

He returned his focus to the stars as I took intermittent sips of whiskey. We stared at the sky in silence for a while, casually drinking. Most people didn't like silence, but I thought of it as a luxury. When you're surrounded by noise and chaos, it's the quiet that makes you feel alive.

An owl hooted from a tree and an animal howled on and off in the distance, probably a wolf or a coyote, but I wasn't sure. From the corner of my eye, I stole a glance at Calvin. He was stoic like more thoughts were running through his brain than there were stars in the sky. I wondered what it was he was thinking. What did a simple man like Calvin have to think about? You could find out a lot about a person just by knowing where their mind went when it was quiet.

"Whatcha thinking?" I asked, interrupting the silence.

He blinked several times and looked over at me. "Just how I managed to get lucky enough to be sitting here with you surrounded by all this beauty." Calvin gave a small smile and lifted his glass to his lips, taking a sip.

See? That answer revealed that he didn't think he deserved this moment. But why? What had he done to believe that?

"What about you, Grace? What are you thinking?" he asked.

"I was thinking the same thing." I smiled back and drained the rest of my whiskey.

"Thank you for the drink," I said, setting the glass down and getting to my feet. I pulled the cardigan from my shoulders and held it out. "And for the sweater."

Calvin took it from me. "Anytime, Grace."

"Night, Calvin."

He told me good night, and I walked inside, letting the screen door close behind me. Just before I disappeared down the hall, I stopped and looked back at Calvin sitting on the porch, giving him a once-over, the outline of his broad, muscular shoulders illuminated by the night sky. He sipped his whiskey slowly, gazing up. His thoughts were a little more on display now, and on some level, I knew he and I were one and the same. I could feel it.

The sound of a woman screaming pulled me from my sleep. I jolted up in bed. The room was bathed in moonlight, and the window behind the headboard was partially cracked open. I tried to control my breathing. Four counts in through the nose. Hold for seven. Exhale through the mouth for eight. I listened closely. The buzzing cicadas were so loud, it felt like they were in the room with me. There must have been a swarm of them because their high-pitched hum drowned out nearly everything else. The hoot of an owl came next. Four counts in through the nose. Hold for seven. Exhale through the mouth for eight. I wasn't sure what I had actually heard now. I laid back down, pulling the blanket up to my chin. I laid awake for a long time, and I didn't hear the scream again. Perhaps I was dreaming, but what if . . . I wasn't?

Day Three

10.
Calvin

I woke up real early today like a kid on Christmas morning, but I wasn't eager for presents, I was eager for Grace—just to see her, to spend time with her. It was the things she said and the things she didn't say that drew me to her. She wasn't like any other woman I had ever encountered. The other girls were like turnips. Sure, they were pretty, but what you saw was what you got, and they were mostly forgettable. Grace, she was like an onion: layered, complex, with so much to offer. Onions could be grilled, sautéed, baked, caramelized, roasted—heck, even eaten raw. They could take a dish to a whole new level with all the flavor they packed. They were unassuming but also surprising, just like Grace. I'd even used them as insect repellent in a pinch—sliced them open and rubbed them all over my skin.

Sitting on that porch with her last night, noticing how she was different than anyone I'd met, made me realize I wanted to spend all my nights with her.

I brewed a fresh pot of coffee and waited at the kitchen table with the local newspaper. I was five pages into the paper, but I couldn't tell you what I had read because my mind could only think of one thing, and that was Grace. I kept glancing at her bedroom door, hoping and willing she'd come out any moment now. I stood outside of it for a while, just listening. The morning chores and some much-needed property maintenance were done, so I had the whole day to devote to her—if she'd allow it, of course. I worried I might be encroaching on her space, but I'd get a good read on her today and decide whether I needed to take a step back or a step forward.

Finally, the door creaked open, and I heard her soft footsteps pad the hallway. I tried to look as casual as possible, sipping at my coffee, flipping through the newspaper like I hadn't been waiting for her to wake up. When she entered the kitchen, it was like all the air got sucked out of the room.

"Good morning," Grace said. Her voice was quiet and raspy like she had just woken from a deep, deep sleep. I'm glad she felt comfortable enough to sleep soundly in my home.

I acted as though I was surprised to see her. "Morning." Her hair was tied up in a ponytail, and she was still in her little white nightgown. Her face was almost fresh, but she had definitely put some of that black stuff on her lashes because it made her blue, blue eyes pop even more.

"How'd you sleep?" I asked.

She paused for a moment, biting at her lower lip. "Umm . . . fine."

Shit. Grace clearly hadn't slept well. Maybe it was the old mattress she was sleeping on. I considered offering her my bed but stopped myself as that might come off as odd.

"Is it the mattress? I could go out and get you a mattress pad or something. Just want to make sure you're comfortable."

"No, the mattress is fine. But . . . did you hear anything last night?" Her body language changed as she asked it like she was scared of the answer.

"Like what?" I tilted my head. "Around here, you'll hear all sorts of stuff at night."

She bit at her lower lip again. "A scream."

"A scream? No, can't say I heard that."

Grace rubbed her forehead. "I must have been dreaming or something."

She poured a cup of coffee and leaned her back against the counter. Grace wrapped both hands around the mug and took a sip.

"Maybe you were, but what kind of scream was it?"

"Like a woman screaming," she said, peering over her mug at me.

"That was probably an animal. The red fox's mating call sounds like a woman screaming. It's near the end of their mating season too," I explained. "It's rather haunting when you hear it because it sounds human."

She stared into her coffee, not acknowledging what I said. It was like she was lost in thought.

"They're another animal I gotta worry about. They come after my chickens too at all times of the day. At least mating season keeps them busy so I don't see too much of them this time of year," I said with a chuckle.

Her eyes flickered as she nodded. Grace glanced at the table and then back at me. "What are you reading?" she asked, changing the subject.

"Just the paper." I flipped a page.

"Anything interesting?"

I scanned the page quickly. I hadn't read a damn single word of this thing. "Not really," I settled on. "Got any plans for the day?"

She crossed her ankle in front of the other. "Relaxing, reading, maybe go for a run."

I raised an eyebrow. "How about some fishing?"

"Calvin Wells, are you trying to turn me into a country girl?" she teased.

I folded up the newspaper and placed it in the center of the table. There she went saying my full name again, sending a shiver right down my spine. I sat tall in my chair. "I just might be." I nodded.

"Well, I'd like that." She brought the mug to her mouth again and sipped.

I stood and pushed in my chair. "Go and get your proper dirty clothes on, and I'll meet you down by the river with the gear."

She started toward her bedroom, calling over her shoulder, "It's a date."

A flush crept up on my cheeks and my heart rate quickened again as I watched her pad down the hallway. Her nightgown just barely covered her backside. I never wanted to see her walk away from me again.

"You've got to put a worm on the hook, silly," I joked.

Grace dropped the line right in the water without casting it or putting anything on it. Her cheeks flushed as she reeled it back in. She was dressed in short shorts, cowboy boots, and a black tank top. I was sure there was nothing underneath it either. Grace definitely made an effort to make herself look good. Her lips were pink and glossy, her lashes long and dark, and her hair was slightly curled.

"A worm?" She crumpled up her face as she reeled the remainder of the line in.

"Yes, ma'am. You ain't gonna catch much without it." I set my pole down and grabbed the little tub of worms beside the tackle box. I pulled out a long, thick one covered in dirt. It squirmed as I tore it in half. I tossed part of it back in the container and held it out for Grace. The other half of it still wiggled. The tail end would die shortly, so I always used that part first. The half with the brain would survive and could generate a new tail if given the time.

"Here you are."

She shook her head and pointed the tip of the rod toward me. Grace made her blue, blue eyes extra big and her lips extra pouty. "Will you put it on?" Her voice was baby-like, and she was definitely working me to get her way, but I didn't mind.

"Of course, I will." I smiled. "With anything in life, you gotta have bait to catch it. The trick is to get it all the way through from end to end, so it can't get off the hook." I poked one end of the worm and threaded it so there was just a half inch hanging off the end. She watched me intently. Her eyes followed my fingers. I thought for sure she'd look away during this part, but she was interested in learning. "This will ensure no fish snags your worm clean off the hook before you get a chance to catch it."

"There you are." I let the hook fall from my hands. "See, it can still wiggle but it can't get off the hook. That's the key. Now, you're gonna cast it in."

Grace held the pole in front of her and faced the river. She flicked her wrist forward, but she didn't open the bail. The threaded worm just spun in circles. She tried again a little harder this time, but once again the line didn't release. I folded my arms in front of my chest and watched her try over and over, and then I let out a husky laugh.

"Are you laughing at me, Calvin?" She squinted and pursed her lips, but her face was soft.

"I would never." I stood a few feet behind her. "Want some help?"

She smiled and nodded. Taking a couple steps to her, I felt her back up, pressing her butt right into me. A big whiff of her sweet-smelling hair made its way to my nose as I wrapped my arms around her. I put one hand over hers on the handle and one hand over the other on the reel foot with a finger on the bail arm.

"The key is to flick your wrists quickly, and when you cast forward, you open the bail."

Grace nodded. She took another small step into me, and I nearly dropped the pole.

"Also, make sure you hold on to the pole firmly." I laughed.

I created a slight bend in my elbow, guiding her with me, and then flicked my wrist forward, releasing the bail. The hook cast through the air, clean across the river.

"I did it," she said with a slight bounce.

"You did." I took my hands off, giving her full control, and stepped back.

"Thanks." She threw a glance over her shoulder at me.

"Anytime, Grace. Now, reel it in slow, and if you feel a tug, you'll want to pull up on the pole quick and with force so you hook the fish. Then, you bring him in. The key to catching anything is patience though." I put my hands in my pockets and watched her slowly reel the line in. When she finished, she cast it just like I taught her—a perfect cast. I could watch her all day. She was persistent as she turned the handle, concentrating on the feeling of the rod in her hands. Each time she cast the hook back in the water, her face lit up. That was the thing about fishing. Every cast was a new possibility of a great catch.

I grabbed two Bud Lights from the cooler and popped them open with a bottle opener. I handed one to her just as she was reeling her line in again.

"It's not fishing unless you have a beer," I said.

Grace clinked her bottle against mine and we both swigged.

"This is really nice." She set the bottle down and cast again. She was a determined woman. I could see that the first day I laid eyes on her.

I picked up my pole and baited the hook, casting right next to her, careful not to cross lines. "Shall we make it interesting?"

She raised an eyebrow and glanced over at me. "What'd you have in mind?"

"First one to catch a fish, the other one has to jump in this river."

"Let's make it more interesting," she said.

"Oh yeah? Like how?"

"First one to catch a fish, the other one has to jump in this river . . . naked."

There she was, surprising me again. I couldn't help but smile.

She cast her line again and looked over, sizing me up. The corner of her mouth lifted in a challenging way.

"You got yourself a bet, Grace," I said, casting my line in again.

Her brows drew together as she focused on her task.

"Hope you like fish because you're going to be swimming with them," I teased as I cast another line.

"I wouldn't be so sure about that, Mr. Wells." She peered up at me through her lashes and bit her bottom lip. If that was the look I'd get from Grace if she won, I'd lose every day of my life for her.

"Hey," a voice from behind us called. Over my shoulder, Charlotte walked across the green pasture toward Grace and me. Her long, silky brown hair blew in the wind, and the sun highlighted her freckles and tan skin. She was dressed in a pair of shorts and her Dubois Super Foods polo, so I knew she'd come straight from work.

Grace glanced over her shoulder. "Who's that?"

"That's Charlotte. She's the one I was telling you about that helps out on the ranch."

"Oh, your girlfriend?" she teased.

"My friend that's a girl," I said in a low voice.

"She's pretty."

I didn't agree or disagree and just kept my mouth shut instead. It was a trap I was familiar with.

"Who's this?" Charlotte asked, raising her chin.

"Hi, I'm Grace, Calvin's Airbnb guest," Grace said, extending her free hand while the other held the fishing pole.

Charlotte looked at her hand and hesitated before finally finding her manners and shaking.

"I'm Charlotte, Calvin's good friend." She pulled away from the handshake rather quickly. "How long you in town for?" Char asked. Her eyes briefly tightened.

"'Til next week." Grace flashed a faint smile at me.

The two seemed to appraise one another like I do with my vegetables, deciding whether or not they're ripe for the picking or, in some cases, rotten from the inside out and needing to be tossed instead.

"That'll be here in no time." Charlotte's eyes bounced to me. "What are you two doing?"

It was obvious what we were doing. Charlotte was acting funny. It was like she had staked some sort of claim to me or thought she was being protective. She and I were friends, and we'd always be friends no matter what happened or didn't happen between us.

"I'm teaching Grace how to fish," I said proudly.

Grace threw a smile at me. "He's a good teacher. I think I'll catch a fish before him."

"We'll see about that," I taunted.

"I didn't realize fishing was included in your Airbnb package, Calvin." Charlotte had a sour look on her face.

"I'm full-service here. Complete hospitality and total accommodations. Whatever my guests want they get." I nodded.

"You sound like one of them annoying local TV ads." Charlotte chuckled. She glanced at Grace and then back at me. When no one laughed with her, she cleared her throat. "You mind taking a break and helping me with the eggs? The store sold out, so I gotta be quick."

"Of course. You okay for a bit without me?" I asked Grace.

"Yeah." Grace turned back and cast her line in again. "It was nice meeting you, Charlotte," she called over her shoulder.

"Likewise," Charlotte said with a neutral look on her face. When her eyes landed on me, they brightened. "Shall we?"

I nodded and just as I started walking with Charlotte toward the pasture, Grace squealed.

"I got something!"

I quickly turned back. Charlotte let out a huff, but I didn't care. Grace flicked her pole up and started reeling it in. She struggled to turn the handle. Whatever fish it was, it was sure putting up a fight. I ran over to Grace and wrapped my arms around her, placing my hands on hers.

"Nice and steady." I helped reel it in with her.

She looked up at me briefly and smiled.

"He's a tough one," I said as we got the fish right near the riverbank where I'd pull it out. "I like it when they fight."

"You coming, Calvin?" Charlotte yelled. "I told ya I gotta be quick."

I glanced over my shoulder. Her hands were on her hips, and her face was twisted up. Char was clearly not pleased, and I wasn't sure if it was because of me or my house guest.

"Go ahead without me. I'll be right over."

She pursed her lips and turned on her foot, marching toward the pond. I redirected my attention back to the fish and pulled it out of the water.

"What is it?" Grace's voice was full of excitement.

"That right there is a walleye. He's big, at least thirty inches, and I can make some of the best fish fry you've ever had with it." I grinned.

She held the pole while I walked over and grabbed the ice cooler.

"We're going to eat it?" she asked.

"Of course. That's some good eating right there, a proper meal." I took the fish off the hook. He flailed and flopped in my hands, trying to get away, but his fate was already sealed. And you can't fight fate. I quickly stowed him in the cooler and closed the lid. He would die slowly on the ice, making for a tastier meal.

"I can't believe I caught one," she said.

"You're a natural." I placed an arm around Grace and pulled her into me, patting her shoulder. She wrapped her arm around my lower back and leaned her head against my chest. She fit perfectly there like a missing puzzle piece. *Fate.*

"Thank you," she said, looking up at me.

I rubbed her shoulder. "Anytime."

"Calvin." She fluttered her lashes.

"Yeah, Grace." My heart pounded, and I felt blood pool to my cheeks.

"Hope you like fish because you're going to be swimming with them." She laughed, and I pulled her in a little tighter, a smile stretching across my face.

She had her catch of the day, and I had mine. Grace just didn't know it yet. She was my catch.

11.

Grace

I stretched out my quad, pulling my foot up to my butt and holding it there for a minute. I could see Charlotte and Calvin out by the pond, collecting eggs and putting them into containers. She had said she needed Calvin's help because she was in a hurry, but it seemed she was now taking her sweet time. Charlotte tossed her head of long brown hair back in laughter. I wondered what it was they were talking about. She grazed up against him each time she passed by. Her hand ruffled his hair and lightly patted him on the arm. Calvin said they were only friends, but I think something must have happened between them. That girl was clearly in love, and I knew love made you do crazy things.

Calvin caught my gaze, and he waved. A huge smile spread across his face. Charlotte glanced in my direction, flipped her hair over her shoulder, and went back to collecting eggs. I gave a little wave back, nestled my AirPods in my ear, and jogged across the gravel driveway toward the road. Pressing play on a downloaded Spotify playlist called Vacay Vibes, the song "Life's for the Living" by Passenger started up.

As my feet pounded against the pavement, I thought of Calvin with each step. The way his white T-shirt stretched over his large biceps and broad shoulders like it was vacuum-sealed around him. The way he let his thumbs hang from the loops of his jeans. The way he shuffled his feet when he didn't know what to say. The way his cheeks reddened when he looked at me . . .

Pound. Calvin's dimples.

Pound. Calvin's scar.

Pound. Calvin's smile.

My heart raced from more than just running. I belted the chorus just to get my mind off of Calvin. Busying the brain ensured thoughts didn't go astray. It kept them in check, corralled like a pasture of cattle.

When the song ended, my mind went back to Calvin.

Pound. Calvin's hands.

Pound. Calvin's body.

Pound. Calvin all over me.

I stopped in my tracks, nearly tumbling over. My breath was ragged as my lungs wanted more air than I could suck in. Staring up at the sky, I leaned back, cracking my spine. I was only here for another week. I had come here for one thing and one thing only: to find the peace and satisfaction my everyday life failed to provide. That's really why anyone packs up a suitcase and travels to a place they've never been. They're searching for something they can't find in their own world.

Calvin and I came from very different worlds. We had different goals, different needs, different wants. We didn't see life the same way. For him, it was more precious because he'd lost so many people close to him. As a result, he didn't take risks. He lived in the same house he grew up in. He knew the same people he had always known. And he had given up his own life for the wishes of his deceased parents. He couldn't possibly be happy or content living the same day every day. I knew I wasn't, hence why I was here. I wondered what it was Calvin did or desired that kept him sane, fulfilled, and satisfied. Because it sure as hell wasn't working on that ranch, doing the same damn thing every single day. The mundane is what drives people mad, and Calvin's life was just that.

I took in my surroundings, appreciating them at the moment,

knowing that appreciation wouldn't last forever. By the end of my time here, the beauty I saw in this place would fade. Everything becomes dull eventually. We just get used to it. The snow-capped mountains towered in the distance. One day they wouldn't look so big to me. The rolling green pasture was bright and inviting. One day I'd see it for what it truly was—nothing. And the black winding road I slithered in on seemed to go on forever with no end in sight. But I knew everything had an end.

12.

Calvin

Grace's hips and behind slightly jiggled as her shoes pounded against the pavement. Her stride was long and fast, so she disappeared down the road quicker than I would have liked. I could have watched her all day. Now that she was out of my line of sight, I could finally get back to collecting eggs.

"You got a thing for that girl or something?" Charlotte twisted up her nose. It was more of an accusation than a question.

I let out an awkward laugh. "Of course not. She's my house guest."

"Hmmph," Charlotte said, pushing out her hip. "Could have fooled me."

I placed my hand above my eyes, shading them from the sunshine, so I could see her better. "What's that supposed to mean?"

"I saw the way you looked at her, the way you put your arms around her." Charlotte pursed her lips and bent down to retrieve a duck egg.

I lowered my hand and shrugged. "I was just helping her, and I look at her like I look at everyone."

"You do not, Calvin, because if you did people would think you were some type of creep." She laughed but she was very serious.

This wasn't a side of Charlotte I had ever seen. We'd been friends since we were young, and even when I came back a year and a half ago, we picked right up where it left off, and it was like I had never left. She was there for me after my parents passed, and after Lisa died in that car accident, we grew even closer. I think Charlotte thought it was her responsibility to protect me. I did appreciate how much she cared but at times it felt like she was suffocating me.

"Fine, I may look at her a little different," I said as I pushed some tall grass aside in search of duck eggs. Sometimes I had to dig 'em up because ducks often buried their eggs to protect them from predators. Coyotes, foxes, raccoons, hawks, owls—heck, even humans. We're all predators to something.

Charlotte closed up another egg container and stacked it in a crate. "I think she's bad news."

A duck egg slipped from my hand and splatted against the ground. Bright blood marbled the golden yolk. Bloody eggs were rare—so rare they came with superstitions. My mother's words sprung to the front of my mind, *See a bloody yolk? It means you're gonna die.* I wondered if she saw one before she died—or two, one for her and one for my father. I closed my eyes for a moment, shaking the memory away. That's the thing about bad memories, they're the easiest to remember.

I opened my eyes and looked to Charlotte. "Why?"

"It's just odd. Why would a woman travel alone and stay at a total stranger's house in the middle of nowhere?" She stood and dusted off her hands.

"Lots of women do that these days. All a part of that feminist movement." I kicked some dirt and grass clippings onto the bloody egg, covering it up.

"No, they don't, Calvin."

I gathered another handful of duck eggs, careful not to drop any of them. If one bloody egg meant death, I sure as shit didn't want to find out what any more of them meant.

"Grace is just independent, and she wanted a break from New York City." I handed them over, and Charlotte placed them in another container.

"She's weird."

"Everyone from New York is a little weird," I smirked.

Charlotte rolled her eyes and closed up two more containers, stacking them in the crate. "She's stiff, like a robot."

"Maybe around you she is. But she ain't that way around me."

Char put her hand on my arm and looked up at me, her face turning serious. "I'm just saying be careful with that girl. I think she's bad news."

Bad news was the only type of news I was familiar with so it didn't make all that much of a difference to me.

A high-pitched scream stole my attention. I knew it was Grace. She screamed again, and I took off in a full sprint toward the driveway. Another scream. My feet pounded against the gravel, kicking up rocks and dirt.

"Grace!"

At the end of the driveway, I looked where the highway extended in both directions over flatlands and rolling fields. Another scream made me whip my head to the tall grass between the road and the property fence. I took a few more quick steps and nearly tossed my breakfast. Grace was lying in a pit of dead animals underneath a lodgepole pine tree. The pit was the size of a car, filled with a dozen animals all in different stages of decay. A freshly dead elk laid on top, its body torn open from one end to the other. Blood and sinew spilled out of it. Several puncture wounds and lacerations covered the neck and head. Grace was on her hands and knees, trying to crawl out of the sticky pit. She was covered in death—from fresh blood to maggots. Tears streamed down her face and her breath was quick and uncontrolled.

"Here, grab my hand," I said, leaning down.

She looked up at me, hesitating for a moment, before extending hers. There were several wiggly maggots stuck to her fingers. I pulled her up, and immediately she swatted her hands against her pants, squishing the maggots. She keeled over and retched onto the side of the road.

Charlotte caught up to me. Panting, she asked, "What is it?"

"Dead animals."

She rolled her eyes but stopped when she saw Grace behind me, covered in blood and guts. Grace gagged again and vomited a splash of brown liquid onto the ground. *Probably coffee from earlier.*

Char twisted up her face. "Gross."

I shook my head and delivered a stern look.

Grace gagged a few more times before standing upright. Even with the guts and blood and vomit and maggots, she was still gorgeous to me.

"What could have done that?" Grace rubbed her hands against her leggings and pulled her shirt up to wipe her face with the underside of it. It just smeared the blood around though. "Why is there a pile of dead animals here?"

"Some animals drag their prey to a place they can safely eat it, so could be anything. We got grizzly bears, wolves, coyotes, you name it." Charlotte raised an eyebrow. "This ain't New York, sweetie."

Grace ignored her, staring at the dead animals instead. Her eyes narrowed as she studied them.

After a few moments of silence, Char turned on her foot. "I gotta finish up with the eggs in the chicken coop," she said, walking back toward the ranch.

I looked at the carcasses and then at Grace. She couldn't take her eyes off of the pit. It was like watching a car crash. Not something you see every day, so your brain becomes fascinated by the mere sight, like it's stimulated a new part of it.

"How'd ya fall in?" I asked.

It took her a moment to register my question and when she did, Grace glanced at me. "I heard something rustling. I got a little too close before I realized what it was. As you can see, it's kind of hidden by long grass and weeds, and the branches off this tree hang low to the ground. I slipped right in." She shuddered.

"I'm sorry, Grace. I'll get animal control out here to clean it up. These bones and carcasses are what's attracting whatever's killing to this spot."

She took her eyes off of the pit and looked in my direction—not at me but beyond, staring intently at the ranch like she was seeing it differently now. I wondered if she felt it. The curse. It was hard not to feel it. Death hung heavy in the air here.

I took a few steps toward her and placed a hand on her shoulder.

She tensed up, so I immediately pulled it back. "I wouldn't let anything ever happen to you, Grace."

Grace didn't say anything, so I didn't either. There was that silence I enjoyed between us. A low nasal whine came from above. We both looked up, watching several turkey vultures circle high in the air, waiting to swoop in for a meal.

"Don't worry. They're harmless," I said. "They actually help keep the environment clean and prevent the spread of diseases."

I wasn't sure why I shared that fact with Grace. I guess I just wanted her to feel safer. My gaze went to her again. The dried rust-colored blood made her blue, blue eyes pop. I wondered what it was she was thinking. Was she upset? Was she intrigued? Was she planning her exit now?

"I'm going to shower," she finally said.

Grace walked apprehensively toward the ranch. Her arms were folded against her chest like she was trying to close herself off from everything around her. Dragging my hand down my face, I blew out my cheeks. This wasn't the Wyoming I wanted to show her. It was beautiful, yes, but even beautiful places were ugly. Flies buzzed around the bloody carcasses, swooping in and picking at the rotting meat. Death wasn't pretty.

I shook my head and made my way up the driveway. Charlotte was loading up her car with the crates of eggs.

"How's the princess?" she asked with a laugh.

"Char, don't," I warned.

"What? I told ya she don't belong here."

I rubbed my brow and let out a deep sigh. "Because she didn't like falling into a pit of dead animals?"

"I mean, that part was gross, and I'd be disgusted too. But animals die all the time out here. This isn't her world, Calvin. Can't you see that?" Char tilted her head.

"Maybe it's not mine either."

"Don't say that." She folded in her lips, waiting for me to speak. When I didn't, she asked, "How did you not report that pit to animal control earlier?"

"Didn't see it. I don't leave this ranch often because I don't have the time to. This place takes up most of my life. Too much to look after. Too much to worry about."

Char gave me a sympathetic look. "I think this place has a hold on you, Calvin, and you're punishing yourself for things you had no control over. We're worried about you."

"Who's we?"

"Betty, myself, and Joe too, I'm sure." Charlotte placed a hand on my shoulder. "I'm here for you. I'll always be here for you." Her hand grazed the side of my face, and when she looked at me, there was an intensity beneath her eyes. I had seen it once before, and I knew what it meant . . . to her. But I didn't feel the same way.

I turned my head and let her hand fall away.

Char finished loading the last crate into the back of her car and looked to me.

"I'll see you on Saturday," she said, closing the trunk of her car.

I drew my brows together. "Saturday?"

"Yeah, Calvin. Your birthday barbecue bash. I told you months ago you weren't spending it alone, and you agreed." She dusted her hands off and walked to the driver's side door.

"Shit. I completely forgot."

"You're the only person I know under the age of forty that forgets about their birthday. It's weird," Char said, getting into her car.

"It's not weird. It's just another day."

"Will Little Miss New York be in attendance?" Charlotte smirked.

"If she's still here, I'm sure. Might have scared her off with that elk cemetery." I kicked at the gravel.

"One can hope," she said with a laugh.

"Char, come on. Be nice. For me?"

"Fine, I'll be nice—only for you." Char tilted her head. "Speaking of nice. Would you be so kind as to come over and fix the leaky pipe under my sink? Pretty please," she begged, pushing out her lower lip.

"Of course."

"You're the best, Calvin." She closed her car door, and I headed toward my truck.

Char rolled down the window and called out. "Hey, Calvin."

I turned back. "Yeah."

"There's something I want to talk to you about after she leaves."

I shifted my stance and slid a hand into my front pocket. "You can tell me now."

"No, it can wait." Charlotte turned the key in the ignition.

"What if she doesn't leave?" I said with a laugh, only half joking.

She put the car in drive and looked over at me. "Then I'll throw her out myself." Her eyes narrowed for a moment but then she flashed a smile that could only best be described as sinister.

13.
Grace

Curled up on the sofa next to the fireplace, I watched the flames dance, switching from hues of orange and yellow to blue. My skin felt hot to the touch because I had scrubbed it raw in the shower. Despite that, I could still feel the sticky blood on me, the maggots crawling over my skin, the rubbery sinew that seemed to grab on and never let go. The smell still lingered at the tip of my nose—a mix of iron, rotten eggs, mothballs, garlic, and feces. There was also a sweetness to it all. No one ever mentions that death has a sweet odor like the smell of a fresh-cut lawn or a ripe banana. Hexanol and butanol are responsible for that pleasant scent just after death sets in.

Every time I blinked, I saw the ragged animal, the blood, the half-eaten guts, the frozen black eyes. Those same dark marbles were all around, hung up on the walls of the living room, staring down at me. I refocused my attention on the thriller I was reading, trying to silence my thoughts, but they were still there. I hadn't read more than a few sentences since I had laid down over an hour ago. My mind kept going back to that feeling I had in the pit of my stomach—the one that tells you something is very wrong. To the lemon of a car sitting outside. The lack of cell phone service and Wi-Fi. The rotting pit of animals at the end of the driveway. The scream I heard last night. I heard it, right? I rubbed my forehead and hoped the thoughts would rub away too. It was odd. One moment, I found the ranch comforting, and the next, it terrified me.

Calvin had driven off in his truck, following Charlotte, hours ago. He didn't even tell me he was leaving or where he was going or when he'd be back. I couldn't believe he had just left me here. But perhaps he was giving me space. I was cold to him, and maybe I pushed him away too hard. He hadn't really done anything wrong . . . that I knew of. I needed to get over the pit of dead animals—no matter how disgusting it was—because it wasn't Calvin's fault. He didn't kill those animals, and he didn't make me slip into it. And the rest of the issues—no cell phone service or Wi-Fi and my car acting up—were inconveniences I'd deal with eventually. But the scream? Well, I can't be sure I even heard it. I was being paranoid. But deep down I knew that paranoia some-times kept you safe.

The clock on the wall opposite the couch said it was after seven. I let out a sigh and flipped a page that I didn't actually read. Headlights flooded the living room window, and the roar of a truck engine rum-bled the house. Calvin's footsteps clamored up the stairs, then across the porch. I heard him wrestle his boots off and drop them on the ground outside before the door squeaked open. I draped one leg over the other and propped my head up with my hand. When he entered the living room, he didn't say anything, and I pretended I didn't hear him. I felt his eyes scan over me—from my toes to my legs to my chest and then they stopped at my face.

"Hey," he said.

I casually flipped a page of the book. "Where have you been?"

He wiped off his shirt the best he could and scratched the back of his neck.

"I was over at Charlotte's helping her with her sink. Then, she had me help her with a window that wouldn't open. Then, I fixed a cup-board door, and so on . . ."

"She kept you real busy." I bit at my lower lip and ran my foot along my leg.

"Umm . . . yeah." It was all he could manage to say. It was like all the energy in his body was going someplace else other than his brain. I knew then he hadn't completely shut me out. I could salvage this and enjoy the rest of my time here. The most pleasurable things in life are temporary. Most people don't understand that. They want to drag it out and make it last a lifetime. I could tell Calvin was like most people. He needed forever, but I just needed right now.

"You all right? Feeling any better?" He shuffled his feet.

I stood from the sofa, lowering my head slightly, and gazed up at him. "I will be after you settle your debt first."

He raised an eyebrow. "Debt?"

Realization hit right away. His eyes went wide, and he cracked a grin as I walked to him. My fingers curled under the bottom of his shirt. I knew it was bold of me, but I also knew Calvin liked bold. He seemed to overthink and overanalyze everything, which was surprising for a country boy like himself. I pulled his shirt up over his head and dropped it on the floor beside him. I could practically see his heart pulsating in his chest. His breath quickened, and he quickly licked his lips like he was preparing for me to kiss him. But I wouldn't, at least not yet. My eyes slithered up his stomach, to his chest, and then landed on his eyes. He swallowed hard, his Adam's apple bouncing up and down.

I patted his shoulder. "You have a river to jump in."

Calvin let out a deep breath and chuckled as I walked to the back door.

I looked back at him with a smirk. "You coming?"

He playfully shook his head and grinned. "Grace Evans, you astound me."

See? He liked bold.

The dewy grass felt refreshing beneath my bare feet. Calvin followed behind almost stumbling like Bambi learning how to walk. I think he was too stunned and too excited for his usual cool, country boy stroll.

At the riverbank, Calvin slid his jeans down and kicked them off. He bent down, slowly removing each sock. When he was finished, he stood in front of me wearing just a pair of navy blue boxers. At that point, I didn't even really want him to jump in. I just wanted to watch him, to study him, to take in every muscle bulge and crevice, every scar, every freckle, every inch of his skin. But a bet was a bet.

"Boxers too."

He looked down at himself and shuffled his feet. "Oh, come on."

"You lost the bet, Calvin. It's time to pay up."

He huffed, but I knew it was just for show. He slid off his boxers and quickly covered himself before I could really see anything. Calvin looked at the dark, murky water, hesitating for a moment. The reflection from the moon and stars glimmered across it, creating a mirror of the sky. There was a small splash downstream, a fish, I presumed. I thought it would scare Calvin, and he'd refuse to jump in. But it didn't. He was used to nature.

"Consider my debt paid in full, Grace," he said, uncovering himself and jumping quickly into the river. Calvin came up for air and tossed his head back, shaking the water from him.

"How is it?" I asked, giving him a pleased smile.

"It's actually nice." He wiped his face with his hand while treading water. "You should come in."

I glanced down at my silk pajamas. "I'm not wearing the right swimming clothes."

"Well, go ahead and take them off," he teased. "I'll turn around, and I promise I won't peek."

I looked down the river one way and then the other. It was endless in both directions, disappearing only behind bends or trees. Calvin had the biggest smile on his face while he waited. I wanted to say no. I had no idea what was in that water, how vulnerable I'd be in there, but I wasn't one to back away from a challenge.

"Fine. But no looking."

"Cross my heart," he said, turning away.

I quickly slid my bottoms off and removed my top. I hesitated for a moment, standing there completely unclothed. Calvin didn't look. I was surprised. He was a man of his word. Most men weren't. I jumped in and let out a squeal. The water was cool but refreshing, just as he said it was. I was underwater for only a few seconds before I reached the surface. Wiping my face, I leaned my head back, letting the water coat and smooth out my hair.

Calvin turned around, and that same smile was still on his face. His eyes flickered with desire—or was it something else? I couldn't be sure.

"You all right?" he asked.

I nodded and playfully splashed a little water at him, letting out a high-pitched laugh. He did the same back. As we swam, the seconds became minutes, and we got closer and closer until we were only a few feet apart. My leg bumped his first.

"Sorry."

"Don't be," he said.

"Thanks for teaching me to fish today."

"It was my pleasure, and I'm glad you caught one before me."

We smiled and continued to tread, swimming around one another until the minutes became an hour.

"How was your night with Charlotte?" I finally asked, interrupting the silence we both were obviously fond of.

"Uneventful. I just worked the whole time."

"You know she likes you?" It was a question, but I didn't think he'd have an answer for it.

"I know," he admitted.

"You know she also doesn't like me?"

"I know that too."

"Why do you think that is?" I asked, already knowing the answer.

He wiped his face and swam a little closer. The moon caught the whites of his eyes, almost making them glow. "I think you know why, Grace."

It was too fast, too soon. And I knew I needed to pull away.

"I'm going to head in," I said, putting an end to where this conversation was heading.

Calvin pressed his lips together, and his eyes lost their glow. Disappointment kept people wanting more. It was fuel for their desires. He didn't say anything and just turned around instead.

"No peeking." I swam to the edge of the river and climbed out.

Picking up my pajamas, I opted not to put them on. Instead, I walked back toward the house unclothed, letting the cool summer night graze my skin. I glanced back once, and I saw Calvin looking over his shoulder, watching me walk away. Perhaps he wasn't as true to his word as I thought he was. *You never really know a person.*

Day Four

14.

Calvin

"That's a good girl, Gretchen." I ran a body brush over her shoulder and down her back. George nuzzled me with his chin. He always wanted extra attention, especially when I was giving it to Gretchen. It was a normal Wyoming day—the sun ablaze with big blue skies that reached the ends of the earth. The air was still and warm—not even a breeze.

"I've already brushed you, George." I scratched his forehead with my free hand, my mind wandering to our houseguest. "It's been an odd couple of days with Grace in the house. I just don't know how to act around her. One minute, she's hot, and the next, she's cold. Makes me nervous, and I'm not sure if it's in a good way or not."

I applied some pressure as I moved the body brush in large strokes along Gretchen's back. She moved into it, signaling that she was thoroughly enjoying it.

"I don't know. Maybe I'm just being silly. I know I fall too hard, too fast. It's how I've always been, and it's probably why my relationships always end. I know I'm not ready for anything—in more ways than one—but I also don't think I can help myself." I looked at George and then Gretchen. They turned out their ears and lowered their heads.

I set the brush down and grabbed two carrots from a bucket, holding them out. Gretchen and George bit at them. I like to think they were chewing on the words I had spoken, but I'm sure they were just chewing on carrots.

"There's something special about Grace. Something different. I know she leaves in six days but maybe she doesn't have to. She and I could get to know one another on a deeper level. She could be the girl of my dreams, and, what, I'm just gonna throw that away because time constraint, location, or not being completely ready? I think Grace is worth fighting for, worth risking it all for."

After they finished chewing their carrots, I scratched both of their heads.

"You two got it easy. You live together. Built-in soulmates. Nothing like time or distance getting in your way." I ran my hands down their muzzles.

"You talking to yourself, Calvin?" a voice called from behind the horses.

I craned my head to get a better look. Grace stood there dressed in Daisy Dukes, cowboy boots, and a blue tank top. Her hair was pulled back in a ponytail and her lips were glossy. I hoped she hadn't heard anything—surely she'd think I was a weirdo if she did.

"Not at all. Just talking to George and Gretchen," I said with a tight smile.

Grace walked around them and grazed her hand along Gretchen's coat.

"That's cute."

Sliding a thumb in the loop on my jeans, I ran a hand down George's forehead and looked back at Grace. In that outfit, I would never have guessed she was from the city. She was fitting in real nice, almost like she was here all along. I actually couldn't picture this place without her now.

"You wanna ride?" I asked.

Grace glanced at the horse and then at me. Her eyes were tight like she was worried. That was the only dead giveaway that she wasn't from around here—the hesitation, the tension. She carried it inside of her.

I raised an eyebrow. "You said you never backed down from a challenge."

She gave a forced nod. "Umm . . . yes." It was almost robotic.

I smiled. "Don't worry. I've got you."

I'll always have you.

15.

Grace

With one foot in the stirrup and one hand on the horn, Calvin hoisted me up on Gretchen. I straightened myself in the saddle, rocking side to side until I was somewhat comfortable—well, physically. There was nothing comforting about being six feet up in the air with nothing strapping you in. I made sure my shoes were firmly in each stirrup and inhaled deeply, holding it for a few seconds before letting it out. I didn't like feeling like I wasn't in control. My personality was Type double A, and right now, I was at the mercy of this thousand-pound horse.

"You all right?" Calvin glanced up at me.

I nodded but I'm sure the look on my face gave way to the fact that I was not all right. Calvin didn't know it, but I had a slight fear of heights. You had no power when you were in the air. One slip and gravity would pull you to the ground. I sealed my nod with a smile just to reassure him.

He handed me the reins, and I held them tightly. Calvin put his foot in the stirrup on George, grabbed onto the saddle horn, and hoisted himself up, swinging his leg over in one fell swoop. He made it look easy.

"Hold the horn," he reminded. Calvin had taught me all the parts of the saddle before I even got on the horse. He also made sure I got to know Gretchen through grooming before he saddled her up. He said it was important to establish a bond before you rode an animal. I grabbed the horn with one hand.

"You ready?" He smiled.

"Yeah."

"Let's go over some of the basics again. I'm applying light pressure with my left leg while pulling on the left rein to get him to turn," he said. George turned to the left. "You try."

I took another deep breath and did the same with Gretchen. She turned her head just like Calvin said she would.

"See. You got it." He smiled proudly. "Now, how do you stop the horse?"

"Pull back on the reins and say *woah*." I readjusted myself in the saddle.

"That's right. Ready to start walking?"

I nodded.

"Hands soft on the reins. Apply some light pressure with both legs."

I did what he said, and the horse started walking. Calvin got George to walk right beside Gretchen and me at a nice slow pace. I was fascinated by the idea of domesticating wild animals. They did as we said because we trained them to forget their nature, to disregard who they truly were. But nature can't be erased. It's always there, lying dormant, waiting for its turn to resurface. Even Siegfried and Roy couldn't keep the tiger in the cage.

"How's it feel?" Calvin sat tall on George, the reins in each of his hands.

"Better than I thought it would."

"You look good on that horse, Grace." He winked.

"You're not so bad yourself."

His cheeks flushed, and he pointed up ahead. "Let's go down by the river."

I nodded, and we walked slowly across the green pasture until we got down to the water. My thoughts rolled like the water babbling over the rocks.

It wasn't so bad here. Actually, it was better than I thought it'd be, despite the few hiccups. And Calvin . . . well, he had been a good host. That hadn't always been my experience with Airbnb.

"You never told me why you picked my ranch," he said. "I know Dubois was, in a way, fate, but why me?"

I glanced at Calvin, trying to get a read on him, but his face was serious.

"Couple reasons, actually. I liked that it was secluded. You know I don't have that in the city. And you seemed nice and attentive, a person I wouldn't mind spending ten days with." I smiled briefly and then re-focused my attention on the horse and the path ahead of us.

"You got all that from my Airbnb profile?" He tilted his head.

"No. I got all that from social media. People basically put their diaries online for the whole world to see," I said with a laugh.

"So, you researched me?"

"A little. It's a dangerous world we live in, and I had to make sure you weren't some creep or crazy person."

He finally smiled back. "You're smart, Grace. I like that about you."

"Why'd you start doing Airbnb in the first place?" I asked. "Doesn't the ranch keep you busy enough?"

"It does." He nodded, continuing to keep George's stride in-line with Gretchen's.

He paused the conversation and had me turn Gretchen to start walking along the bank. Between the sounds of birds chirping and the babbling river, I finally felt relaxed. The sun's rays warmed every inch of my exposed skin.

When Calvin was beside me again, he continued. "It costs a lot of money to run a ranch, so Airbnb helps keep the whole thing afloat."

"Ever think about giving it all up and starting over somewhere else?" I asked.

"No." His answer was curt, and I think it had to do with his parents.

I noticed he didn't say much about them, just that they'd passed and they had wanted him to take over. His shoulders would tense and his body would briefly stiffen at the mention of them. I could tell he was carrying a darkness inside of him. But I guess we all were though. Calvin just didn't carry his well.

"Ready to trot?" he asked, changing the subject.

I reminded myself to ask him more about his past and his family. It felt like he was hiding something, something sinister or shameful.

I looked at Calvin and then Gretchen. "I think so."

"All right, you're gonna want to get loose like a noodle so you flow with Gretchen's movements." He shimmied his upper body dramatically. "Sit deeper in the saddle. Hands are still soft on the reins, and the cue is applying pressure with the legs or a little tap with your heels. You ready?"

I followed all of Calvin's instructions but was still rigid. Gretchen went from a slow walk to a trot, bouncing me up and down as she scampered. It was jerky and uncomfortable, so I tried to loosen up and flow with her—but my body just wouldn't. Calvin caught up, trotting alongside us. He moved with George nice and smooth—not like me. I held onto the horn tightly, trying to keep my balance and make the ride smoother.

"You got this, Grace. Loosen up a little more. You're doing great." He smiled.

I appreciated his encouraging words, but they weren't working. I couldn't seem to get in tune with the horse's movements. Gretchen's ears swiveled, and she started trotting faster.

"Woah, girl," I said.

All of a sudden, she burst into a full run. I pulled back on the reins, but she just ran faster and faster. Nature had resurfaced.

"Gretchen," Calvin yelled. "Yah, yah," I heard him say, trying to get George to catch up to us. He sounded like a cowboy in one of those old John Wayne films my dad used to watch.

"Pull on the reins!"

"I am!" My voice was panicked.

"Pull just one side then," he yelled.

I did, and Gretchen reared, lifting her front legs off the ground. My eyes went wide, and I screamed as she bucked me off. My body hit the ground first with a thud, followed by the back of my head smacking against the hard, dry dirt. I saw stars, and the world around me faded quickly. The last thing I saw before it went dark was Calvin standing over me.

16.

Calvin

"Are you okay?" I knelt beside Grace, pushing her soft blond hair out of her face. She was stiff like a board and covered in dirt. Her lids slowly opened, revealing those blue, blue eyes—now clouded with confusion.

She winced when she tried to sit up.

"Careful. That was a hell of a fall." I gently pulled her into a sitting position and ran my hand across her cheek.

She turned her head away from it. "Owww." Her eyes struggled to stay open.

"We should get you to the clinic and have Doc check on you to make sure you're all right. You might have a concussion."

"No, really. I'm fine."

I pulled her chin up and looked her in the eyes. "Grace, I am taking you to the doctor. There's no sense in acting tough."

She didn't say no but her eyes did. She was a stubborn woman, which is also what I liked about her. I enjoyed being challenged. It made life worth living. I helped Grace to her feet, and she winced again, putting her hand on her lower back and rubbing her butt. "Owww."

"Looks like you need to be carried." I picked her up in one fell swoop before she could resist.

"Put me down. I can walk," she argued, but there was the faintest smile on her face so I knew she wasn't serious.

"Now's not the time to be stubborn, Grace." I looked back at George and Gretchen and made a *click, click* with my mouth. They followed, in step with each other.

They always listened well so I don't know why Gretchen freaked out the way she did.

I made my way along the bank, carrying Grace in my arms. She was light, and I rather liked having her this close to me, thankful, for just a moment, that Gretchen had bucked her.

"You're not seriously carrying me all the way?" She raised an eyebrow. The sun highlighted her button nose.

"I most certainly am. I'll carry you around for the next six days if I have to."

A small laugh escaped her mouth, and she rested her head on my shoulder. I felt her body finally relax in my arms. "You smell nice, Calvin," Grace said, looking up at me through them long eyelashes of hers.

"I think that fall might have rattled something loose and messed with your sense of smell," I joked.

When we reached my truck, I gently set her down beside it and opened the passenger door for her. Grace stood in front of me, her hands resting on my chest to steady herself.

"I'm going to put the horses away quick, and then I'm taking you to the clinic."

She let her fingers slither down my chest and stomach and then she brought them to her side. I thought she was going to protest, but she just nodded instead. She knew she didn't have a choice.

Grace was seated on the examination table, fidgeting with her fingers and stirring her dangling legs. She seemed nervous, but I supposed a doctor's office wasn't the most comfortable place to be, especially on vacation. Dr. Reed stuck up his pointer finger and moved it in front of Grace's face, asking her to follow it with her eyes. I had known Doc all my life. He was a short man, now in his sixties with a comb-over to cover up his bald spot. I think he thought he was pulling it off, but it looked like a bird's nest was perched on top of his head. I'd never tell him that though. After all, he was the only decent doctor in nearly a hundred miles.

"Do you know what you were doing before you hit your head?" he asked.

"Horseback riding."

He looked to me for confirmation, and I nodded.

Dr. Reed picked up his clipboard and jotted down some notes. "Do you know what day of the week it is, Grace?"

She looked around the room and a blank stare came over her.

"She's on vacation, Doc. No one knows what day it is when they're on vacation."

He chuckled. "That's true. It's Thursday, in case you were wondering."

Grace smiled tightly.

"What's your full name?" he asked.

She squinted her eyes like she was trying to conjure up the answer, and a pang of worry flashed through me. Dr. Reed paused his note-taking and studied her. "You do know your name, don't you?"

Doc shot me a worried look and pulled a penlight from his front pocket. He shined the light from the outer corner of each eye to the inside. Grace squinted but kept them open.

"Grace Evans," she blurted out like she had just woken from a trance.

"Your pupils responded quickly to the light, so that's a good sign," he said, pocketing the penlight. "Where do you live?"

She hesitated again, looking up toward the ceiling, searching for the right answer.

Dr. Reed scribbled down more notes.

"New York City."

"All right, good. Any dizziness or nausea?"

She shook her head.

"Hear any ringing in your ears?"

"No," she said.

Dr. Reed tilted his head. "Can you tell me the three words I asked you to remember when you first sat down on this examination table?"

"Red, house, fish," Grace said without hesitation.

He nodded. "Very good."

"I'll be honest, Doc, I didn't remember them myself," I joked.

"Well, we'll have to get you up on this examination table next then," he said with a laugh.

Grace cracked a smile.

"I didn't hit my head though."

"I've known you all your life, Calvin. No doubt in my mind that you got some screw loose up there," Dr. Reed teased. "Let me have a quick look at your lower back," he said to Grace.

She pulled up her shirt just enough for him to have a look. He pressed on the skin along her spine and then pulled her shirt back down, retaking his place in front of her.

"You've got some swelling and bruising on your back, so you'll want to ice it and take Tylenol for the pain. As far as your head goes, you have a mild concussion. I'm a bit worried because of some of your delayed responses, so to be safe I'd suggest an MRI to ensure there's no brain damage." Dr. Reed pursed his lips together and capped his pen.

"Brain damage?" Grace asked. Her eyes bounced from the doc to me and back to him again.

"Although unlikely, I like to err on the side of caution when it comes to head injuries."

"No, I'd rather not," she replied. "I feel fine."

"Is an MRI necessary, Doc?" I asked.

It was clear Grace didn't want one, so I wanted her to know I was on her side . . . I'd always be on her side.

"It's my professional opinion, but it is your choice, Grace."

She hopped down from the exam table. "Thank you, Dr. Reed, but really, I feel fine."

Dr. Reed raised an eyebrow. "Okay. You'll want to take it easy then.

Like I said, Tylenol and ice. If you have any nausea, vomiting, extreme fatigue, or anything like that, please call me right away."

"I will," she said.

"Hopefully, you should be feeling good as new in a day or two. But in the meantime, no driving."

Grace's eyes flickered with worry, but she thanked the doctor anyway.

"Oh, Calvin," he said, looking at me.

"Yeah, Doc."

"A nice massage would do her good." Dr. Reed winked at Grace, and she smiled back.

He patted me on the shoulder with a smirk. Doc was still just as sharp and smooth as he was in his forties.

"You can see Patsy up at the front to handle payment." He gestured to the door. "It was great meeting you, Grace, and I hope you get to enjoy the rest of your time here."

Dr. Reed looked to me. "And it's always a pleasure seeing you, Calvin." He gave a firm handshake. "You take good care of her."

"I will, and thanks, Doc."

Patsy, a petite woman in her sixties with thin lips and curly hair, sat at the front desk, knitting something out of navy blue yarn. I had known her since I was a kid and aside from the gray hair, she hadn't changed.

"Hey, Calvin. Everything okay?" Patsy asked, setting down her knitting needles. She glanced at me and then at Grace, who looked a little off. I couldn't tell if she was dazed or just worried about the doc's orders to take it easy the next couple of days.

"Yeah. Just a mild concussion," I said.

"That's good—well, not good. But better than . . . You know what I mean," Patsy said with a nod. "I'll just need your insurance card then, sweetheart." She smiled warmly.

Grace glanced down at her feet and then back at Patsy. "I don't have my purse with me. I left it back at the ranch."

"Well, that's all right. Just write down the insurance company and your information, and I can contact them to submit your claim." Patsy held out a pad of paper and a pen. Grace took the items from her and wrote out her full name then stopped. She gazed up at the ceiling.

"You all right?" I whispered to her. "Sure you don't want that MRI?"

Grace's eyes bounced to me and then back at the pad. She pressed the tip of the pen against the paper. The ink bled, forming a large circle. When you held on to something too long, it always left a mark. The same was true for people.

"No, I just can't remember the name of my insurance company," she said.

Patsy gave a worried look and reached for the phone. "Maybe we should get Dr. Reed back up here."

"No, I'm fine really. I just haven't had to use it in a while." Grace studied the paper. She tapped the tip of the pen on the ink blob. "I think it starts with a *B*."

I slid the pen from her fingers and set it down on the desk. Her brows drew together and she stared up at me.

"I'll just pay for it." I pulled my wallet from my back pocket. "What's the damage, Patsy?"

She clicked several buttons on her calculator.

"No, Calvin. I'll take care of it," Grace urged, putting her hand on my arm. I liked her hand on me.

"Nonsense. My horse. My problem," I said.

"Two hundred and thirty-one dollars."

"You really don't have to." She gently pulled on my arm.

I could have swum in those blue, blue eyes of hers. "I really do, Grace." I smiled and handed my card to Patsy.

Her fingers caressed my arm, sending a shiver down my spine. She mouthed, *Thank you.*

I'd take care of Grace every day of my life if she'd let me and even if she wouldn't.

17.

Grace

"We don't need all this stuff," I said as Calvin placed an ice pack and a bottle of Tylenol in the cart. So far, we had ice cream and chocolate because he said that makes everything better, flowers to brighten up my mood, chicken noodle soup—"for my soul" as he put it—and lotion for the massage the doc ordered.

"But we do." He smiled, putting a stuffed teddy bear in the cart. "I told ya. I'm going to take real good care of you."

"What do I need a teddy bear for?" I held it up and gave him a crooked smile. It was soft with a big belly and a tan chest patch.

"For your comfort." He snatched it from me and set it in the cart's child seat.

Up at the register, he tossed a couple packs of beef jerky on the counter. "That's for me," Calvin said, flashing a toothy grin.

The cashier rang everything up, and Calvin didn't hesitate to pay for it all, which I thought was odd. He told me earlier the ranch was barely staying afloat. But he'd covered the doctor's visit and all this without blinking an eye. Either he was bad with money or he had more of it than he was letting on. Calvin grabbed the bags and pulled the teddy bear from one of them, handing it to me.

"The comfort starts now," he said.

I smiled, held it against my chest, and followed him out of the store.

In the parking lot, I spotted Charlotte dressed in a Dubois Super Foods polo with her head down, focused on her phone.

"Hey, Char," Calvin called out.

Charlotte looked up, and her face instantly brightened. When she saw me, it dimmed a little, but she forced a smile—so I did too.

"What brings you two here?" Charlotte stopped right in front of us.

I didn't have the energy to respond. My brain felt like it had been put in a blender, and my back was killing me. I couldn't wait to lie down.

"Just getting some things for Grace. She got bucked off Gretchen pretty hard."

I squeezed the teddy bear a little tighter.

"Oh my. Are you all right?" She looked concerned, but it also seemed like she was putting on an act, forcing herself to be nice to me. It was her tone that gave it away, almost like a customer service voice reserved for a rude shopper.

"Yeah. Just headachy and sore," I said.

"That's so odd and not like Gretchen at all. She's so calm."

I wasn't sure what she was insinuating. That it was me who caused Gretchen to buck?

"She is." Calvin nodded. "But we were down by the river, and I'm thinking an animal or something spooked her."

"Well, sorry that happened." Charlotte briefly glanced at me. Her eyes were tight and her brow was furrowed. She relaxed her face, returning her focus to Calvin. "I've got work, so I better get going. But I'll see you Saturday." Her hand grazed his arm as she walked past him.

"See ya, Char."

"Saturday?" I looked up at Calvin.

"Oh yeah, I forgot to tell you. Actually, I forgot about it myself. Char planned a get-together with my friends and family for my birthday. You'll join us, right?" He said it in such a casual way, but his eyes widened while he waited for my answer.

I really wasn't interested in meeting Calvin's friends and family. It felt like something a girlfriend would do, and I was just his houseguest. But with how he was looking at me, I knew I couldn't say no.

"I wouldn't miss it." I smiled.

"Perfect. Let's get you home." He grinned and led me across the parking lot.

Home? It wasn't a home to me. It was a house, a dwelling, a building with four walls and a roof. There was a difference between a house and a home—but Calvin had already decided what it was for me.

My eyes sprung open, and for a moment, I forgot where I was and who I was. I blinked several times, my surroundings slowly coming into view. On the walls of the living room, the dead animals loomed over me. Their carcasses and black beady eyes stared directly at me as though they were taunting me. I must have fallen asleep after we got back.

"Calvin," I called out.

The house was silent.

I called his name again, this time a little louder. Again, I was met with silence. He wouldn't have left me here, not with a concussion. Would he? I heard a growl like the sound of an oversized cat. My body ached, and I sat up on the couch, snapping my head in all directions, trying to find where it was coming from. From my peripheral view, I saw something move. The head of an elk on the wall. I had seen it move, twist its neck toward me. I watched, waiting for it to move again. Was I going crazy? Standing from the couch, I stumbled toward the wall of creatures, staring at each of them. The low growl grew louder. My eyes went to the head of a mountain lion hung in the center of the far wall. Its mouth was frozen open, fangs permanently on display. The house creaked and groaned.

"Calvin," I yelled.

Again silence.

The wall cracked, splitting from the ceiling to the floor. I took a step back, and the house began to shake. I nearly tumbled over, but I held my hands out to steady myself. All at once, the animals broke through the wall. They leapt through the air, their bodies now fully intact, no longer mounted heads. Claws extended, teeth bared, horns and antlers aimed, ready to strike. I screamed and fell onto the coffee table. *Crack*. I threw my arms up in front of my face, trying to protect myself from them.

"Grace!"

My eyes shot open. I swatted my hands through the air. Calvin grabbed my arms and held them. "Grace, you just had a bad dream," he said, trying to calm me. "You fell asleep."

My breaths were short, panicky. I could feel my heartbeat in every part of my body. My eyes went to the walls of the living room. The animals were still there, mounted, staring at me with their cold, dead eyes.

"Are you okay?" Calvin asked. I looked up at him, focusing on the specks of brown that dotted his green eyes. I hadn't noticed them before. I inhaled deeply and nodded several times.

"Yeah, sorry."

"It's all right." He pushed a strand of hair out of my face and tucked it behind my ear. "We all have bad dreams."

He was right. We all did have bad dreams, but I always believed they were warnings, the subconscious trying its best to alert you that something in your waking world was amiss.

Calvin helped me lie down and repositioned a fresh ice pack under my back. He tucked the teddy bear beneath my arm.

"You didn't have him here to protect you," he said with a smile.

I rested my hand against my forehead. "How long was I out for?"

"Couldn't have been long. I was just cleaning up after dinner." He gestured to the coffee table. "And I brought you these." A glass of red wine and a Lindt chocolate bar were set out for me.

"Thanks."

"Don't mention it. I'll be right back." He quickly disappeared into the kitchen.

I sipped the wine and popped a piece of chocolate into my mouth. It melted instantly and paired well with the dryness of the merlot. Calvin had cared for me nearly all day, never leaving my side for more than a few minutes—well, except after dinner apparently. He brought me Tylenol, fresh ice packs, and water. I asked him earlier if he'd ever cared for someone because he was a little too good at it. He said no. But I thought he was lying. Maybe he had taken care of his parents.

I sipped slowly, peering over the rim of the glass to keep an eye on the mounted taxidermy. I knew it was just a dream but it felt real, and sometimes there wasn't a difference between the two.

Calvin strolled back into the living room holding a glass of wine and a bottle of lotion.

"Did you talk to your brother about my car?" I asked.

My mind kept going back to that. There was nothing worse than feeling stuck. The mounted animals reminded me of that. Actually, I didn't *feel* stuck—I *was* stuck, just like them. Maybe that was the warning.

"No, haven't been able to get ahold of him yet, but he should be here tomorrow," Calvin said, setting his glass of wine on the coffee table.

I chewed at my lower lip.

"Don't worry, Grace. Let's take your mind off of that." He smiled. "Massage?" Calvin held up the bottle of lavender-scented lotion. His cheeks reddened to the same shade of merlot we were drinking.

"You did promise." My voice was low.

He smiled and knelt beside the couch while I rolled over on my stomach and pulled my shirt up. I heard him take a deep breath, and even though his hands weren't on me, I could feel them there like burns on my skin. I pulled my shirt farther up past my bra clasp. He swallowed hard, making a gulping sound. I slid my shirt up over my head and tossed it aside. I could practically hear his heart beating, fast and loud like the applause of an overenthused audience. I tensed up when the cold lotion splatted against my skin. His hands pressed against me, first gently and then he applied much more pressure, working up and down my back. This was clearly not his first massage. The hairs on the back of my neck stood, and my heart raced. His touch stopped at the clasp of my bra and then his hands worked their way back down. I undid the clasp, letting my straps fall down my shoulders. His hands left my body for a brief moment and then returned, pushing on my skin, moving up and down and side to side.

Several pounds on the front door interrupted us. Calvin jumped to his feet, and I quickly sat up and redressed. Goose bumps covered my skin, but they had nothing to do with the temperature of the room.

"Fremont County Sheriff's Department," a man called from the other side of the door. His voice was hoarse like a smoker.

Calvin opened the drapes partially and peered out. Red-and-blue flashing lights danced across the ceiling and walls.

"What is it?" I whispered, but my voice cracked.

His mouth opened and closed twice before he spoke. "I don't know."

Three more pounds on the door. The man on the other side had grown impatient. Calvin dragged a hand down his face.

"Maybe the dead animals. Did you call about that?" I asked. My eyes bounced from Calvin to the flickering lights.

"Yeah, yeah. That's probably it." A look of relief rushed over him. Placing his hand on the door handle, he hesitated for a moment. Another pound shook the door. Calvin jumped, then threw it open.

"Evening, what can I help you with?" Calvin's voice was calm.

"Good evening. I'm Sheriff Almond from the Fremont Sheriff's Department. Are you Calvin Wells?"

I shifted to the side so I could get a good look at the officer. He was a large man with a full beard and weathered, sun-damaged skin. He wore a campaign hat and a belt buckle the size of a deck of cards. The sheriff's dark eyes bounced over to me for a moment. He gave a slight nod of acknowledgment and returned his gaze to Calvin.

"Yeah. How can I help you, sir?" Calvin shifted his stance.

"I'm following up on a missing person's report for a woman by the name of Briana Becker. Her sister from Michigan reported her missing early this afternoon. Apparently, she was traveling alone on a cross-country road trip, and they expected her home three days ago but hadn't heard from her in over two weeks." Sheriff Almond slid a piece of paper from his front pocket and held it out. "Have you seen this woman?"

Calvin took the photo. His eyes lingered for a few moments before he shook his head and handed it back. "Nope, she doesn't look familiar."

"What about you, miss?" The sheriff extended his hand out.

I closed the distance and glanced at the photo. The woman was striking. Long, wavy blond hair. Blue eyes. A pearly white smile. And dimples so deep, you could hide a penny in them. I looked up at the sheriff and shook my head. "No, I've never seen her."

He flicked the corner of the photo in disappointment and slid it back into his pocket. His eyes returned to me. "And you are?"

"Grace Evans."

"You run an Airbnb, Calvin?" Sheriff Almond pulled at a thick strand of his mustache and twirled it.

With his attention off of me, I backed up a couple steps. He wasn't here for me. He was here for Calvin.

"That's right."

"According to Miss Becker's Airbnb account, she was supposed to arrive here two weeks ago and stay a few days. Does that sound right to you?" Sheriff Almond raised an eyebrow.

I wished I could see Calvin's face, but I was standing slightly behind him. I focused on his back where his lungs expanded. He didn't twitch or tense up.

"She must have been a no-show. It happens on occasion. Someone books a room to rent and then radio silence. I marked a person as a no-show two weeks ago."

Sheriff Almond tilted his head. "Yes, we were able to access her account and see that she checked in and out at a previous place over in Sioux Falls, South Dakota, but she never checked in here."

Calvin nodded. "Must have never made it here. That's a long way to travel, and it's easy to get lost."

If she hadn't checked in, why was the sheriff here? Perhaps he had nothing to go on and was grasping at straws, trying to turn over a lead.

Sheriff Almond shuffled his feet, glancing to his left and right, up and down the long porch. "Beautiful place you got here."

"Thanks." Calvin folded his arms in front of his chest. "It was my parents. I took over about eighteen months ago."

"Did your parents do the rental thing too?" The sheriff scratched at his chin.

"Oh no. I started that up about a year ago when I realized the finances weren't in that great of shape. It brings in extra money to keep the ranch afloat."

I still didn't believe that, and I reminded myself to ask him about it later.

Sheriff Almond nodded. "And you, miss." He directed his attention to me. "You live here too?"

I shook my head. "No, I'm a guest. I got in a few days ago."

"You traveled alone?"

"Yes," I said.

"Humph." He shifted his stance. "Where from?"

"New York."

Sheriff Almond let out a low whistle. "You're a long way from home."

I nodded.

His eyes bounced from me to Calvin. "Well, all right." He pulled a card from his front pocket and handed it over. "Mr. Wells, if you think of anything else, please give me a call. Otherwise, I'll be in touch if I have any more questions."

Calvin slid the card into his pocket. "Will do, Sheriff. I hope you find her."

He tilted his hat, and his eyes lingered on me for a little too long. "Sorry to bother you. Y'all take care and stay safe." The sheriff turned on his foot and walked slowly back toward his vehicle. He held his head high and scanned the property before getting into his SUV.

Calvin gave a small wave and closed the door. His hand lingered on the handle, and I watched his head fall forward briefly before he picked it back up.

He turned toward me with a smile. "Where were we?"

I rubbed my lower back. The pain radiated, extending nearly to the middle.

"Is it all right if I head to bed early? I just need a good night's rest. That fall wrecked me." My voice was low, and I brought the palm of my hand to my forehead, pressing against it.

Calvin's face crumpled for a moment and then relaxed. "Yeah, yeah, of course. Do you need anything?"

I gave a tight smile. "No, you've done enough," I said, turning on my foot.

"Good night, Grace," he called out as I headed down the hall.

The door with the padlock that supposedly led to the basement made me stop in my tracks. I stared at it, wondering what was on the other side.

A shiver ran down my spine as a thought crossed my mind. The missing woman. The scream I heard the other night. The woman's clothes in the dresser. Maybe they weren't his ex's. Maybe they were Briana's. I made my way down the hallway and closed the bedroom door behind me. When I went to turn the lock, I realized there wasn't one.

Day Five

18.

Calvin

My knuckles rapped against Grace's door. Usually, I'd wait out in the kitchen until she woke up, but I wanted to make sure she was feeling all right, especially after getting that concussion. Our night didn't end how I intended it to. After the sheriff showed up, Grace seemed to have built a wall between us. It didn't make any sense why he came around here anyway. That girl had never even checked in. He said so himself. I was glad he left quickly. But I think the damage was already done. He spooked Grace. She'd already been on edge with the riding accident and the issue with her car. Now, who knows how she was feeling? I laid awake nearly all night thinking about her, and when I finally fell asleep, I dreamed about her.

Footsteps padded across the room, something slid across the floor, and then the door opened. Her hair was messy, and she was dressed in a tiny silk robe.

"Hey. Sorry to wake you. Just wanted to make sure you were all right. How ya feeling?"

"A little sleepy and foggy-brained."

I placed my hand against her forehead. "No fever." I smiled.

She shook her head. "I'm not sick."

"Gotta make sure. You could have caught a bug when you were rolling around in that dirt." I teased, pulling my hand away. "There's a fresh pot of coffee and some oatmeal in the Crock-Pot. Brown sugar is beside it."

"Thanks."

"Well, I've gotta go mow the lawn and check on some things. Glad to see you're feeling better." I tipped an imaginary hat.

She opened the door a little wider, and I couldn't help taking her all in: her smooth tan legs and partially open robe that revealed her sculpted collarbone. All this made my smile grow wide. The corner of her lip perked up as she watched my eyes. She knew exactly what she was doing to me.

"Do you need any help?"

"Absolutely not. You're on vacation, miss. There's a hammock down by the river. It's the perfect place to lay out and read, and I insist you do so."

"Is that an order?" she teased.

"You bet your behind it is," I said with a laugh and a wink. My flirtation was getting downright ridiculous. I just didn't know how to act around Grace. Thankfully, she laughed too, and I hoped it was with me and not at me—but I wouldn't blame her if it was the latter.

"Your wish is my command." She smiled and closed the door slowly.

Goddamn, that girl was going to be the death of me.

19.

Grace

Lying in the hammock, I closed the book and held it against my chest. The branches above looked like hands and arms reaching in all directions. The white fluffy clouds beyond appeared to be tangled in the trees but I knew they weren't. That was the thing about point of view—you saw things the way they presented themselves but that didn't make them true. I wondered if this ranch was how I saw the tangled clouds.

There was a sense of dread I had been carrying with me since I arrived. This place was different. Was I being paranoid or was there really cause for concern? There were too many coincidences. Too many things going wrong or just not how I thought they'd go. I should be completely relaxed, not on edge with thoughts running through my brain like a Rolodex. The scream I heard. The lack of Wi-Fi and cell phone service. My car acting up. And the missing girl. The sheriff said she never checked in. He verified it himself. But then why did he come here asking questions he already had the answers to? Unless he didn't believe the answers.

Swinging my legs out of the hammock, I decided I was going to find Calvin. I needed to at least ask him about the car. It'd been three days and his brother still hadn't shown up. I got the feeling that maybe there was a reason for that. I knew I couldn't just go marching around, demanding he fix my car. I needed to be tactful, and despite everything, I liked Calvin. I was drawn to him like a cat to a mouse.

Lunch was a perfect excuse to approach him. Before running into the house, I glanced at the field, spotting an idle tractor and Calvin nowhere in sight. My eyes flicked to the barn, the pond, the pasture. He was around here somewhere. Inside, I quickly threw together two PB&J sandwiches and snagged cold beers from the fridge.

Walking out to the pasture, Calvin was now driving the John Deere tractor with a lawn mower attachment on the back of it. I wondered where he'd been before. He mowed the area the sheep and cows didn't get to, where the grass was longer than the rest of the field. I knew the moment he laid eyes on me—because his face went from expressionless to excited. His smile was big, and he sat up a little straighter. He wore cowboy boots and a pair of ripped-up jeans that were torn from working on the farm. I held up the beers and the plate just as he pulled up in front of me. He immediately killed the engine.

"What are you doing out here, miss?" Calvin lifted an eyebrow and turned up the corner of his lip.

"Figured you needed a drink and something to eat."

"Well, climb on up here."

I handed over the beers and plate of sandwiches. He placed them beside him and grabbed my hand, pulling me right up onto his lap. His skin was wet, hot to the touch.

"What do you got here?" he asked, holding up the plate. Jelly oozed out of the corners and part of the bread was torn from trying to spread the thick peanut butter.

"PB&J," I said.

Calvin grabbed one and handed it to me. "My favorite." He smiled and bit into the other sandwich. We didn't speak until we finished eating. Calvin wiped off his hands and popped the caps off the beers on the side of the tractor. I clinked mine against his.

"Thank you, Grace," he said just before taking a swig.

"I presumed you needed some taking care of too." I tipped back the beer and drank.

Awe transformed his face as if I had struck a chord. I assumed no one had taken care of him in a long time. My back still ached, not as bad as yesterday, and my head felt a little full but maybe that was because it was bursting with worry.

"Shall we ride?" he asked.

"Yeah."

The tractor came to life and jolted when he put it in drive. He drove it slow and steady through the pasture while the mower cut and spit out grass behind us.

"Calvin, I wanted to ask about the car. It's been a few days." My face was expressionless, carefully hiding the fear I had of feeling stuck.

"I phoned my brother, Joe, last night after you went to bed to remind him and again this morning. He'll be over today to take a look at it."

I nodded.

Calvin glanced at me, tilting his head slightly "Joe forgets things sometimes. Hence why he doesn't come around as often as he used to. But he'll be here. You trust me, right, Grace?"

I hesitated but forced my head to go up and down. "Yeah."

"Good." He pressed down a little harder on the gas pedal.

The change in speed caused me to fall back into him. Calvin caught me and kept me steady, our faces only a few inches apart. I thought for sure he was going to kiss me right then and there, but he didn't. He pushed a piece of hair behind my ear and looked ahead, leaving my eyes lingering, staring at his profile—a strong chin, a carved jawline covered in stubble, and full lips that I was sure told lies.

20.

Calvin

The ice-cold water slithered down my hot skin but it was doing little to cool me off. It was like the heat was radiating from my insides. I screwed up again. Grace practically gave me an opening, but something stopped me. I think it's the way she'd look at me. One moment, it was like she was falling for me, and the next, it was as though she was scared of me. Maybe she felt both ways. I didn't know why. I hadn't done anything to make her fear me.

I shut the water off and looked out the ill-placed window in the shower. Apparently, when this house was built, privacy was something that people didn't care too much about. Grace walked by in a tiny red bikini, carrying a towel and a book. She didn't notice me watching her. Every part of her was perfection, even the bruise on her lower back. Her bottoms didn't fully cover her backside. Her top looked as though it was made out of just a few pieces of string. Girls 'round here didn't wear things like that. I watched her until she disappeared around the house, and then I turned the shower back on, letting the cold water run over my skin again. It was either that or I'd have to rub Grace out of me.

Pulling open the curtain, I stepped out of the tub and dried myself off. The roar of a truck and a loud exhaust made me quicken my pace. I knew exactly who it was. I threw on clothes and jogged out of the house before my brother was able to introduce himself to Grace.

He was always too friendly too quickly because he wanted everyone to like him. I think growing up in my shadow made him that way. People were immediately drawn to me, but they weren't the same with Joe. Even our father was more drawn to me than him. Joe had done everything to try to get Dad to love him, to be proud of him—that's why he knew about fixing cars, and I didn't. Joe learned it all from Dad, thinking it would make them grow close, be a bond between them. But Dad was like a thorn. You got too close, you got pricked. What hurt my brother most was our parents leaving the ranch to me. While I up and left for years, he stayed and worked every day on it. I knew he resented me for it.

Joe hopped out of his lifted Dodge Ram just as I got outside. I told him not to have it lifted because it made him look like a douche. He spent his money on silly things as though they'd make him happy. They never did. As long as I was alive, I didn't think he'd ever be happy.

"What's up, bro?" Joe called out.

He puffed out his chest and raised his shoulders as he walked toward me. We shook hands and half hugged, punctuating it with firm pats on the back. Joe was shorter, only around five foot ten, but he was muscular. He worked hard for his body at the gym, and I think he had some sort of complex about being the shorter one—so he tried to make up for it with muscle mass.

"Same-o, same-o," I said, glancing over at the pasture.

"Sorry I haven't been over this week to help out. There's this girl I've been hanging out with," he said with a small smile. I couldn't remember the last time I saw him smile. Maybe he felt guilty being happy around me.

I raised my brows and gave him a pat on the arm. "Oh, really. Am I going to be meeting her sometime soon?"

"Probably not. Can't bring her around the stud just yet. Gotta get her to fall in love with me first." He laughed but I knew he was serious. "Whoa!" Joe took a step to the side and looked behind me. "Who is that?"

I turned around and saw Grace laying out a towel on the ground. She bent over, her whole behind in view, and placed a book on the ground. Then she straightened the towel and laid down on her back.

Joe's eyes slithered over Grace. I didn't like the way he was looking at her.

"Hey." I patted the side of his cheek. "That's my guest. I told you about her last night. She's the one with the car trouble."

Joe let out a high-pitched whistle. "They don't make them like that around here."

I shifted and stood in front of him, blocking his view. "Stop. She's a lady."

"She's a knockout." He tried to get another look at her, but I blocked him.

I folded my arms across my chest. "I'm going to knock you out if you don't stop making eyes at her."

Joe's face turned serious. "You like her?" he said in a low voice.

"She's only here 'til Wednesday."

"That didn't answer my question."

I shrugged. "Maybe."

Joe patted my shoulder, and his eyes glistened. "I'm glad you're moving on."

I didn't say anything and just nodded. I knew Joe wanted me to date again. Probably more for his sake than mine.

He tilted his head. "Introduce me, so I can find out what's going on with her car."

"Fine, but don't say anything weird," I warned.

He ran his fingers through his hair and straightened out his belt buckle. "I'm cool as a cucumber, bro."

"I'm serious." I narrowed my eyes at him. "I don't want you scaring her off."

"I won't."

I relaxed my face and led him toward Grace. A pair of oversized sunglasses covered her eyes, and her nose was in a book. It was obvious she spent time in the gym because her body was toned from her arms down to her legs.

"Grace," I called out.

She looked up from her book and pulled off her sunglasses, revealing those blue, blue eyes.

"This here is my brother, Joe." I pointed to him.

He bent down, extending his hand.

"Nice to meet you." Grace shook his hand.

"The pleasure is all mine," he said, emphasizing the word *pleasure*. He did that sometimes now—put emphasis on the wrong word when he spoke.

She gave me an odd look. *Sorry*, I mouthed.

"You here to look at my car?" Grace asked.

Joe clasped his hands in front of him and his biceps flexed. His little-dog complex was at work.

"Of course. Calvin here couldn't handle it without me," he teased.

I rolled my eyes. "Let's take a look at that car."

Joe redirected his attention to Grace. "Tell me what happened to it."

She sighed. "It was fine all the way here, and I drove a long way. But when I left Betty's Boutique, the check engine light came on. It started vibrating and shaking, even more so when I accelerated," Grace said. I could see the worry on her face.

Joe nodded. "All right, I'll take a look at it."

"Thanks," Grace said. "Keys are on the kitchen table."

"Don't worry. I'll make sure you're not stranded here with my big bro." He laughed.

Grace's eyes bounced from me to Joe and back again like a pendulum swinging. My jaw tightened but I smiled anyway and steered my brother toward the house. The less he said to her the better.

21.
Grace

I watched the two of them walk away. Joe was nearly six inches shorter than Calvin, but they were different in more ways than just height. A lump sat in the pit of my stomach. It had begun to form a few days prior, and grew with each passing moment. It was like a tumor; maybe benign, maybe cancerous. Regardless, I'd find out soon enough. Joe's presence was like Miracle Grow for the lump. There was something off about him. He seemed like a man with a guilty conscience. It gave me that sinking feeling like when you sense something bad is going to happen—a primal instinct for impending doom. Like a cold sweat. Hairs that stand upright. Goose bumps on hot skin.

It wasn't just Joe though. It was this ranch. It was Calvin too. He seemed apprehensive about his brother's very presence—like a zookeeper with a wild animal, careful to keep their guard up while also anticipating the ferocity of the creature. The two walked side by side, playfully pushing each other and laughing like a pair of brothers would.

Then again, looks could be deceiving. I'm sure Abel loved Cain right up until the very end.

22.
Calvin

Joe fiddled under the hood while I sat in the driver's seat, waiting for him to tell me to start the car, press on the gas pedal, or shut it off. Now, I was wishing I had taken the time to learn more about cars growing up. It seemed the only thing I knew how to do was wreck them.

"Turn it on," he called out.

I turned the key in the ignition. It sputtered a few times before it started.

"Give it a little gas."

I slowly pressed down on the pedal, causing the engine to roar and the vehicle to shake.

"All right, kill it," he yelled, poking his head around the hood. Joe pulled his shirt off, wiped his sweaty face, and tossed the shirt in the driveway.

"What's wrong with it?"

"One more time. Turn it on."

This time when I turned the key, the engine didn't flick on. The car sputtered. The starter clicked over and over. "Shit," I yelled, slamming my hand against the steering wheel.

I joined my brother at the front of the car. He was still elbow-deep under the hood, fiddling with wires and caps. I wasn't sure what I was looking at.

"The alternator housing's got a crack in it and the battery's dead."

He pointed to different parts of the engine. "I could get it fixed in a few days. Gotta order some parts." Joe scratched his chin. "Probably be around six hundred dollars." He dropped the hood back into place.

"All right, go ahead and do that. I'll take care of the cost." I wiped my sweaty forehead with the back of my arm. Grace probably wasn't going to feel comfortable with me paying for it, but I needed her to know I cared and that I'd do anything for her.

Joe raised his thick brow. "You're paying to get her car fixed? You must really like her."

I kicked at some loose gravel. "Just want her to feel at ease."

"If you say so," he said, picking up his toolbox. He walked to the back of his truck, hoisted the toolbox up, and closed the tailgate. "You down for grabbing a beer?"

He and I hadn't had a beer together in a long time. I think Grace being here made him think we could do brotherly things again, that we could move forward, put the past in the past, as they say. But *past* was just a word. The memories we carried kept it alive, and memories were just stories we told ourselves. Joe and I had two very different stories. He had forgotten his, but I hadn't forgotten mine.

"Yeah. That sounds good right about now. I'll let Grace know we're taking off."

Joe shook his head and let out a chuckle. "She's already got you whipped."

"No, just being courteous."

"All right." Joe made a whip noise as I headed out to find Grace.

She wasn't lying by the river anymore. I scanned the surrounding area but Grace was nowhere to be seen. I checked the back deck. Not there either. Joe met me on the side of the house.

"Where'd your girl go?"

"She's not my girl," I said. It was a lie because it felt like she was my girl.

He patted my shoulder. "I'm just messing with ya."

Grace came back into sight as we rounded the front of the house.

Dressed in a blue jean skirt and a white tank top, her face was serious. My jeans felt a little tighter just looking at her.

I didn't like the way Joe was looking at Grace, so I gave him a slug in the shoulder.

"What the hell?" He rubbed his arm.

"Stop looking at her like that."

"Like what?"

"You know," I said as we walked up to the porch. Grace's big sky-blue eyes nearly burned a hole through me.

"Is my car fixed?" she asked.

"Not yet." Joe shifted his stance. "You got a bad alternator and a dead battery. I can get it all fixed in a few days."

Grace bit at her lower lip and ran her hand down the side of her arm. She looked defeated.

"Don't worry. My brother here will have it good as new before you leave, I promise," I said, trying to calm her worries.

She hesitated. Her eyes flicked from us to her lemon of a car. "A few days." She nodded. "Okay."

"Want to join us for a beer?" Joe asked. "It'll take your mind off the fact you're stranded on this ranch with my bro." He chuckled.

I groaned and wanted to slug him again but resisted. I wanted Grace to come just so I could spend more time with her. But I also didn't want her around Joe, which was why I even agreed to grab a beer with him.

"Sure. I'd love to."

I forced a smile and hoped her tagging along wouldn't be a mistake.

Joe put his truck in park in front of Rustic Pine Tavern. Grace sat between us but leaned toward me. I wasn't sure if it was because I made her comfortable or Joe made her uncomfortable. Grace looked ahead at the old saloon. It was the largest bar in town—one of the only ones, actually. They were known for their pool tables, cheap beers, and good music. The tavern attracted everyone, from the old to the young and from the good to the bad.

"This is it?" she asked.

"Yes, ma'am," I said, shifting out of my seat. I held Grace's hand as she jumped out of the lifted truck.

"You're probably used to a swanky bar." Joe peered over the hood of the truck. "I'm sure they can fix you a cocktail."

Grace gave him a challenging look, narrowed eyes paired with a tight smile. "Beer's just fine for me."

There were a few local farmers smoking outside of the bar and right when they spotted Grace, they fell silent from their mundane conversations. They watched as she walked, and when she saw them staring, she simply gave a little wave with her fingers. That got them going. She really knew how to work people.

"She was waving at me," one of them said.

"No, it was me," another one said.

"She's too young for both of you."

"Oh, hush. My body may be weak, but my mind is still strong."

"Hey, Calvin and Joe," one of them called out with a nod.

"Who's the girl, Calvin?"

"That's his Airbnb guest," Joe said.

"Airbnb?" The old man looked confused.

"Like a hotel at your house," Joe explained.

"I should start me one of those," the old man said with a chuckle. "Pretty girls only."

Their conversation continued as we disappeared inside. Grace was already at the bar ordering three beers when we walked in. It wasn't too busy yet, just around ten people at the bar and a few playing a game of pool. Nearly all of them noticed Grace—even the women. We didn't get a lot of visitors out here, so any new person always sparked intrigue. Several patrons bobbed their heads at Joe and me. Many looked surprised to see the two of us in here together. Maxie, the bartender, smiled. She was practically a fixture of Rustic Pine Tavern, which had all the trimmings of a dive bar: slot machines, neon signs, pool tables, dartboards, and old men bellied up to the counter.

Joe picked up his pace and helped Grace with the drinks.

"Here you are, Calvin," she said, handing one over. "First round's on me."

"Thanks." I tilted the glass back, drinking nearly half of it in one big swig. Nothing better than a freshly poured beer.

Joe stood between us—always in the way. "You two down for a game of 301?"

"What's 301?" Grace asked.

"Darts. It's easy. Let me show you." Joe took her hand and led her toward the dartboard in the back. I didn't like that. He was being overly friendly with her. *Typical.*

I followed closely behind and picked up a set of darts from Maxie, the thin woman in her fifties who had been tending the bar since she was old enough to drink. "Glad to see you and Joe here," she whispered. I nodded but didn't say anything and made my way to Grace.

"You throw a dart before?" Joe asked.

Grace glanced over at me and smiled before answering his question. "Kinda. It led me here."

He gave a quizzical look. "Well, all right. Let's see whatcha got."

Grace took her spot and concentrated on the dartboard, holding her dart up and squinting her eyes. When she was ready, she fired it off. Bull's-eye.

"Holy shit," Joe said. "We got a shark on our hands."

Grace jumped up and down and threw her arms around my neck for a hug. I held her for a moment, breathing in her sweet scent. Maybe it wasn't fate that brought her here. Maybe it was skill. When she pulled away, my eyes lingered on her lips for a moment too long.

Joe held out another dart for her. "Let's see if you can do it again."

"All right."

She went back to her spot. Her fingers pinched the barrel. She brought the dart in front of her eyes, concentrating for a moment before throwing. Bull's-eye. Grace turned around with eyes wide open.

Joe shook his head in disbelief. "Well, damn. Shots are in order after that." He clapped his hands and walked toward the bar.

"Am I gonna hurt your brother's ego?" Grace teased.

"He'll be fine." I chuckled. "He is competitive though, so get your game face on."

She raised an eyebrow. "Oh, it's on."

Grace drank the rest of her beer in one swig and wiped her mouth with the back of her hand. The girl I met five days ago wasn't the girl I was seeing right now. She was like a chameleon, fitting in with whatever backdrop she happened to be a part of. I liked it but it left me wondering who the real Grace was.

"Here you are." Joe handed us each a shot.

"What is it?" She eyed the amber-colored liquid filled to the rim.

"My friend, Jack." Joe winked. He clinked his glass against mine and hers, tapped it against the table, and then threw it back. "Cheers," he said, placing the shot glass upside down. Joe drank Jack Daniel's like it was water, evident by the lack of reaction he had after slamming it.

Grace looked to me. Together, we tipped back the shots. She shook her head and swallowed hard after the liquid hit her tongue. Whiskey, like most people, wasn't something you enjoyed right away.

"Not your cup of tea, City Girl?" Joe teased.

"I'm more of a vodka girl, Country Boy," Grace hit back with a small smirk.

"You're up, bro," I said, patting him on the back. Joe smiled, gave a quick nod, and took his place in front of the dartboard.

"Having fun?" I asked.

"Always." Grace batted her eyelashes.

"I figured that much, since reading and running are fun for you." I let on a smile.

"Oh, stop." She playfully patted my shoulder.

I laughed and picked up our empty beer glasses. "Want another?"

Grace nodded, and I left her standing there. After I ordered another round, I turned back and spotted Joe leaning against the table beside Grace.

"Here you are, Calvin," Maxie said, setting the beers down.

"Thanks. Go ahead and put it on my tab."

"You got yourself a looker there." She pointed over at Grace. I followed her finger and found that Joe had moved a little closer to her. "Glad to see you out and about." She tilted her head. "But you might want to keep Joe away from her," Maxie warned.

"It was an accident," I said in a low voice.

"Some people around here don't believe that."

I shook my head. "Don't go on believing them rumors."

She squinted her eyes, and I knew then that some of her famous advice was coming my way. Maxie was more than the town's barkeep; she was the town's therapist too. Unofficially, of course—she didn't have a degree. She just knew everyone's problems and knew what everyone needed to hear.

"What one person calls a rumor, another calls the truth. I wouldn't be so quick to determine which one it is." She slapped the palm of her hand against the bar top, picked up a wet rag, and started wiping it down.

"He's my brother, Maxie." I tilted my head.

"Ted Bundy had a brother," she quipped.

"Half brother." I turned back toward Grace and Joe, watching him closely.

Maxie had a point. Maxie always had a point.

When I reached the table, I wedged myself between the two of them.

"Whoa, bro," Joe said as he fell back a step or two.

"Didn't see ya there, little guy," I jabbed.

I handed him the beer, but his eyes lingered on me for a few seconds. The golden liquid finally distracted him, and he brought the glass to his lips.

"Here you are, Grace."

"Got another one of those?" a high-pitched voice called from behind me. I turned around to find Charlotte. Her long, silky brown hair hung freely and her freckles were prominent. She must have been outside today.

"Hey, Char," I said, pulling her in for a half hug.

"I saw Joe's truck when I drove past and decided to stop. Didn't think I'd find you here too." She tilted her head.

"Didn't think I'd find myself here either," I said.

"What's up, Char-Char? Long time, no see." Joe swooped in and gave her a hug just as I released her from mine.

"Yeah, I know. You've been skimping out on the ranch chores. Got me picking up your slack," she teased.

"Sorry about that." He looked at me briefly and swallowed hard. "I've been tied up."

Joe pointed at Grace and Charlotte. "You two meet?"

"We have," Grace said. "Nice to see you, Charlotte."

"Yeah, you too."

"Let me get you a beer," I offered.

"I got it," Joe interrupted, immediately walking over to the bar. He needed to be liked. People that didn't like themselves always sought approval from others. And I knew Joe hated every fiber of himself. Guilt will do that, rot you from the inside out.

Charlotte took a seat across from Grace at the high-top table and cleared her throat. "You feeling better from your fall?"

"Much better. Calvin took good care of me." Grace smiled, and her blue eyes almost seemed to twinkle when they met mine.

"Yeah, he sure knows how to take care of all types of animals," Charlotte teased.

If Grace realized the dig, she didn't react to it. She simply grazed her hand against mine as she reached for her glass of beer. She brought it to her lips and took a long, slow drink.

"You're leaving soon, right?" Charlotte asked as if she were just making small talk, but there was nothing small about this exchange.

"Five more days, but who knows? Maybe I'll extend my vacation." Grace smiled, or maybe it was more of a smirk. I couldn't tell if she was serious or if she was just being catty with Char.

Before either of us could respond, Joe set down a beer for Charlotte and a tray of shots for the table.

"Let's get this party started," he said.

Without saying a word, Grace picked up a shot and tipped back the whiskey. This time her face was expressionless. Char narrowed her eyes, picked up a shot, tipped it back, and made a refreshing sound when she was done. Grace grabbed another. These two were going to kill themselves trying to outdrink one another.

"Whoa, slow down." I took it from her and drank it myself.

Joe did the same, slamming the other one.

"I'm just trying to keep up," Grace said in a cutesy voice.

Char rolled her eyes.

"Don't try to keep up. Set your own pace. That's the key to life." I tilted my head.

"Let's play pool," Joe said. "Teams. Grace, you can be on mine."

"Sounds good to me. Calvin and I are undefeated. Aren't we, Calv?" Charlotte smiled.

I brought the glass to my lips and took a big drink. "We actually are."

A couple of hours later, we were on our third game of pool. Char and I had won the first, but Grace surprised us all by pocketing six balls in one turn. I got the feeling she was holding back on the first game, a true shark. We were neck and neck on game three, which would decide the winning team. Joe's words slurred and his eyes were about three-quarters open.

"You're up, Charlotte," Grace said, taking a sip of her beer. Her eyes were glassy.

"I know." Char stepped up to the table.

When she went to shoot, her pool cue slipped off the white cue ball and it only moved an inch. "Damn it." She had drunk a little too much. I'm the only one that slowed down because I knew I had to get Joe and Grace home in one piece.

Joe placed his stick behind the cue ball. "Let me show you how it's done." He shot and knocked in a solid.

"Knocking in the other team's balls? That's how it's done?" Grace teased.

"Shit." Joe rubbed his brow.

Charlotte laughed and fell into me, but I held her up. "Easy there,"

I said. Her hand rested on my chest and she looked up at me with a small smile.

The song "Save a Horse (Ride a Cowboy)" ended, and Char's face lit up as her mind registered the next song the jukebox started playing. "Amazed" by Lonestar.

"I love this song. Come dance with me." Before I could answer, Char was pulling me toward the dance floor where several couples had already started dancing. I was about to protest because I didn't want Grace to get the wrong idea about us. We were just friends. But before the words left my mouth, Joe was asking Grace to dance.

We were all on the dance floor in a matter of seconds. I rested a hand above Char's hip and took her other hand in mine—just a friendly dance. But I knew she thought it was something more. I thought I made it clear there was nothing between us, but it was obvious it fell on deaf ears. My eyes went to Joe and Grace. They were positioned the same way as us. Grace looked like she was having fun. She was smiling and laughing while Joe clumsily tripped over his own feet and hers. He was going to make a fool of himself.

"Hey," Char said.

"Hay is for horses," I said.

She pulled me in a little closer. "This is nice."

"Yeah, tonight's been fun." I looked at her and then back at Grace.

"No, this," she said, caressing my shoulder.

I raised an eyebrow. She was clearly drunk. Her eyes were glazed, and I was sure she was seeing two of me. A sudden movement off to the side caught my attention. I turned to see Grace pull away from Joe and then give him a hard push. I couldn't hear what they were saying over the music. He looked stunned, and he stumbled back toward her, closing the new distance between them. Grace slapped him right across the face, leaving a red mark where her hand connected with his skin. I dropped Char's hand, and in three big steps, I was in front of Joe.

I pushed him back so hard that he nearly fell over. "What the hell are you doing?" I yelled. He got to his feet, staggering toward us. Anger took hold of me like a volcano erupting all at once. I pulled my fist back and thrust it forward, connecting with Joe's jaw. Something cracked, and he fell to the ground like a pile of bricks.

"Out!" Maxie screamed from the bar. "I won't have that in here."

My head snapped in her direction, and I mouthed, *I'm sorry*. Whispered conversations ensued and all eyes were on us.

I turned to Grace. "Are you okay?"

Her eyes were clouded with rage, something I hadn't seen from her. If looks could kill, well, Grace's would have blown up that whole damn bar. It was like she was in a trance.

"I'm fine. It was just a misunderstanding," she finally said, shaking her head slightly and massaging the hand that had slapped Joe. I shook out my own. My knuckles were raw and beet red.

Joe spit blood on the ground as he got to his feet. Blood wasn't always thicker than water. He rubbed his swollen jaw.

"You're drunk, Joe. Let me take you home." I tried to guide him to the exit but he pushed me away.

"Don't fucking touch me," he seethed and unceremoniously made his way out of the bar. All eyes followed him. Maxie shook her head and tossed a rag on the bar. She was right. I should have kept Joe away from Grace.

23.

Grace

The winding dark road was lit up by the headlights of the truck. The moon illuminated the mountainous backdrop, shimmering along part of the Wind River. It was all a dark blur around me. Everything had been a blur since I got here. I was seated in the front while Charlotte sat quietly in the back. No one had said a word since we got in the vehicle. I knew Calvin wanted to ask what Joe did to piss me off but he stayed quiet instead. He pulled into a gravel driveway. From what I could see by the glow of a dim porch light, Charlotte took good care of her property. The nicely pruned shrubbery, colorful flower beds, and array of trees all distracted from how dumpy the actual house looked—clearly a fixer-upper that hadn't been fixed up.

"I'm gonna help get her inside," he said to me.

I didn't say anything.

Calvin walked Charlotte up the sidewalk. His hand hovered by the small of her back. She stumbled a little, but he was careful to keep her upright. At the door, she struggled with the keys and ended up dropping them. Calvin bent down, scooped them up, and unlocked the door. The house slowly lit up as they made their way from one room to the next.

Something about their dynamic was strange. It was clear Charlotte was in love with Calvin, but was Calvin in love with her?

The outlines of their bodies came back into view through the large living room window. Charlotte's body leaned into Calvin's and his arms wrapped around her. Then they disappeared again. Another light flicked on, then off. Something must have happened between them at some point.

I looked at my cell phone. I had one bar of service but just as I typed in my password, the bar went away, replaced with the words No Service. *Of course.* I just wanted to check some emails but I couldn't even do that. At the start of the trip, I liked the isolation. But now, I didn't know how to feel about it. Ten minutes had passed since Calvin went inside with Charlotte. Just as I placed my hand on the steering wheel to blare the horn, he exited the house, gently closing the front door behind him. He jogged back to the truck and hopped in.

"Sorry that took so long." Calvin slid the key into the ignition and started it up. "She was pretty drunk, and I wanted to make sure she was all right. I've never seen her like that." The vehicle backed out smoothly onto the main road.

"It's fine. Is she okay?"

"Yeah. I got her some water and Tylenol and put her to bed." Calvin stepped on the gas gently.

I didn't say anything. Instead, I stared out the passenger window at nothing. It was all a dark blur.

A few minutes down the road, he spoke. "What did Joe say to you?"

I glanced over at him. "It doesn't matter. I told you, it was just a misunderstanding."

Even though it was dark, I could see his jaw tighten. He swallowed so hard that his Adam's apple visibly rose and fell. Calvin shook his head.

"I knew I shouldn't have brought him around you."

"What's that supposed to mean? Did he do something?"

His eyes were tight just like his jaw now.

I knew I was stepping over a line that Calvin didn't want to cross but I needed to know. Was Joe dangerous? Was I safe at that ranch? I looked at my phone again. *No service.*

"I really don't want to talk about Joe," he said firmly.

My eyes lingered on him. He focused on his driving as if he were studying for a test. It was far too much concentration for driving on an empty country road in the middle of the night. His hands gripped the steering wheel a little too tightly. I hadn't noticed how large and strong his hands were before. The knuckles on his right hand were an angry red from hitting his brother. I knew something was off with Joe. He was like a peach whose pit had been eaten out by insects, still supple and appealing on the outside, but no substance left on the inside. How Calvin acted around him—tense, anxious, worried—confirmed my suspicions. What had Joe done? And why was Calvin keeping it from me?

Day Six

24.

Calvin

It was just after nine in the morning when I threw open the screen door and reentered the house. All the morning chores were done, feeding and watering all the animals, milking the cows, tending to the coop, and some spring cleaning. I was up by four in the morning, barely sleeping a wink. My mind kept going back to the conversation in the truck with Grace. Why had I reacted like that? Why hadn't I opened up to her? I think I upset Grace more than Joe did because she trusted me. When we got back last night, she got out of the truck and went straight to bed without saying a word. I stood outside her door, listening. I finally went to my own room after some time—could have been minutes, maybe hours.

Surveying the kitchen, I saw the mug that I left out for Grace was still there, unused. She either wasn't up yet or she was avoiding me. Slipping off my farm boots, I padded down the hall and stood in front of her bedroom door. It was always calling me like metal to a magnet, pulling me in. I stared for a moment, then leaned my ear against it, listening closely. It was quiet. I pressed my ear against the door harder. Still quiet.

"What are you doing?"

Startled, I stepped away from the door and turned toward Grace. She pulled an Air Pod from her ear and stared at me with those big blue eyes. Dressed in a sports bra, tiny spandex shorts, and a pair of Nike running shoes, she also wore a look of concern. Her hair was pulled back in a high ponytail, and her chest, stomach, and face were glistening with sweat.

"Sorry. I was just checking to see if you were awake. I made a pot of coffee and wanted to see if you were hungry," I stammered, feeling like a fool and maybe a little bit of a creep.

"I'm not hungry." Grace was curt as she walked toward me with a blank look on her face.

"You must be feeling better if you were out for a run," I said.

"Yeah." She grabbed the door handle to her room and opened it. "Do you need anything else?"

I hesitated, glancing down at my feet and then back at her. "Listen, I'm sorry about last night. I shouldn't have shut you out. It's just . . ." I paused, sliding my thumbs in the loops of my jeans.

"It's just what?" she asked. Those big blue eyes became slits.

"It's just Joe. I've been dealing with his bullshit my whole life, and I don't like talking about him. I'm sorry, and I understand if you want to take off early. I'll reimburse you for the whole stay."

I locked eyes with her, trying to convey that I was serious and sincere. If she wanted to leave, I suppose I could respect that. Deep down, I actually thought she should leave. My family brought nothing but trouble. Bad things happened to us and to the people we cared for most. We were cursed. Our ranch was cursed, and our land was cursed.

"I can't just leave, Calvin, and you know that. My car doesn't work." She tilted her head in a challenging way.

"I know. I know." I held my hands up. "I'll get someone to come down here and work on it—someone from the auto shop so you don't have to deal with my asshole brother."

She wiped the back of her hand across her brow.

"Fine," she said. "I'm going to shower. If there were eggs and bacon made when I got out, I suppose I'd eat them." Her face was still stern but her tone had a small amount of lightness to it.

I nodded as she closed the bedroom door behind her. I hurried to the kitchen to fix her breakfast. She should have left then, but I was happy she was considering staying, or at least a part of me was—the selfish, greedy side of me.

An hour later Grace emerged from the bathroom dressed in jean shorts and a crop top that showed off more than a sliver of her midriff. Her hair was tousled to the side, still partially damp. Her cheeks were rosy, her lashes dark and long, and her lips glossy. She was still making an effort to look nice for me. That was a good sign. Always a sight to be seen Grace was. I quickly put a cheesy omelet and a few slices of bacon on a plate and set it on the table beside a fresh cup of coffee. Grace took a seat and began picking at her plate while I served myself. I sat across from her and drank a big gulp of coffee.

"How was your shower?" I asked, not knowing what to say. It was a weird question, and I cringed as soon as the words left my mouth.

She chewed on a piece of bacon. "Fine."

"How's the food?" I asked, still not knowing what to say. It was better than the shower question.

"Fine," she said.

I nodded and shoveled a forkful of cheesy eggs into my mouth, chewing carefully on the words she had said and not said. She hadn't mentioned leaving, and I was scared to ask, scared to find out if she was. Grace took a sip of her coffee and then another. She placed the mug down and twirled her fork around her plate.

"I can cancel that barbecue today if you'd like," I offered.

She shook her head. "No, you don't have to do that." Grace swallowed hard and her face softened as her eyes met mine. "Happy birthday, Calvin."

It was almost like she didn't want to say it, but thank God it was my birthday. You can't be mean to someone on their birthday, and you can't leave them either.

"Thank you." I smiled.

She picked up a piece of bacon and bit into it. For a few minutes, we ate in silence. I knew she was upset with me because I hadn't told her more, but it wasn't the right time. Plus, I didn't know what to say or even how to say it. Some stories were just hard to tell for one reason or another. When I was finished with my plate, I brought it to the sink. My eyes went back to Grace. She picked at her food and sipped her coffee. I scrubbed up my dishes, put them in the drying rack, and then proceeded to clean up the kitchen. I made a mess in my rush to have breakfast ready for Grace. There was dried egg on the burners and bacon grease on the counter and stovetop. When I turned around, I nearly knocked Grace over. She was standing right behind me, holding her plate and fork. I didn't hear her get up from the table or walk over to me. She was quiet like the early mornings in Wyoming before the sun rose and the birds woke up.

"Didn't mean to scare you," Grace said, looking up at me.

"I can take care of these." I collected the dishes from her.

We stood there for a moment only six inches apart, frozen like we were in a standoff. She dropped her chin and glanced back up at me.

"Calvin."

"Yes."

"I'll stay for now."

My mouth spread into a large grin.

"Really?"

Grace nodded. "Yeah. But promise me one thing."

"Anything."

"No more secrets."

I swallowed hard and then nodded a little too vigorously. I didn't know if it came off as sincere or forced, and I also didn't know how I intended it. Well, actually, I did.

"Good," she said, placing her hand on my chest as if she were trying to feel the beat of my heart. I'm not sure she felt it because I wasn't sure it was even there.

"Want to come to the store with me?" I asked.

Grace glanced around the empty house and then back at me, twisting up her lips as if she were pondering her answer. "Sure," she said. It wasn't enthusiastic, but I'd take it anyway. I didn't need her enthusiasm. I just needed her here . . . with me.

25.
Grace

We rounded the corner of an aisle in Dubois Super Foods. The shopping cart was overfilling with food and drinks for the barbecue, and Calvin was being extra attentive, almost too attentive. I knew he was worried that I'd leave early—that Joe, the pit of carcasses, the slaughtered chickens, Gretchen bucking me off, the isolation of the ranch, and the sheriff showing up asking about a missing woman would scare me off. Fortunately for him, I didn't scare easily. I really didn't want to leave, at least not yet. I wasn't ready to go back to my life. Despite the issues here, there was a lot I was fond of in Dubois, including Calvin. I enjoyed the way he looked at me like I was the only person that existed in the world. It was also odd though because I had only been a part of his world for six days.

"You like Oreos?" Calvin asked, holding up a package of the double-stuffed kind.

"Does a horse eat hay?"

"Perfect." He smiled and tossed them in the cart.

"Do you think Joe will show up today?"

Calvin shrugged. "Not sure. I haven't heard from him, but I have his truck—so he'll turn up."

He must have noticed the worried look on my face because he walked to me and pushed a piece of my hair behind my ear, gazing into my eyes.

"Don't worry about Joe. He probably doesn't even remember what he did last night, which is no excuse for his behavior. But I'll keep a close eye on him if he does show up," he said it all in one breath as if it wasn't the first time he had to say it.

"Okay," I said.

Calvin nodded and glanced around the store, then back at the cart. "I think we got everything. Is there anything else you wanted?"

I shook my head and proceeded to push the cart toward the front. Calvin picked up a bouquet of roses and set them in the cart.

"Who are those for?"

"Oh, just some Airbnb guest of mine."

"I should be the one buying you a present. It's your birthday."

"You're my present, Grace." Calvin smiled wide.

I knew he intended it to be sweet, but I found it kind of sad. I smiled back anyway.

There was only one checkout lane open, and Charlotte was working it. Her hair was pulled back, her skin was dull, and her eyes were blood-shot. She was clearly nursing a hangover as a half-drunk Gatorade and a bottle of ibuprofen sat beside her register. I felt fine as I never really got hangovers. I was one of the lucky ones. Genetics, as they say. I placed items from the cart onto the belt while keeping an eye on Charlotte.

"Hey, Calv, happy birthday!" Char said. Her voice went up an octave.

"Thanks. How ya feeling today?"

"A little headachy but I'm looking forward to your party. I'm gonna need a little hair of the dog." She laughed.

"I bet," he said.

Charlotte slid the bouquet of roses across the price scanner and shoved them into a bag without any care for the delicate flowers. Her eyes scanned Calvin and the groceries, and then they finally landed on me. She gave a small insincere smile.

"Didn't see you there, Grace." It wasn't a greeting, just an acknowl-edgment that I was alive and present.

Charlotte reverted her attention to Calvin. "I didn't embarrass myself last night, did I?" Her voice was flirty.

"No, not at all. I think everyone had a little too much to drink." He pressed his lips together.

"Has Joe stopped by?" she asked.

Calvin shook his head. "Nope. Haven't heard from him."

"Oh, well he was in here earlier. Bought a couple twenty-four packs of beer for the barbecue." She continued to scan and bag the groceries.

"He's still coming?" he asked.

Charlotte nodded. "I'll be honest, I don't remember much of last night." She rubbed her head, trying to conjure up the memory that was long gone. "What exactly happened?"

"It's best we just put that behind us then."

In the little bit of time I had been in Dubois, I noticed things frequently got swept under the rug. But the problem with sweeping things under a rug is eventually it all spills out. What else was hidden around here?

"Okay," Charlotte said. She hit a few keys on the register. "That'll be one hundred ninety-six dollars and twenty cents."

Calvin stuck his card into the machine without any hesitation. Someone with money problems would hesitate.

"I thought that was you, Grace," a voice from behind called. I turned back to find Betty, the woman I met at the clothing store earlier this week. She was dressed in a floral print dress with a high neckline and sleeves that went to her elbows.

"Oh, hi. How are you?" I wasn't sure why she was being so friendly toward me. At her boutique she seemed suspicious of my very presence.

"Just fine. How are those clothes working out for ya, hon?"

"They're holding up. Calvin's got me riding horses and fishing in them."

Calvin slid his card back into his wallet and pocketed it. He gave Betty a hug and whispered, "Missed you."

"Happy birthday, sugar. I know today's a complicated one but you enjoy it best you can," she whispered back.

A complicated one? Why? Was it because of his parents?

"Thanks, Betty. Grace here has been keeping me happy." He smiled and took a step back to put his arm around me. "Not sure what I'd do without her."

Betty collected some items from her basket and placed them on the belt. "Look at you two getting along so well. You're not going to want to leave, Grace." She looked at me with a tight smile.

Charlotte let out a cough. "But you *are* leaving . . . right? In four days?"

I ignored her.

"Anyway," Betty said, steering the conversation. "I was just here to pick up a few items for my famous honey cake, but I don't wanna tie you two up. I'll see ya later this afternoon."

"I can't wait. Your honey cake is heaven," Calvin gushed.

"Oh, Calv. You sure know how to make an old lonely woman feel good about herself." Betty blushed.

"You're not old and you've got me," he said, giving her a half hug. "I'll see ya later."

"Not if I see you first," she said back with a wave and a small laugh.

The dynamic between Betty and Calvin was like mother and son, but Betty wasn't his mother. His parents were dead. But Calvin never told me how they died. What happened to them, and were they the reason Calvin's birthday was, as Betty put it, complicated?

26.

Calvin

I entered the kitchen with a towel wrapped around my waist—fresh from a hot shower. Grace stood at the stove with a wooden spoon in her hand. The smell of bacon and garlic entered my nose, and I breathed deeper, trying to get more of the best scents a kitchen could offer. I knew she'd ruin it soon with those brussels sprouts.

"Whatcha doing?" I asked.

She looked over her shoulder, and I think I almost saw her mouth drop open. Her eyes scanned my dripping wet body. I had done a poor job of drying off.

"Cooking up those brussels sprouts you love so much," she said with a flirty smile.

Grace continued to stir her wooden spoon slowly, moving around the sautéed bacon and garlic, but her eyes stayed on me. I liked those eyes on me. That's where they belonged.

I took a few steps into the kitchen. "Want something to drink?"

"A beer would be great."

"You got it." I pulled two cold ones from the fridge and popped the caps off. "Here."

She took it from me, and we both tipped the beers back and drank—our eyes never breaking contact.

"Need any help?" I offered.

"No, Calvin. It's your birthday. Let me worry about everything."
She smiled, and it was inviting.

I took a step closer to her, pretending like I was trying to get a better
look at the food she was cooking up, but what I wanted was more of
Grace. She backed into me a little and turned her head, looking over
her shoulder. When she didn't jolt away or apologize, I knew this was
the moment—our moment. I leaned down a few inches and kissed her.
My lips were on hers, and all of a sudden, she was kissing me back. Her
body turned toward me. Her hands went to my back, my chest, my
stomach. Her mouth opened, and I slid my tongue in, circling around
hers. She practically moaned. I wrapped my arms around her, pulling her as close as she could possibly get to me. I could have crushed
her to ashes—that's how bad I wanted her. My hands ran through her
hair and down her back, settling on her firm backside. She pushed me
hard, and I let her, until I was thrust into the kitchen wall. The Sheet-
rock cracked behind me but I didn't care. I'd fix it later, or maybe I'd
leave it there to serve as a reminder of this very moment. The moment
Grace became mine. One of my hands moved from her backside to her
breast, grabbing it, caressing it. She moaned again. Her hand traveled
down my chest, my abdomen, through the opening of the towel, and
I grunted in pleasure when she gripped me. I moved my mouth to her
cheek, then her neck, her ear—sucking and kissing—while her hand
stroked and pulled.

Grace was all I wanted and all I needed. She was everything between the sun rising and the sun setting. She was the sensation you
get after you felt a jerk on your fishing pole (literally). She was the
smell of coffee and the burn of whiskey. She was a hard day's work
and a well-earned lazy Sunday. She was a garden full of ripe vegetables and a field of overgrown grass. She was everything and she was
nothing, which made her the perfect amount of something. I couldn't
get enough of her.

Her pull became a little harder, essentially in sync with me. My
towel fell to the ground. I brought her lips back to my mouth, and she
kissed me harder. Her tongue entangled mine like barbwire, hooking

me, holding me. Where her tongue couldn't hold, her mouth sucked and her teeth clenched, creating a subtle but pleasurable pain. The sounds that escaped me were new, but I would remember them forever, for they marked a moment in my life . . . a moment that split everything I knew in two: a beginning and an ending. Grace was the middle, the good part—the white cream between Oreo cookies, the heart of a medium-rare steak, the center of a Tootsie Pop. She was all those things and more. My hand slid down the front of Grace's jean shorts, beneath her panties, my fingers crept along her pelvic bone and just as they touched her center, the screen door flung open.

"Happy birthday, bro!" Joe yelled.

She quickly backed away from me as I bent down to pick up my towel. Joe put his hands over his eyes.

"Sorry," he said as Grace scurried to the stove, and I covered myself.

After I was covered and Grace had stirred the pan a few times, Joe moseyed into the kitchen.

"Can't you knock?" I practically seethed.

"Sorry," he said again.

I shook my head, shaking away the anger. I didn't want to scare Grace by pummeling the shit out of my brother.

"How much do you remember of last night?" I asked, quickly changing the subject.

He shrugged. "Not much."

"Sounds about right."

"I'm not sure what happened. I hadn't even drunk that much. It was weird. Like I was in a daze." He rubbed his forehead. "Felt like I had been drugged or something."

"I think you drank more than you thought you did, Joe." My eyes narrowed. "You owe Grace an apology," I added.

"I know." He nodded. "Grace," he called out.

She turned toward him, feigning interest. I had a feeling she'd already made her mind up about Joe, and I didn't blame her. I should have my mind made up about him too, but he was my brother. No matter what he did or what I thought, my brain was wired to always,

always, always give him the benefit of the doubt—whether he deserved it or not.

"Yeah, Joe."

"I apologize for last night. I can't remember what I said or did but
I know I was an ass, and I know we haven't known each other long, but
I am sorry for having to say sorry and having to have something to say
sorry about."

Grace nodded and glanced briefly at me. "It's fine, Joe. I accept
your apology."

I knew what *fine* meant. *Fine* meant it wasn't fine, but it was fine
for now. She paused and squinted. "Actually, it's fine if you get my car
fixed in the next three days."

So—she was done with me, done with whatever this was. I felt my
face frown and forced my muscles to relax, maintaining a neutral look.

"You got yourself a deal," he said. "And I really hope what I did last
night doesn't get between you and Calvin." He gestured toward me. "I
think you two are great together."

Grace simply nodded, and Joe turned to me.

"Calvin, I'm sorry about the way I acted last night. It was out of
line and it won't happen again."

I wanted to ask what was out of line and what behavior he wouldn't
do again but he didn't remember what he had done, and Grace wouldn't
tell me either. What could he have done or said to make her slap him
across the face? What made Grace tick? I really wanted to know.

"It's fine, bro. We're good."

Joe was just apologizing to apologize, to make everything good again.
He was my brother, so forgiveness was built into our bond.

"Are you doing okay today?" Joe whispered. He glanced at his boots
and then back to me and then at his boots again. It was shame and guilt
that made it hard for him to look me in the eyes. Grace peered over her
shoulder at us.

"Yeah, I'm good," I said. "Why don't you fire up the grills?"

"Sure thing, bro." He nodded, pressing his lips firmly together. "I'm
gonna grab the coolers from Wyatt's truck quick."

"Wyatt's here?" I asked.

"Yeah. How else would I have gotten here? You have my truck," Joe called over his shoulder as he disappeared outside.

Grace turned toward me. "Who's Wyatt?"

"Charlotte's ex."

And if I was being honest, I'd tell Grace she was technically my ex too . . . if one-night stands counted for anything.

27.

Grace

I went back to stirring the brussels sprouts that had partially burned during our make-out session. I figured they were still salvageable. Most things were salvageable if you put in a little extra effort. A bit of burn would give them a nice, charred flavor. My lips were swollen, and my heart was still racing from the moment we shared. I wanted more. I wanted to cancel this whole barbecue and spend the day exploring Calvin's body rather than the ins and outs of his family and friendship dynamics. Every alarm inside me was going off, saying, *don't get involved*—but there was a part of me that needed him like one needs water or food or shelter.

Calvin kissed my ear and neck. "To be continued . . ." he whispered.

I had forgotten he was still in the kitchen. I didn't say a word, and he scurried down the hallway toward his bedroom. I turned off the burner and added a honey-balsamic mixture to the pan. The sliding door off of the deck squeaked open.

"Hey," Joe called from behind me.

I took a deep breath before turning around.

"Want one?" He stood there holding two beers, one outstretched to me.

I accepted and took a swig, turning back toward the stove to continue stirring the brussels sprouts. I couldn't see his eyes, but I could feel them. I set the beer down and pushed the food from the pan into a serving bowl, pretending I didn't notice that Joe was still there.

"Whatcha making?" he asked.

"Brussels sprouts." I finally looked over at him. His eyes were right where I thought they'd be—on me.

"That's odd," Joe said. He swigged his beer.

"Why?"

"Because Calvin hates brussels sprouts."

My lips parted but I quickly pressed them together. "Oh. I didn't know that."

Calvin had lied to me about something as stupid as liking brussels sprouts. I'm sure it was because he didn't want to hurt my feelings. But it left me wondering what else he was lying about.

"Is there something I should know about today, Joe?" I lifted my chin.

"What do you mean?" He leaned against the counter and slouched his shoulders like he was trying to make himself look smaller. Maybe that's how he felt—small.

"I've noticed people have been treating Calvin like he's glass today, like he could shatter into a million pieces at any moment. Why?"

Joe swallowed hard. His eyes bounced around the room, deciding what and what not to tell me.

"Joe." I said his name sternly, probably how his dad used to say it.

His eyes now had a sheen to them. "Calvin's girlfriend, Lisa, died one year ago today. That's why we're all treating him like glass, as you put it."

I took a deep breath and nodded. "I'm sorry to hear that."

I knew about Lisa, but I didn't know it had happened on his birthday. That must have been tough. One thing stuck out though—Joe's choice of words and Calvin's. Joe had called Lisa his girlfriend, while Calvin had referred to her as his ex. Maybe it was easier to mourn her that way.

Joe swigged his beer again. "I'm glad he has you today but I'd be careful if . . ."

Before he could finish his sentence, Calvin appeared in the kitchen dressed in jeans and a T-shirt. "What are you two talking about?"

Joe straightened up and cleared his throat.

I smiled at Calvin. "Just deciding who's going to lead the happy birthday song."

He eyed both of us for a moment but then cracked a smile. "Please, please no singing."

"I guess you'll have to use your birthday wish to stop that from happening," I teased.

"That's fine. I don't need it for anything else. I already got everything I want." Calvin winked at me, then turned to Joe. "Did you get the grills going?"

"Not yet," he said.

Calvin gave him a pat on the back. "Let's get to it," he said, steering him outside. Calvin was like a sheepdog with his brother, always herding him away from me.

Joe gave me a long look but didn't say another word and left the kitchen through the sliding door.

"Need any help in here?" Calvin planted a kiss on my cheek.

I scooped three brussels sprouts onto a spoon and held it out. "Just for you to try this and tell me how great it is," I said with a coy smile, thinking, *The punishment fit the crime.*

He looked at the brussels sprouts and then at me. "I can do that," Calvin said with a gulp. As soon as he opened his mouth, I shoved the spoon right in there. He chewed quickly and swallowed hard. "So good," he lied.

He planted a quick kiss on my cheek. "Come join us outside when you're done," he called out before hurrying outside and closing the door behind him.

As I finished up in the kitchen, my thoughts went back to Joe. Why had he been so apprehensive about answering my question? *I'd be careful if . . .* If what? The words cut short swirled around my brain.

The sound of laughter pulled me from my thoughts and the kitchen. I grabbed a beer and made my way to the back deck.

Joe and Calvin were side by side, preparing the grill. Another guy, who I presume was Wyatt, stood with his legs slightly apart and his back toward me. A stream of liquid hit the patch of grass in front of him. He was as tall as Calvin but much broader in the shoulders. Calvin glanced over at him.

"Jesus, Wyatt. I have a bathroom. Stop pissing in the grass."

Wyatt shrugged and wrestled with his zipper. After he straightened himself, he leaned down and grabbed the beer sitting in the grass beside him.

"Sorry, Calv. This beer is going right through me." His voice was as thick as molasses. He took a long swig and then turned, facing me.

"Oh, shit. Sorry, I didn't realize you were standing there." The tops of his cheeks flushed.

His beard was thick and his hair was scruffy, going in all directions. Wyatt was dressed in a faded flannel shirt, ripped jeans, and dirty cowboy boots. Overall, he was unkempt in both his appearance and his manners.

"Hey there. I'm Deputy Wyatt Miller," he said, taking a few steps toward me. He extended his hand. I hesitated, not wanting to shake it since he had just urinated, but not to be rude, I put my hand in his. I had touched grosser things in my life.

"I'm Grace," I cringed. His skin was tough and tan like leather hide that had been left out to dry. "Deputy?"

"Yep, Dubois's finest," he said with a chuckle.

"Around here, they'll give anyone a badge and a gun," Joe teased.

"Except for you, Short Stack." Wyatt let out a husky laugh.

Joe flexed his thick bicep. "I come fully equipped," he said, turning his wrist in and out. The veins on his arms bounced.

I noticed Joe and Wyatt acted more like brothers than Calvin and Joe did.

"Put those away before you hurt yourself," Wyatt said. He redirected his attention back to me. "Calvin here tells me you're his Airbnb guest?"

"That's right." I glanced over at Calvin, who was busy replacing the propane tank on the gas grill.

Curiosity got the best of me and I asked, "Did you guys ever find that missing girl? Sheriff was over here the other night."

"Nope." Wyatt shook his head. "But we did find her car broken down on a back road a couple of miles outside of town yesterday. The car was cleaned out—except we found her cell phone under her driver's seat, hence why her sister wasn't able to get ahold of her. We're thinking she hitched a ride with someone, and hopefully, she's just having a hard time getting back home with no cell or car." He took a swig of his beer and slid a hand in his pocket.

Calvin put the empty propane tank to the side and dusted off his hands. "I hope you find her, but not sure why the sheriff was here asking me questions when he knew she never even checked in."

"That's the new sheriff for ya." Wyatt nodded. "He does things a little differently. I wouldn't take offense to it though, Calv. We had nothing to go on until we found her car."

Calvin shrugged and started up the grill. "Yeah, I figured that much."

"They just now found her car?" I tilted my head, making eye contact with Wyatt. "That seems odd since she's been missing for a couple of weeks, right?"

Wyatt parted his mouth, about to respond, but his head snapped toward the side of the house. I turned my head to see what suddenly stole his attention. It was Charlotte.

"Happy birthday," she called out.

Her face was bright, her smile was wide, and her makeup was apparent, unlike the other times I'd seen her all fresh-faced. Actually, wait—her makeup looked exactly like mine: long, dark eyelashes, glossy lips, and rosy cheeks. On top of that, she was dressed like me, in blue jean shorts and a black crop top.

"Hey, Char, grab yourself a beer," Calvin said, pointing to the coolers.

"You don't have to tell me twice," she said with a laugh. "Betty went in through the front with her honey cake," she added as she plucked a beer from the cooler.

"Hey, C. I missed you," Wyatt said.

Charlotte's face went sour when she laid eyes on him. "Don't call me C. That's a letter, not a name."

"Damn, Charlotte. Did you bring anything else other than your nasty attitude?" Wyatt sniped back.

Charlotte simply dismissed him by shaking her head, so I assumed this wasn't the first time he had said something like that to her. She popped the cap off her beer and took a swig. Her eyes went to me. "Have you started packing yet, Grace?"

Apparently, her nasty attitude wasn't reserved just for Wyatt. It was for me too.

Before I could speak, Joe cut in. "She's here for another four nights. Why would she start packing?" He gave her a peculiar look and shook his head.

Joe clearly didn't understand that Charlotte wanted me out of Calvin's house. The sliding door opened and out walked Betty, dressed in a full bee suit.

"What are you doing?" Joe laughed.

"Well, I figured while I was here, I may as well check on my honeybees."

"Betty, you're never not working. Make it quick, I'm about to throw the meat on the grill." Calvin flipped a spatula in the air and caught it again.

"I'll be back in a jiffy." Betty carefully walked down the steps of the deck and headed toward the apiary just in front of the woods.

I took a seat and watched Calvin work the grill while Charlotte stared at him longingly. How could he not see how she felt about him? That girl was more than in love. She was obsessed. Maybe he knew that. And maybe he liked the attention. But why the hell was she dressed like me? I looked down at my clothing, then back at hers, and considered changing into something else. But imitation was the sincerest form of flattery. Joe and Wyatt tossed around a football. Every time Wyatt threw or caught the ball, he looked over at Charlotte. He was like a child seeking his parent's attention to show off how talented he was—but she was paying him no mind.

Charlotte walked over to Calvin, engaging him in a whispered conversation. She playfully tapped his forearm and giggled like a schoolgirl.

Wyatt, realizing he wasn't getting the attention he desired, stopped playing catch and took a seat on the love seat across from me. Joe sat down next to him, putting his feet up on the coffee table. I was about to ask about the missing girl again, but Wyatt spoke first.

"So, you got a man back home?" he asked.

I shook my head. "No."

Wyatt flashed a smile and nudged Joe with his elbow.

"You like my brother?" Joe asked.

I cleared my throat and glanced at Calvin, who was still in whispered conversations with Charlotte.

"I think I might."

Joe let on a small smile. "Well, like I was trying to say earlier, I'd be careful with my brother there. He tends to fall hard."

I tilted my head. "How hard?" I wasn't looking for anything serious.

Joe's eyes narrowed slightly and he quickly glanced back at his brother.

"Joe, what are you telling her?" Calvin called from the grill.

He cleared his throat and relaxed his eyes. "Just that you're a big softie."

Calvin's face turned a little red. "Get over here and man this thing."

Joe stood from his chair. "If I don't mess with him, he'll be at that grill all night and you won't have any time with him. You're welcome." He winked, grabbed the spatula and tongs from Calvin, and took his spot in front of the grill. It was like Joe felt he owed Calvin something, but I wasn't sure why that was.

Calvin picked up two beers and sat down beside me, handing one over. Charlotte was only a few steps behind him like a puppy following its human. She took Joe's open seat right next to Wyatt. He sat up a little taller. Charlotte glanced at Wyatt and gave him a challenging look, but he just smiled back.

"Anyone else coming?" Wyatt asked.

Calvin placed his hand on my knee and gave it a gentle pat. I leaned a little into him. "Yeah, Dr. Reed and Patsy."

I looked to Wyatt and Charlotte. "So, you two are exes?"

"Don't remind me," she scoffed.

"We are not exes. We're just taking a break," Wyatt challenged.

She jutted out her chin. "We're not getting back together, Wyatt. That means we're exes."

"I'm not giving up on us." He shifted in his seat, angling himself toward her. "You randomly broke up with me for no good reason."

"You two are really cute together," I chimed in with a grin. Sometimes you just had to stir the pot.

"See, C? We're good together."

Charlotte elbowed him in the side and swigged her beer. I knew he thought she was just being flirty because he smiled and patted her knee like Calvin had done with me. He probably thought he saw a spark re-ignite between them. I knew there was nothing flirtatious about it. It was a spark . . . a spark of violence. Charlotte didn't want to flirt with Wyatt. She wanted to hurt him. I wondered what exactly had gone wrong between them. Wyatt seemed like a nice enough guy, a little rough around the edges, but I'd expect that from a country boy. Perhaps nothing went wrong between them. Perhaps something went right between her and someone else.

"Why did you two break up?" I asked, deciding to continue to poke the bear named Charlotte.

"I don't know." Wyatt shook his head. "One day we were good and the next she was breaking it off."

"We were not good together," she spit.

Wyatt narrowed his eyes. "We were."

Betty let out a yell. "The bees are so agitated!" Her voice was panicked.

Calvin stood quickly and helped her out of her beekeeping hat, gloves, and suit.

I noticed red splotches on her hands and neck. The bees had made their way inside her suit. It's ironic how the ones you care for most are the ones that are most easily able to crawl inside you and do damage.

"What happened?" Calvin asked.

"It seems like they had been messed with. They were buzzing all around, trying to sting me, and they ain't usually like that."

"Betty, they're bees. They're not trained. What do you expect?" Joe crumpled up his face and flipped a burger patty on the grill.

Betty scratched at her neck and shot him a glare, but quickly softened it. "You wouldn't understand, Joe. Your dog doesn't even know its own name."

Joe shook his head and chuckled, turning over the brats.

Charlotte set her beer down and stood. "Let me help you apply something to those stings."

Betty nodded, and Charlotte helped her into the house, closing the sliding door behind them.

"What's with Betty?" Joe asked.

Calvin put his thumbs in the loops of his jeans like he usually did when he was apprehensive or didn't know what to say. I had only known him for six days, and I had already picked up on that little tell of his. He would never do well in poker. Too many tells.

"Don't go saying this to anyone else." He lowered his voice. "But when I took Grace to Dr. Reed after she fell off the horse, he mentioned Betty hadn't refilled her prescription in two months."

Joe's eyes went wide. "Have you talked to her?"

"Of course not. Dr. Reed shouldn't have told me that in the first place. He could lose his license to practice." Calvin rubbed his forehead.

"Chicks be crazy, am I right?" Wyatt said, swigging his beer.

Calvin rolled his eyes.

Joe shrugged. "This is a small town. Who really has a license around here?"

"I would hope a doctor would. Dr. Reed removed my appendix." Calvin gave a look of dismay.

"Yeah, and you've never been able to do a full sit-up ever since." Wyatt let out a laugh.

Calvin rolled his eyes and flicked a hand at him. "Everyone knows crunches are more effective."

"Says the guy with a four-pack."

Joe shuffled to the side and peered in through the patio door before settling back into place. "What are you going to do?"

"I'll say something to her, but not today."

Joe shook his head and straightened up, flipping a burger again. "Grace, you like . . . meat?" he asked just as the sliding door opened. Betty emerged, followed by Charlotte. It was clear he had intended to ask something else but quickly changed the subject.

"How ya feeling?" Calvin asked.

Betty's neck and hands were covered in red splotches. There was a slight jelly glisten over each mark where Charlotte had rubbed Neosporin. It felt like this whole town had Neosporin rubbed over it—something to conceal it, make it feel better, look better—but beneath the jelly glisten, there was irritation, pain, maybe even venom.

"Yeah, much better, darling." Betty's eyes bounced over all of us like a pinball in an arcade.

"Hello," a voice called from around the corner.

Calvin, Wyatt, and Joe all yelled, "Hello." Dr. Reed rounded the side of the house, carrying a large package covered in white butcher paper. Patsy, his secretary, walked beside him holding a bottle of sauvignon blanc.

"Whatcha got there, Doc?" asked Calvin.

"A dozen New York strip steaks. Happy birthday," he said with a smile.

"Thanks, Doc. You didn't have to do that."

Dr. Reed patted him on the back. "I don't have to do anything, doesn't mean I won't." He then greeted each of us.

"Nice to see you," I said when his eyes landed on me.

Dr. Reed closed the distance and gave me a half hug, eyeing me in a doctorly way. "You feeling all right?"

"Perfectly new, thanks to you." I nodded and smiled at him.

"And Calvin took good care of you?"

"Only second to you."

He smiled back and glanced over at the boys. "Calvin, you didn't tell me my favorite patient would be here." Dr. Reed put an arm around me.

"Damn, Doc. I thought we were close." Joe dramatically grabbed at his chest.

"Oh, we are . . . a little *too* close." Dr. Reed's eyes widened and then he let out a hefty chuckle.

"Ha ha." Joe uncapped a beer and handed it to the doc.

Dr. Reed took a swig and his eyes found Betty. "Oh no, what happened to you?"

She shook her head and looked at her blotchy hands. "Bees got me. Not like them at all."

Dr. Reed gave her a concerned look. "You put something on them?" He was clearly worried about her well-being, and it went beyond the bee stings.

"Of course," she said.

He pulled her off to the side and they continued a whispered conversation. The boys bantered back and forth while Charlotte looked on.

I moseyed over to Patsy who was still holding that bottle of wine.

"You look much better than the last time I seen you," she said.

"Thanks." I smiled. "Would you like me to open that?"

"Oh yes, please. Dr. Reed picked this up for me." Her grin widened. "He's so good to me."

"He seems to be good to everyone."

"He takes care of this whole town. Without him, we'd all be dead," she chuckled.

I gave a small awkward smile and told her I'd be right back.

I spotted a wineglass on the top shelf of one of the cupboards in the kitchen. Standing on my tippy toes, I reached up, barely grasping it with my fingertips. The glass slipped from my hand and hit the floor with a crash, shattering into pieces.

I let out a heavy sigh. "Shit."

"Don't you hate when things like that happen in places you don't belong?" Charlotte's voice was like a knife being dragged along concrete.

I turned to find her standing with one hand on her hip and a smirk on her face. She was clearly pleased with her comment.

I ignored what she said and asked where the cleaning supplies were.

"I know where everything in this house is," she said, walking to the fridge and pulling out a broom and dustpan from beside it.

When I extended my hand for them, she shook her head. "I got it. I wouldn't want you to get hurt."

I rolled my eyes and tiptoed out of the way, sliding open a drawer in search of a corkscrew. Charlotte acted like the ranch was her territory. But the question was, how far would she go to protect it, and what would she do if she couldn't?

She pulled one from a drawer I hadn't yet rummaged through. "Here," she said, handing it to me.

Charlotte opened the cupboard and grabbed another wineglass, placed it on the counter, and then went back to sweeping.

I brought the glass and corkscrew to the kitchen table to uncork the bottle. My eyes bounced back and forth between Charlotte and the task at hand. I didn't trust her.

"I'm curious," she said, pausing her sweeping. "Why would a girl from New York City vacation alone in this blip of a town?"

I glanced back at her.

She raised her brows and stared into my eyes. "And why this ranch? Why Calvin?"

I tilted my head. "People want what they don't have. I have the bustling and loud concrete city. I don't have the quiet countryside. The rest was random . . . or fate, as some would call it."

The cork made a *plop* when I removed it from the bottle, and I poured a hefty glass for Patsy.

Charlotte leaned down and swept the broken glass into the dustpan. "I don't believe in fate."

"I don't either."

She walked to the trash can, dramatically stepped on the pedal to open the lid, and looked to me. "It's funny how something that once had a purpose can end up in the trash." Charlotte tipped the dustpan, letting the broken glass fall into the garbage.

I'm not sure if she was threatening me or just trying to be theatrical. In my experience, insecure women were other women's greatest enemies because they'd do anything to further mask their own uncertainties. I brought that out of Charlotte. She clearly wanted Calvin but couldn't have him. Perhaps she had convinced herself that Calvin just wasn't interested in anyone, but with me here, her previous notions were proven false.

"Did something happen between you and Calvin?" I asked.

She narrowed her eyes and pursed her lips together. "Why? Did he say something?"

If I told her yes, I knew she'd tell me more. If I told her no, I knew it would anger her. Did I want to know more, or did I want to just piss her off right now? I was tired of her hanging around, and I wasn't sure how much longer I could bite my tongue.

"No, he doesn't talk about you at all."

Charlotte's eyes looked like glass. She inhaled and exhaled sharply. Her hand clenched into a fist by her side.

"You know what. In four days, you'll be gone, and I'll still be here." She raised her chin and smirked.

"I wouldn't be so sure about that."

Charlotte let out a huff and returned the broom and dustpan to their place. She stomped across the kitchen and threw open the sliding door. Before exiting, she turned and looked at me. "I hope Joe keeps you here permanently."

I drew my brows together. But before I could ask her what she meant by that, she slammed the door closed behind her.

28.

Calvin

Grace walked out onto the deck with a full glass of wine and handed it to Patsy. She had a worried look on her face, and I wondered what it was she was bothered by. Maybe it was spending the afternoon with my friends and family. But she was fitting in real nice here. I took a long swig of my beer while I watched her. She had no problem talking to anyone. Some people enter your life and it's as if they were always there. Grace was one of those people, and I hoped she would always be there.

Betty tapped me on the shoulder. "You knocking boots with Grace?"

I coughed and choked on my beer as it went down the wrong tube. "What?" I asked. My voice croaked.

Betty patted me on the back. "You heard me, Calvin. Are you knocking boots with Grace?"

I looked over at Grace. She bent down and grabbed two beers from the cooler. My attention went back to Betty. "Why would you ask that?"

"Just want to make sure you're protecting yourself. She's gone in, what, four, five days, so don't go falling in love with her, Calvin. She don't belong." Betsy spoke softly and sternly.

"I know you mean well. But I'm grown, and you don't need to watch out for me anymore."

"I'm always going to watch out for you, Calvin, like you were my own," she said, raising a brow. "And that ain't ever gonna change."

"Thought you could use another." Grace interrupted, handing me a beer. She smiled at Betty, and I saw Betty's mouth twitch as she forced one back.

Betty backed away. "I'm going to put all the food out."

"Let me help you," Grace offered, taking a step toward her.

Betty put her hand up in protest and then lowered it. "On second thought, I'd love the extra help." Her smile twitched again.

I wasn't sure what she was up to, but she was clearly up to something. With Betty off her meds, her behavior could be quite unpredictable.

"Char, come help us with the food," Betty called out, beckoning her with her hand.

Charlotte nodded and followed them inside.

"Damn, Calvin. You look at her as if the sun won't rise tomorrow," Wyatt said with a laugh.

Joe smacked him in the arm. "Since when are you poetic?"

"Since I've been trying to win Charlotte back." Wyatt slugged Joe's shoulder. "I've been reading a lot of them Colleen Hoover romance books while I'm working speed traps. Ain't no one getting tickets, but I'm learning a lot." He swigged his beer. "And that lady sure can make me cry," Wyatt said, shaking his head.

I laughed and turned to the grill, lifting the cover. Some of the meat was done so I started taking it off and placing it on a platter.

"What happened between you two anyway?" Joe asked.

"I don't know. Just one day she told me she didn't want to be with me anymore. No reason given." Wyatt sighed.

"Think she was cheating?" Joe asked.

I glanced over my shoulder at them.

Wyatt frowned. "Well, I *didn't* think that. But now I do."

"Why would you say that, Joe?" I shot daggers at my brother for putting that thought in his head.

Joe shrugged. "Girls don't just go breaking up with guys for no reason."

I flipped the steaks again, ensuring they had nice grill marks on both sides.

"Enough about C and me before I get weepy. What's going on with you and Grace?" Wyatt patted my shoulder.

I slid a thumb into the loop of my jeans and rocked back and forth on my heels. "That, I don't know."

"You kidding me?" Joe laughed. "I walked in on you two. You were naked."

Wyatt smirked. "You hound dog."

I pulled the steaks off and felt my face get warm. I was surely blushing.

My eyes went to the house after I closed up the grill. I couldn't see Grace, but I knew she was in there—probably heating up her nasty brussels sprouts or helping Betty with the honey cake. She was in my house, and I liked her there. It's where she belonged no matter what Betty or anyone in this town thought, and I was determined to keep her.

"Look at you. My brother's falling in love with a city girl."

"That girl is going to rip your heart out," Wyatt said. "Trust me. Charlotte did the same to me."

"I hate to say it, but Wyatt has a point." Joe lowered his chin. "She's leaving in four days."

"Not to sound cliché, but I think I can get her to stay." I immediately regretted the words as they left my mouth.

Wyatt and Joe glanced at one another and then gave me a puzzled look.

I knew Grace wanted me. And I wanted her. And at the end of the day, there was nothing complicated about that.

"What are you going to do? Lock her in the basement?" Joe chuckled.

"I got an extra set of handcuffs," Wyatt teased.

Shaking my head, I laughed with them but it was forced because I was dead serious. I swigged my beer, imagining a life with Miss Grace Evans. I hoped I wouldn't have to imagine it for much longer.

29.

Grace

While Betty sliced her honey cake, she hummed "Tiptoe Through the Tulips" by Tiny Tim; I found it quite unnerving. Charlotte brought the coleslaw, potato salad, and condiments out of the fridge while glancing over at me every twenty seconds as if on cue. I wanted to ask her what she meant by what she said earlier, but not in front of Betty. Betty seemed like a busybody and that was the last thing I needed. I poured the skillet of sizzling brussels sprouts into a large serving bowl. It was the second batch I heated up, and there was far too much for this size of barbecue, especially since Calvin hated them.

"So, Grace . . . do you feel like you got what you were looking for out of this vacation?" Betty slid a knife through her cake. It slapped against the cutting board, punctuating her question that was thinly veiled as innocent but I knew it was anything but.

Charlotte paused and looked to me, waiting for an answer.

"Not yet. Still have lots to do." I brought the pan to the sink and turned on the faucet. The hot skillet sizzled under the water while a cloud of steam filled the air around me. It felt like I was in some sort of standoff with these two women—like they were Calvin's protectors. Charlotte, the wannabe lover, and Betty, the stand-in mom. I understood wanting to protect the people you love, but they went beyond that. It had to be because of his parents and ex. Death made people paranoid and cautious—to a fault.

Betty gave a slight nod while Charlotte went back to unsealing the condiment bottles.

I decided this was the time to find out more about Calvin because he hadn't been exactly forthcoming.

"What happened to Calvin's parents?" I asked.

Betty squeezed her eyes tight, and Charlotte's head shook from side to side. I had hit a nerve. Something bad had happened to them—that I was sure of. I could see it in Calvin's eyes and Joe's excess drinking.

Betty opened her eyes, flicking them toward me. "That's not really a topic of conversation I'm interested in discussing."

I had a feeling she wouldn't tell me what really happened. These people were full of secrets, and it seemed they intended on keeping it that way. I shut the water off and put the pan in the drying rack.

"Sorry," I muttered.

"No need to apologize. Just know your place," Betty said matter-of-factly.

The sliding door opened, and Calvin popped in. "Food's ready, ladies." He walked to the counter and leaned over the honey cake. "It looks as good as it smells, Betty."

"Thanks, Calvin. Only the best for the birthday boy." She smiled.

He strolled to me and slung an arm around my shoulder. "Your dish looks great too," he whispered, planting a kiss on my forehead. I knew he was lying.

Charlotte's eyes darkened. "Calvin, can you help carry some of this?" She collected the containers of potato salad and coleslaw.

Her eyes brightened when he glanced in her direction, always changing colors like a mood ring. Calvin couldn't see it but I could. I knew what she was doing. She was the type of woman who would do whatever it took to get what she wanted. And what she wanted was Calvin. But I was in the way.

30.
Calvin

Carrying in empty serving bowls and a bag of trash, I found Grace at the sink washing dishes with her back turned to me. The barbecue had gone well, and it was actually nice getting everyone together again. I think Grace enjoyed herself too, which was all that mattered. I stopped in my tracks and observed her. I could watch her all day. The outline of her body curved in and out in all the right places. Her long blond hair was tied up in a high ponytail, giving me a glimpse of her slender neck. I wanted my lips on it, on every part of her, leaving no inch of her skin untouched or unmarked by me. She must have sensed me standing there because she snapped her head in my direction. Her shoulders tensed.

"Hey," I said. "I didn't mean to startle you."

"It's fine." She relaxed her face and exhaled deeply. "I'm just a little jumpy."

I wasted no time strolling over to her, wrapping my arms around her waist, leaving a trail of kisses along her neck and jawline.

Grace pushed into me and laughed. "Did everyone leave?"

"Yeah."

She turned, facing me. Her teeth sunk into her lower lip. "Good." Those blue, blue eyes seemed to double in size.

I leaned down and kissed her again. Wet, soapy hands wrapped around my neck but I didn't mind. Grace kissed me back like she was hungry.

The sound of someone clearing their throat interrupted us. *Damn it.* Grace and I immediately pulled away from one another. Char stood in the entryway, holding a wire basket with less than a dozen eggs in it. Grace turned toward the sink and submerged her hands in the dishwater.

"Hey Char, thought you left," I said nonchalantly.

She looked angry—actually, more hurt than anything. Her eyes were shiny and red, which could have been from drinking beers all afternoon, but I hadn't noticed them like that when she was leaving earlier.

"Yeah, I was but decided I may as well gather the eggs before I left." She tossed the basket onto the floor. A couple eggs fell out and splattered against the tile.

"Jesus, Charlotte." I threw my hands up.

Without another word, Charlotte stomped out the back door. Grace glanced over her shoulder and raised her brows.

"I'll be right back," I said, letting out a sigh.

I caught up with Charlotte just as she was getting into her car. My hand blocked her from closing the door, and I grabbed it, pulling it open. Tears streamed down her face while she scrambled with her keys.

"What is your problem?"

Char looked up with narrowed eyes and leapt out of her seat at me. "Me? Me? What's wrong with *you?*" She shoved a finger into my chest.

"Nothing." I took a step back, putting my hands up.

"What are you doing with Grace?" She seethed.

"It's none of your business." I shook my head and stared off at the setting sun. That's how I felt. Half here, half gone. I'd felt that way for a long time.

"It is my business." Her voice cracked. More tears escaped her eyes.

"Char, are you drunk? I can take you home."

"No, I'm not fucking drunk, Calvin!" She kicked at the gravel and peered up at me. "Can't you see it?"

A blank look came over me. "See what?"

"Grace. There's something not right about her." Char's eyes widened as she spoke. "Why is she here? It doesn't make any sense."

"She's on vacation. How many times do I have to say that?"

"A million because it doesn't make any sense." She took a small step toward me and put her hand on my forearm. "Please, tell me you see that."

I sighed. "I don't."

Char pulled her hand away and folded her arms in front of her chest. "Is that it then? Are you with her now?"

"If I say yes, are you going to stop all of this?" I gestured to her with my hands. I was tired of Charlotte. She was walking a fine line.

"What about us?"

"There is no us."

Her bottom lip trembled. "But . . . we slept together."

"One time. I'm sorry, Charlotte, but that's all it was for me—one time." She just didn't understand no matter how much I told her. She even broke up with Wyatt, thinking there was a chance with me. I regretted sleeping with her right after I finished. It was a moment of weakness, and my one moment of weakness had left her permanently weak. I knew I had to be mean to get Charlotte to understand that she and I were never going to be anything other than friends. I let out a deep breath and stared directly into her eyes.

"Charlotte, I want every night with Grace, but with you, one night was enough."

In her weakened state, she immediately broke. Her face crumpled and tears poured out of her eyes like a faucet in her brain just turned on. When an animal was suffering, the most humane thing you could do was put it out of its misery. I hoped this was enough for Charlotte.

Without saying a word, she got into her car, turned on the engine, and slammed on the gas. Her tires did the rest of the talking as they spit up dirt and gravel.

I let out a sigh of relief as I watched her car disappear down the road. I wouldn't be made to feel guilty for liking Grace. I had four days left with her, and I wanted to make them the best four days of her life. I didn't care what Char thought, or Joe, or Betty, or any of them. This town wasn't good to outsiders. They didn't like people that were different

than them. But I did. I'd always been much more welcoming to strangers. Perhaps because I knew what it felt like to be different, and I myself
felt like an outsider sometimes.

Back inside, Grace was finishing up by wiping down the counters. She took care of everything, and it was my turn to take care of her.

"How'd it go?" she asked, wringing out the dishrag over the sink.
She looked back at me, waiting for me to speak, but I was just in awe
over her.

I shrugged and looked down at my feet. "We both said some things
we shouldn't have."

Grace dried her hands off with a towel. "It's probably best she doesn't
come around here for a while," she said, tilting her head.

I nodded and walked to her, lifting her chin with my hand. "Let's not
talk about anyone else. I just want to focus on you." I sealed it with a kiss.

"I like that idea." She smiled.

"I have a surprise for you. Come with me." I took Grace by the hand
and led her outside. Out on the porch, I picked up a picnic basket I put
together earlier in the day.

"What's that?" she asked.

"Shhh . . . it's a surprise."

We walked out to the pasture with only the light from the stars
guiding us. It hadn't rained in a while, so the grass crunched beneath
our feet. The night would have been completely silent if it weren't for
the buzzing cicadas. I never understood how such small creatures could
make so much noise. I held her hand tightly to keep her steady on some
of the uneven ground. Grace leaned her shoulder into me as we made
our way to the spot I prepared earlier.

"Stand right here," I said, letting go of her hand. From the picnic
basket, I pulled out a lighter and lit a circle of ten tiki torches. Grace
gasped as the area came to light. I smiled and pulled a blanket from the
basket, laying it out in the center of the torches. Her blue, blue eyes
looked like crystals.

"Have a seat," I said as I unwrapped a plate of grapes and sliced
cheese and set out two glasses and a bottle of red wine.

Grace smiled, slid her shoes off, and sat down while I uncorked the wine and poured it.

"Here you are, Miss Grace Evans," I said, extending a glass to her.

"Thank you, Mr. Calvin Wells."

I slid my shoes off and took a seat next to her. "Cheers, to you, Grace. Thank you for being not only a guest in my home but a guest in my heart too." It was a cheesy toast, and I regretted it as soon as the words slithered out of my mouth, but she didn't seem to mind it.

She clinked her glass against mine and smiled. "Perhaps I'll take residence up in both."

Maybe I wouldn't have to convince her to stay. Maybe she had already convinced herself she wasn't leaving. We both sipped slowly.

Grace pulled the glass from her lips and glanced around the pasture. "This is really nice."

"I'm glad you like it."

She scooched a little closer, leaning her head on my shoulder. A loud whistle came from the mountains. Grace jumped, her eyes bouncing in all directions.

"What was that?"

I put my arm around her and pulled her into the crook of my shoulder. "Just a mountain lion."

"Just a mountain lion? Are we safe?" Her voice was higher pitched than usual.

"Yeah. They don't come out this far," I said with a laugh. "And if they did, I'd protect you."

Her body relaxed a little and she took another sip of her wine.

"Oh, one more thing. I almost forgot." I pulled the teddy bear from the basket. "For your comfort."

Grace bumped her shoulder into me. "Mr. Snuggles." She held it against her chest.

"You gave him a name?"

"Of course, I did."

"It's cute." I kissed her on the cheek, and she sank further into me.

We sipped at our wine, listening to the sounds of the night. Crickets chirping. Coyotes howling. And mountain lions whistling. I refilled both our glasses, and we clinked them together again. My skin pulsated just being this close to Grace, like a bee buzzing near a flower. I wanted Grace more than I had ever wanted anything in my life. Actually, I didn't want her. I needed her.

"I really love it out here," she said.

"I really love you out here."

She raised an eyebrow but didn't say anything.

I let out a cough and drained the rest of my red wine. "You know what I mean," I corrected with a laugh.

Grace finished her drink in one gulp. "I think I know exactly what you mean," she said, and then she didn't hesitate to put her lips on mine.

I kissed her again and again. She wrapped her arms around me and pulled me on top of her. I pushed a few pieces of blond hair from her face and traced her full lips with my finger. Her eyes reflected the flame from the nearest tiki torch. She had fire in her eyes. I looked at her, wondering what she was thinking. The flame danced in her irises, but she quickly extinguished it when she closed her eyes and pulled me to her.

Just like the last time I kissed Grace, her tongue grabbed onto mine and her teeth sank into my lower lip, delivering that subtle feeling of pain meets pleasure. I moaned, and she bit a little harder. She ran her hands through my hair as she kissed me. I tore my mouth from hers and kissed her neck and ear, biting and licking. She lifted her hips to me, giving me the green light.

"I want you, Grace." I whispered hot breath into her ear.

A gentle breeze blew out six of the tiki torches, leaving just enough light to see only part of her face. Grace brought her hands to the bottom of my shirt. Her fingers curled beneath it, and she tugged it over my head. Running her nails down my neck, chest, and abs, she smiled.

I grabbed her shirt and she lifted her arms, allowing me to remove it. She was wearing nothing underneath. My hands immediately went to her breasts, cupping them, squeezing them.

Grace pushed me off of her and rolled me onto my back. She straddled me and then leaned down to continue kissing but only for a moment. Her lips left mine and left a wet trail going down my body. She unbuttoned my jeans and pulled part of me out of them. I laid under the stars while the most beautiful woman in the world devoured me. How did I get so lucky?

I stopped her before I finished. I couldn't have the first time with Grace end so quickly. I wanted it to last forever. I wanted us to last forever. I'd never need another woman again if I had her, I told myself. I pulled her back up to me and kissed her again. Grace rolled onto her back, and I settled in between her legs, sliding her bottoms down. Kneeling in front of her, I took her all in. She was like a piece of art. She begged to be looked at, examined, studied. Grace smiled up at me. Her lips were swollen from our kisses. The fire returned to her eyes. I parted her legs a little more and brought my face to her center. I wanted to taste all of her. She moaned when my lips brushed against her most sensitive skin. She gasped as I went to work. Grace tasted sweet like a strawberry. Her back arched, and I ran one of my hands up her stomach, settling onto her breast. She grabbed a fistful of my hair as my tongue quickened.

"Calvin," she said breathlessly. "I want all of you too."

That excited me more, and I wanted her to lose control. I wanted her body to shake and tremble. I wanted her heart to race. I wanted her skin to sweat, her legs to quiver. I wanted her to explode, to cry out, to beg me to stop. I squeezed her breast hard. Everything I wanted out of her; she gave. She moaned so loudly, it sounded like the howl of a wild animal. Her whole body tightened, and she grabbed at my hair, yanking up on it.

And then she nearly collapsed. "It's too much," she gasped.

I went a little longer, making sure she felt more pleasure tonight than she had in her whole life.

Grace opened her eyes as I crawled up her. She panted while I kissed her neck and ear. When she was ready, she let her legs fall farther apart, inviting me inside.

I grabbed a condom from the picnic basket and held it up with a smile. "Packed it just in case."

"Good," she whispered.

It took a few seconds to unwrap it and put it on. "Are you sure?" I asked.

She nodded. I kissed her again and then settled between her legs. I stared into those blue, blue eyes where the fire danced and slowly lowered myself into her. She moaned when I was inside and so did I. Her hands grabbed at my back, the scarlet red fingernails digging into my skin as I thrust in and out of her. I cried out when she drew blood, but I kept going. Sometimes pain felt just as good as pleasure.

"Don't stop," she said.

"Never."

I wrapped my hand around a clump of her blond hair and yanked it. I felt her center clench me, and I nearly lost it right there.

Grace felt so good—like the feeling of a warm bed on a chilly night, or the cold side of your pillow on a hot evening. I let go of her hair and ran my hand up and down her body. She orgasmed more than once. I could feel it like a jolt of electricity. My body tensed up. This was it. Grace felt too good to hold back and all at once I collapsed. She kept pushing up into me, our sweaty skin gliding against one another. It was too much, too sensitive, and I pulled completely out of her.

"You're goddamn amazing, Grace," I said in between breaths. I rolled on my side to face her.

Grace laid on her back and looked up at the stars. There was no point in looking at them now. They paled in comparison to her.

"That was incredible."

She didn't say anything. She just nodded.

I had never felt that with anyone else. We were in tune with one another. Our bodies craved the same touch, the same energy. We were like animals tearing into one another. Grace was the best I ever had. And thinking that made me wonder if I was the same for her.

"Whatcha thinking?" I asked, immediately regretting my question. It was something girls who were hung up on boys asked. I couldn't help it. I wanted to know.

Grace turned her head toward me. The flame intensified in her blue eyes. "I'm thinking . . ." She bit her lower lip. "That I don't want this to end."

I smiled. "I was thinking the same thing."

"Calvin."

"Yes, Grace."

"There are no secrets between us."

I wasn't sure if it was a question or a statement, but I nodded. "No secrets," I said. But I wondered what made a secret. Was it having information that you hadn't yet shared with the other person, or was it intentionally lying and withholding information? If she didn't ask, was it a secret?

"What happened to your parents?"

I let out a sigh. It wasn't something I liked talking about but I agreed to no secrets, and she did ask. "They died in a fire."

Her mouth dropped open. "I'm so sorry, Calvin."

We sat in silence for a little while. I didn't know what to say. The past belonged in the past, and there was no sense in talking about it.

"Can I tell you something?"

I scooched a little closer toward her. "You can tell me anything, Grace."

"Earlier today, Charlotte said something that I didn't understand, but it made me uncomfortable." She tucked her chin in.

"What did she say to you?"

"She said she hopes Joe keeps me here permanently." Grace furrowed her brow.

I looked up at the sky and screamed internally. Char and Joe were going to mess all this up for me.

"What did she mean by that?" she asked.

"I don't know."

"You said no secrets."

I let out a sigh. "I told you about my ex, Lisa."

Grace nodded. "Yeah, she died in a car accident."

"One year ago today. Joe was driving that night."

Her eyes widened.

"We had gone out for my birthday. He drove us back because Lisa and I had a little too much to drink. He hit an elk going sixty not far down the road from here. Lisa was gored by the elk. She died before the paramedics arrived. I walked away with cuts and bruises. Joe suffered a traumatic brain injury. He was in a coma for a week. He doesn't remember anything about the night of the accident. Doctors said he probably never will." I looked to Grace, gauging her response.

"That's awful. But why would Charlotte say something like that?"

"Some people think Joe hit that elk on purpose."

"What? How could they think that?"

"Because the police didn't find any tire marks, meaning he never hit the brakes." I folded in my lips.

"I don't understand. Why would he even do that?"

"Joe's always resented me. I don't blame him though. Dad was harder on him even though Joe did everything he asked. He stayed here working on the ranch while I left. And when they died, they still left it to me." I let out another sigh.

Grace pulled the teddy bear to her chest. "Do you remember anything? Do you really think he would do that on purpose?"

I laid back and stared up at the sky full of stars.

"I just remember the car going sixty and then not going at all. I was in the back seat, half asleep, so I didn't see it. I wish I could sit here and say there's no way my brother could have done that, but I really don't know."

"And he's not in jail for vehicular manslaughter?"

"He got a year in county but was released after six months. Since it was an animal-related accident, they went easy on him. If he hadn't been going five over the speed limit, they wouldn't have charged him at all."

"I don't know what to say, Calvin." Grace laid beside me, staring up at the sky.

"That night changed Joe." I looked over at Grace. "When he came out of the coma, he wasn't the same."

"How so?" she asked.

"He's angry, reckless, impulsive. It's like there's a darkness in him,

festering. I'm not sure what he's capable of now. I think killing someone changes you."

She swallowed hard.

Joe had demons. Deep down, we all did. The things we think we're
the least capable of are the things we end up doing, and they are what
define us. The town redefined Joe that night. To some, he was a victim.
To others, he was a murderer.

"I really wish Charlotte hadn't said that to you."

Grace glanced over at me. "Me too, but I'm glad I know," she said,
sliding her hand into mine.

I squeezed it tight. "I wouldn't let anything ever happen to you.
You're safe here with me. I promise." I had every intention of keeping
that promise, but intentions were just partially laid plans, and they were
subject to change.

Day Seven

31.

Grace

It wasn't the birds chirping that roused me or the burning sun on my bare skin. I think it was the almond-shaped part of my brain, the amygdala, that woke me. The part that senses fear. My eyes burst open like a star exploding, and I quickly sat up—discovering I was alone in the pasture, naked, with only a picnic blanket covering me. I snapped my head to the right, nothing. To the left, nothing. I looked ahead toward the ranch, my hand shading my eyes from the sun, and I saw nothing. Where was Calvin?

From behind me a raspy loud purr grumbled—the sound of an overgrown housecat. Slowly, I turned my head, and there it was, the thing Calvin said I had nothing to worry about, the creature that never came this far. Its coat was tan with black markings decorating the tips of its ears and snout. Its head was lowered, and its shoulders raised as if it were hunting its prey. Its eyes were yellow like the fresh flame of a candle. Ten yards separated me from the mountain lion. I stood up deliberately, keeping the blanket wrapped around my body, trying to make myself look bigger. It didn't budge. It crept closer, a few more steps. Without taking my eyes off of it, I bent down and picked up the platter of cheese and grapes. I tossed it at the animal like I was throwing a Frisbee, hoping that it would distract it or scare it away. But all it did was bring it closer. The creature sniffed the food but lost interest immediately. Eight yards away. It returned its gaze to me, dropping its head, creeping closer. Never breaking eye contact, I picked up an empty bottle of wine and threw it as hard as I could. When it hit the ground just in front of its paws, the mountain lion jumped back and paused for a moment—like it was considering retreating, but it didn't. It kept tiptoeing toward me. I picked up the full bottle of wine Calvin and I hadn't drunk. Winding my arm back, I hurled it. It must have hit a rock because as soon as it touched the ground it shattered, red wine splashing everywhere. The animal crouched back, but curiosity got the best of it. And it walked to where the wine bottle had crashed, only seven yards away. I started backing up as it sniffed and licked at the spilled wine, hoping that would give me the time I needed to get away. Where the hell was Calvin?

I backed up several more steps before it looked up again, losing interest in the spilled wine and regaining curiosity in me. I glanced around in search of a rock or something to throw, but there was nothing.

"Calvin!" I screamed as loud as I possibly could. My voice cracked, my heart raced, and my skin perspired. Is this what it felt like to be hunted?

I continued edging backward while it persisted toward me. It had its mind made up.

"Calvin!" I screamed even louder.

How could he have left me out here? Was everything he told me a lie?

My heart rate increased as the creature's steps doubled mine. I tried to make my movements bigger and bigger. I refused to turn around and run. I knew it could easily outrun me, so if it was going to attack, I wanted to see it coming. My heel caught on something large and hard, and I fell to the ground—only realizing it was a rock after I hit the earth with a thud. The mountain lion went from a walk to a jog to a full-on sprint when I was horizontal, knowing that I was at my weakest, an easy prey.

I forced my eyes open, waiting for it. It must have leapt or pounced or whatever it was that large cats did because it was in the air flying at me. Its dandelion yellow eyes fixated on its prey. Its retractable claws fully emerged. Time slowed down. I think time slows down for every-one's final moments.

Then there was a burst of red followed by a loud, echoing *bang*.

The mountain lion slammed onto my lower half. Red sticky blood sprayed all over me. The smell of iron invaded my nose. I shimmied away, pushing the corpse off while keeping the blanket wrapped around my body. My breaths were quick and uncontrolled as I crab-walked away, digging my heels into the ground, propelling myself farther from the dead animal.

Turning my head, my eyes found Calvin. He stood twenty yards back, looking down the scope of a hunting rifle, dressed in only blue jeans and untied farm boots. He lowered the gun and ran toward me, screaming my name.

"I'm so sorry. Are you okay, Grace?" he said, kneeling beside me. His hands wiped at the blood that covered my skin, but I'm sure it just smeared it around.

I gritted my teeth. "You said mountain lions didn't come this far."

"They usually don't." He shook his head, looking at the animal and then back at me. "The barbecue or the food out here must have attracted it or maybe it's infected with rabies." He leaned down and kissed my forehead. Blood clung to his lips.

"Are you okay?"

"Yeah," I said, but I was still shaking. I was not okay. How could he have left me out here? "Where were you?" My eyes narrowed, moving from the fallen beast to Calvin.

"I was inside making breakfast. I was going to bring it out to you." He pushed my blood-soaked hair out of my face. "I'm sorry."

I shoved away from him and stood, wiping my skin with the corner of the white sheet.

"I'm going to shower." I wrapped the blanket tighter around my bust and started off toward the ranch.

"I really am sorry, Grace," he called out. The words rang hollow.

As I reached the driveway, a sheriff's vehicle turned into it. I knew when they spotted me because the vehicle went from five miles per hour to thirty in a few seconds. *Shit.*

The driver slammed on his brakes just in front of me and jumped out of his vehicle. I recognized him immediately—Sheriff Almond.

"Good lord! Ma'am, are you all right?" He drew his gun and scanned all around, his eyes like pendulums.

I knew how it looked. This was the man looking for a missing woman and here I was, covered in blood and practically naked.

"Put your hands up!" the sheriff yelled, pointing his gun just over my shoulder.

I turned to find Calvin walking across the pasture with his rifle slung over his shoulder. His eyes went wide and his face paled like a ghost. Calvin dropped the rifle to the ground and shot his hands up toward the sky.

"Get behind me," the sheriff said as he put himself between me and Calvin. "Down on the ground," he yelled.

Calvin dropped to his knees.

"Sir, it's not what it looks like!" I shouted. The last thing I needed was to get wrapped up in a police shooting. "A mountain lion attacked me."

Sheriff Almond glanced at me and then back at Calvin. He didn't look convinced at all.

"It's true," Calvin said. "The body is in the field. I can show you."

He hesitated, keeping his pistol pointed at Calvin.

"He's telling the truth," I added.

Sheriff Almond let out a sigh and lowered his weapon. "All right, show it to me." He gestured with his hand.

Calvin reached for his rifle. "Leave it for now," the sheriff commanded.

He got to his feet and walked slowly, heading in the direction of the dead animal. Sheriff Almond and I followed behind. I was sure he didn't believe we were telling the truth. He probably thought Calvin was my captor, and I had developed Stockholm syndrome.

The flies had already gotten to the mountain lion. They wasted no time when it came to death. A swarm of them buzzed around, dropping into the sticky blood. Its eyes were black, still marbles, and its tongue hung out from the side of its mouth.

"Well, shit. This thing has to be two hundred–plus pounds," the sheriff said as he walked around the carcass, taking it all in. "You said it attacked you?" He looked to me.

I nodded. "Yeah, it was leaping in the air when Calvin shot it."

A shiver ran down my spine. I'd be the one lying dead in the dirt if it weren't for him. I never had that close of an encounter before. The closest I'd come to death was nearly getting swiped by a cab in the city. Now I understood how others who had faced it felt.

"You'll want to contact the DNR, since it's outside of hunting season, and let them know what happened," the sheriff said.

Calvin nodded. "I was just about to do that before you showed up."

"Mountain lion attacks are extremely rare." He glanced at me. "You're lucky to be alive."

I pressed my lips firmly together and wrapped the sheet a little tighter.

"Something must be wrong with this one," Sheriff Almond added as he gestured toward the animal.

"That's what I was thinking," Calvin said. "I don't think I've ever seen one on my property before." He scanned the surrounding area.

"Glad you're safe, ma'am." He tilted his head and gave me a sympathetic look.

Redirecting his attention to Calvin, the sheriff raised his chin. "Now, the reason I came out here was about that missing woman Briana Becker."

I wasn't sure if Calvin tensed up or if I was imagining it. "Yeah, what's up? Did you find her?" He shifted his stance, folding his arms across his chest.

"Unfortunately, no." He cleared his throat. "But we did find her car broken down two miles from here on a back road."

Wyatt had already told us about the car, so what was the sheriff doing here? Calvin looked down at his feet and back at him. Where was the sheriff going with this? From his tone and how he looked at Calvin, it seemed there was an accusation coming.

"Are you sure didn't see her?" Sheriff Almond pulled the photo from his front pocket and held it out. "Get a good look," he added.

There she was again, the bright eyes, long, blond wavy hair, dimples, and a pretty smile. Calvin examined the photo for a moment. "No, like I said before, I haven't seen her. And she never checked in."

"And you?" Sheriff Almond put the picture in my line of sight.

I shook my head. "No, I haven't seen her."

He gave a slight nod and pocketed the photo. "After seeing this I'm starting to wonder if something like this happened to her?" The sheriff looked down at the dead animal.

"Nature is unforgiving," Calvin said.

Sheriff Almond gave him a peculiar look.

"You mind if I have a look around your property?"

I couldn't see where the sheriff was looking because his aviators covered his eyes, but he swiveled his head to the left and to the right—like he was already searching. Did he think the woman was here? If she was, I would have surely stumbled across her. Or did he think Calvin had done something to her? My mind went back to the night I heard the woman's scream. Was it her? I opened my mouth and was about to mention it but stopped. What if I was wrong? What if I had been dreaming? What if I actually hadn't heard anything? It would further complicate things, so I kept my mouth shut.

"Have at it. I can show you around if you'd like," Calvin offered.

"Yeah, sure. That'd be great," Sheriff Almond said.

The two of them walked toward the barn, keeping their distance six feet from one another. Calvin glanced back at me with a tight smile, not his usual smile. I turned, heading back toward the house. And then it hit me. The ranch had no cell service, and if the Wi-Fi was down then, Briana wouldn't have been able to check in even if she was here.

The warm water cascaded over me as I attempted to let fear and anxiety wash away with the blood. It swirled down the drain, a pinkish-red liquid. I knew there was something off when I got here. I felt it in the house. I saw it in Calvin. Perhaps it's what attracted me to him. The danger of it all. The unknowing. Everything in my life had always been planned. There was never any room for spontaneity or things that weren't a part of my schedule. That included fear. You don't plan for fear. It was obvious the sheriff believed Briana had been here. I was starting to believe it too. But where was she now?

I turned off the water and wrapped a towel around me. My hand swiped the condensation buildup from the mirror, revealing a clean face but I could still somehow see the blood on it. Perhaps it was a part of me now. I took a deep breath and pulled open the bathroom door. As soon as I stepped into the hall, I crashed into another person.

"Calvin . . ." But it wasn't Calvin.

"Sorry, ma'am. I didn't expect you to spring out like a chicken."

I wrapped the damp towel tighter around my body. "Who the hell are you?"

The man was hefty, dressed in dirty overalls. He had to have been in his sixties. His peppered hair was shaggy but not intentionally—just as if he didn't take good care of himself. His nose was large, and his skin was covered in rosacea and patchy facial hair.

Loud footsteps made their way toward us. "Grace! Ahh," Calvin paused as his eyes caught the scene before him "I see you two have met. This is Albert. He's another Airbnb guest who will be staying here for the next couple nights."

A wave of emotions flooded over me.

"I didn't know another guest was coming, Calvin. On my booking, I actually requested to be the only guest." I narrowed my eyes.

"I must have missed that, and I do have two rooms listed. So sometimes, although rarely, they can overlap. Albert here was a last-minute booking."

"That's true, little lady. I'm just passing through but needed a place to stop off to get some rest." His smile revealed a dead front tooth.

"I see. Where's Sheriff Almond?" I redirected my attention to Calvin.

He cleared his throat and slid a hand into his front pocket. "He left."

"Already?"

"Yep, didn't find what he was looking for." His eyes bounced from me to Albert and back again.

I wasn't sure how long I had been in the shower. Time didn't seem to exist here in Wyoming. But he left rather quickly for someone looking for a missing person, especially on such a large property. Perhaps Sheriff Almond wasn't convinced Calvin had been involved.

"I'll be in my room."

I needed distance so I could try to think clearly.

I walked around Albert and closed my bedroom door behind me. I didn't even look at Calvin. Something didn't feel right. Between the rare mountain lion attack, the missing woman, and now this strange guest. Why wouldn't he tell me there was another guest staying? I collapsed onto the bed, letting out a groan. I highly doubted a man like Albert would even have an Airbnb account, let alone know what it was or how to use it. Picking up my cell phone from the nightstand, I verified that I was still screwed. *No service.* I groaned again. In the hallway, I heard whispers, but I couldn't make out what was being said. Why were they even whispering?

I tiptoed to the door and pressed my ear against it.

"Sorry about her. She's just a little rattled. Mountain lion nearly attacked her earlier," Calvin said.

"That's terrifying. She all right?" Albert whispered back.

"She will be, I think. You can stay in this room," Calvin said.

The door to the room next to mine creaked open. Everything in this house creaked. Boots clomped a few steps—first Calvin's, then Albert's. I could tell the difference between them. Albert's steps were too heavy, like he was more stumbling than walking. Calvin's were hard but controlled, like a slow beat on a drum.

"Thanks. I'll be out of your hair in a few days," Albert said.

Calvin whispered something back, but I couldn't make it out. The door creaked again and closed. Then, there was a knock on my door. I scrambled back to the bed and took a seat looking at my red fingernails nonchalantly. The paint had chipped off on several of them.

"Come in," I said.

The door opened, and Calvin popped his head in.

"Hey," he said. His eyes scanned my face, evaluating if it was safe to take another step into the room. My face was unchanged though. I simply glanced over at him for a moment and then returned my attention to my chipped nails.

"I'm heading into town. You want to come with me?"

I thought for a moment, pretending to consider his offer. I didn't want to go into town, and I didn't want to stay in this house with Albert either. What I wanted was my car fixed.

"No," I said.

He dropped his head a little and shuffled his feet, disappointed.

"Are we okay?" He worked up the courage to take another step toward me.

"Sure." I turned my head, staring out the cracked window. We weren't okay. I wasn't okay. I should have gone with my gut feeling on day one and left. Something was off with this house, with this town, with Calvin. He took another step toward me and sat on the edge of the bed.

"You sure, Grace?"

"I'm sure."

He scooted a little closer and rested his hand on the bed in the space between us. There was more than physical space between us now. There was distance. What added to the distance were all the uncertainties, the unanswered questions, the answers I could not or did not believe. Calvin moved his hand on top of my bare knee, and my body instantly tensed up. Last night when he touched me my skin warmed, now I felt a coldness run through me. They say love makes you blind. This wasn't love though. This was lust, and it makes you downright stupid.

"I'm really sorry, Grace. I'm going to make this up to you. I want this to work. Us, that is. We still have a few days together. Please don't shut me out yet." His voice was deep yet soft. He patted my knee. "You haven't shut me out yet, have you?"

I looked at his hand resting on my body. A shiver ran down my spine. I shook my head.

He smiled and leaned in, planting a kiss on my cheek. "I'll be back soon." Calvin's eyes lingered on me while he stood. I thought he'd say more but he turned and left the room, closing the door behind him.

I took a deep breath. Calvin was right about one thing: we only had a few more days left, he only had a few more days left . . . and then I would leave all of this behind me.

32.

Calvin

I pulled my truck into a parking spot in front of Betty's Boutique and grabbed the empty cake pan from the passenger seat. Only a few people walked the downtown area because it was still early in the day. I exchanged greetings with them as I made my way inside.

"Hey, sweetheart. To what do I owe the pleasure?" Betty asked, standing from her seat behind the register. The store was empty, another slow day for business.

I held up the cake pan. "Just returning this," I said, setting it down on the counter.

Betty came around and wrapped her arms around me, pulling me in for a tight hug. "How ya doing today?"

"Not great."

She took a few steps back and looked me up and down. Her brows pinched together. "What's wrong, Calvin?"

I ambled around the store, glancing at some of the men's clothes. I didn't really need anything, just needed to talk. "A mountain lion nearly attacked Grace this morning."

Betty's eyes widened, and her hand sprung to her mouth. "Nearly?"

I nodded. "Yep. Shot and killed the thing just as it was coming at her."

"Oh dear," she gasped. "Lucky you know how to shoot. Must have been quite the scare for her."

It wasn't the first time I'd shot an animal, and I knew it wouldn't be the last. I pulled a red-and-black flannel shirt from a stuffed rack and held it up. "Grace is real shaken up." I put the shirt back and continued flipping through a few others.

Betty looked as though she wanted to say something but was holding back. Her mouth closed and opened and closed again.

"What?" I asked.

She waved her hand at me. "Oh, nothing."

"Go on and say it."

"Well, in my experience mountain lions go for easy prey, the weak. That girl don't belong here and even nature is trying to tell you that." She shook her head.

"That's a strange thing to say, Betty."

"She ain't built for Wyoming is all I'm saying." She raised her chin and shrugged.

"I don't think I am either."

"You are, Calvin. That girl has gotten in your head like brain-eating amoeba. You ain't thinking right."

I cocked my head. "Grace has done nothing wrong."

I was tired of the way people were treating her, and I could see why she was acting so strange now. I'd be the same way.

"I just have a funny feeling about her," Betty said.

"Well, maybe that funny feeling is because you haven't filled your prescription in the last two months."

I didn't mean to say it. It just came out. When Betty was off her meds, she was the one not seeing things right.

Her mouth dropped open but she quickly closed it, pursing her lips into a thin line. She narrowed her eyes at me. "Who told you that?"

"That doesn't matter. Why haven't you been taking your pills?"

"Because I don't need them."

"You clearly do. You're paranoid. First about the bees and now about Grace."

I took a few steps toward the counter.

Betty folded her arms in front of her chest. "I think you should take a hard look in the mirror, Calvin. She's changing you. You're smarter than this, so don't go losing your head for some girl."

"She's not just some girl," I scoffed.

Betty shook her head like a parent who'd been disappointed by their child. "After she leaves, you'll start seeing things a little more clearly."

"She's not leaving. I want her to stay."

"Oh, Calvin." She placed a hand on each of my cheeks and pulled me in, planting a kiss on the top of my head like she used to do when I was a young boy. "You're a fool. You're a damn fool."

If she only knew. I pulled away, letting her hands fall to her sides. She frowned at me.

"I really hope you start taking your medication again. You know what happens when you don't."

She twisted up her lips and started straightening up random things around the store, busying herself. "Sheriff stopped in today, asking about you and a missing woman."

I let out a sigh. "Yeah, he stopped over at the ranch earlier and a few days ago too. What did you tell him?"

"That I've never seen that woman." Betty straightened a row of cowboy boots, ensuring each was in line.

"What did he ask about me?" I raised my chin, my eyes following her as she moseyed around the store.

"Just wanted to know more about you and the ranch. Apparently, this girl was supposed to stay with you for a few days."

"Yeah, and I told him she never showed up." I felt my jaw tighten. Betty wouldn't even look at me. I couldn't tell if it was because she couldn't or she wouldn't, and there was a difference.

"Him coming around is going to screw things up with Grace."

"I think that's the least of your worries. In three days, Calvin, you better let that girl leave." Betty didn't look at me or say another word. She just walked to the back of the store and disappeared into the storage room.

33.

Grace

From a backbend, I went into a downward-facing dog pose. The sun felt good on my skin, and it made the coldness running through me a little warmer. I was out front on a yoga mat, trying to relax and not think about how much had gone wrong. This wasn't how it was supposed to go. I hadn't seen Albert since we were introduced earlier, but I knew he was around here because his station wagon sat alongside the driveway. I glanced around the pond area, the porch, beside the house, toward the barn, trying to pinpoint where he was. He was somewhere watching me. I could feel it. After several deep breaths, I lifted myself into a handstand position. My breathing slowed as I held myself up and closed my eyes, trying to picture nothing, only listening to the sounds of nature.

When I opened my eyes, I came tumbling down. Sitting about twenty yards from me was Albert. He drank from a small bottle of Jack Daniel's, watching me. Rather early in the day for Jack. The corner of his mouth perked up. *Creepy old man.* I closed my eyes and went back into a handstand, attempting to forget about Albert and his lingering eyes.

"You're really bendy," he said.

My eyes shot open, and I tumbled over again. Albert stood a few feet away from me. How had I not heard him? He wasn't graceful, and he was rather large—but perhaps like that mountain lion, he could be quiet when he needed to be.

"I think the word you're looking for is *flexible*." I stood up from my yoga mat and pinned my shoulders back.

He took a swig, and his eyes scanned over me.

"Can I help you with something?" I jutted out my hip and threw a hand on it.

"Nope, just taking in the view." His thin, crusty lips turned into a grin.

I rolled up my yoga mat and tucked it under my arm. "Enjoy your view," I said sarcastically as I stormed into the house.

What started out as an enjoyable and relaxing vacation seven days ago had turned into a nightmare I couldn't wake up from. In the living room, I walked to the bookshelf Calvin had pointed out on the day I arrived. He said he loved to read, but I realized I hadn't seen him pick up a book once in the past week. My fingers ran along the spines. They were all classics, the ones you were forced to read in a literature class, not at all what I thought Calvin would be into. I slid one out and fanned through the pages. A piece of paper fell to the floor. I bent down and picked it up. It was a receipt from a bookstore dated two days before I arrived. The total at the bottom was over five hundred dollars. And every book on the shelf was listed on it.

An engine outside sputtered. I shoved the book back into its place and peered out the window. Albert's station wagon crept slowly down the driveway. I let out a sigh, and my eyes flicked back to the bookshelf. It was all a lie, like Calvin had designed a set for my arrival.

I could see nearly the whole ranch plus the road I had driven in on from the porch. It felt like the safest place on the ranch, so I took a seat with a beer and one of Calvin's "favorite" books. I tried to concentrate on reading but the words jumbled together on the page, swirling around. I couldn't focus. My eyes kept going back to the road and then my broken-down car parked off in the grass. How was I going to get out of here?

Tires crunched over gravel. It was either Calvin or Albert, but I didn't look up and continued to pretend to read instead. I wasn't in the mood to talk.

I flipped the page. The car shut off. A car door slammed. Footsteps padded up the porch stairs. They weren't Calvin's though or Albert's. They were lighter.

"Calvin here?" Charlotte asked. She sounded drunk, and I knew she was looking for trouble. "I didn't see his truck."

"No," I said.

"Good, I wanted to talk to you." She stumbled toward me, plopping down in a rocking chair.

It creaked every time she rocked back.

"Calvin didn't tell you about us, did he?" She raised one of her thick dark eyebrows.

I didn't say anything. I just looked at her, waiting for her to spill whatever it was she wanted to spill. Charlotte's eyes were bloodshot and her lipstick was partially smeared.

"He and I slept together about a month ago. I thought you'd want to know," she said, and then she stared at me, waiting for a reaction.

I grabbed the beer from the table and took a long swig. It wasn't a surprise to me. I figured something happened between them. It was obvious and explained why she'd been so cold and territorial. I didn't care that they had slept together. I just wanted her gone.

"Calvin told me he didn't want you coming around anymore," I said.

She clenched her jaw, moving it side to side.

"When did he say that?" Charlotte raised her chin. She tried to relax her face, but there was so much tension in it. It was like she was going to explode depending on what came out of my mouth.

I took another swig and glanced at her, choosing my words carefully—or carelessly, for that matter. "Last night," I pointed the top of the beer bottle toward the field of grass beyond the barn, "when he fucked me over in that pasture."

Her face turned red like she was going to cry and scream at the same time. Before she could react, Calvin's truck pulled into the driveway. She stood unsteadily and marched across the porch and down the steps.

He closed the door of his truck behind him and spun the keys in his hand.

"What are you doing here, Charlotte?" Calvin slid his hands into his pockets and leaned against his vehicle while she closed the space between them.

I walked toward the steps, standing at the top of them, deciding whether to intervene or to just go inside.

"I told Grace about us," Charlotte spat.

He shook his head and ran his hands down his face. Calvin's eyes swung to me.

"I'm sorry, Grace," he said. "It was nothing, just a one-time mistake."

I offered no expression because he didn't deserve one. His lip trembled when I turned on my foot.

"Grace, wait!" he called out.

Without looking back or saying anything, I went into the ranch house and let the door close behind me. It was the last place I wanted to be but I didn't have a choice. Calvin was a liar. That much was clear. But I wondered now . . . was he something worse than that?

34.

Calvin

I considered running after Grace, but I needed to get rid of Charlotte once and for all. I thought I already had, but some animals put up a fight. She was ruining everything. Grace was right. I should have made sure Charlotte didn't come around again. She looked at me the same way I looked at Grace, and I knew that was dangerous because she couldn't have me.

"A mistake?" Charlotte's voice shook. Tears gathered at the corners of her bloodshot eyes.

I nodded. It wasn't new information, so I didn't understand why she was back here again.

Her skin flushed as she glared at me. "I'll show you a mistake." It came off like a threat, but I wasn't sure what she was threatening.

I raised my chin. "What's that supposed to mean?"

"I slept with Joe," she seethed. "Last night." Charlotte pushed past me "And I told him everything!"

My eyes went wide.

"Told him what?" I yelled, reaching for her. My fingers gripped her arm, pressing into her skin. She swung her other arm, thrusting her balled fist into my eye.

I pushed her hard—too hard. She fell back onto the ground, her skull hitting the gravel with a thud. She laid there for a moment, stunned.

When she sat up, Charlotte pressed her fingers against the back of her head and brought them in front of her face. There was blood.

"Char, I'm sorry. I didn't mean to." I tried to help her up. She swatted my hand away and stood on her own, wobbly and unsteady. She touched the back of her head again and looked at her fingers. More blood.

"Let me take you home," I pleaded.

She looked at me through her splayed, bloodstained fingers.

"I'm done keeping your secrets."

"Secrets? What are you talking about? What did you tell Joe?" My hands ran over my face, pulling at my skin. I took a deep breath.

She backed away as if she were afraid of me, afraid of what I would do. Then she turned and marched angrily back to her car, the back of her head saturated with blood from the gouge.

I thought she would speed out of here, but she took her time starting her car and driving off. I looked down at my own hands. They weren't still. They shook like an addict going through withdrawals. I tried to steady them but they wouldn't. Her vehicle disappeared down the road, and my mind went back to her parting words. *I'm done keeping your secrets.* What did Charlotte know?

35.
Grace

I needed to get out of here. Away from this ranch, this town—hell, the whole state of Wyoming. Charlotte was a problem, a major one at that. Then there was the sheriff and the missing woman. Could Calvin have done something to her? That changed everything. I packed up most of my things in case I needed to make a quick escape. Without a working car or phone, I didn't know how I'd get out of here. I could steal Calvin's truck or call from the house phone—if it even worked. I hadn't heard it ring once since I got here. A new plan was needed. Maybe the best way to go about this was to act as though I was fine, at least until my car got fixed.

A knock on the door pulled me from my thoughts.

"Can I come in?" Calvin asked.

I took a seat on the bed and grabbed a book from my nightstand, pretending to read. "Yeah."

The door opened and Calvin walked in carrying that damn teddy bear. I wanted to rip the stupid thing's head off.

"This was on the couch." He took a seat on the bed, handing it over. I tossed it aside.

Calvin hung his head. "I'm sorry I didn't tell you about Charlotte. It really was a one-time thing. I was just feeling sorry for myself and, well, she was here. One thing led to another." He shrugged. "It's no excuse though. I should have told you."

He placed a hand on the blanket. My thigh was just beneath it. I nearly shuddered but slowed my breathing to calm myself down.

"What else are you lying about?" I studied his face. I knew a few things he had been dishonest about. Would he fess up to them? Or would he keep lying?

"Nothing, I swear."

Lie.

He exhaled sharply.

"She told me she slept with Joe." Calvin glanced over at me. "Last night after the barbecue."

I knew he was only telling me this so I'd feel sorry for him. I didn't. But why had Charlotte implied that Joe was dangerous? If he truly was, she wouldn't have slept with him. Right? Or maybe she was that crazy. Crazy enough to sleep with a potentially dangerous man just to try to make Calvin jealous.

I grabbed the glass of water from my nightstand and took a sip. There was shame in his eyes, but there was also anger. Where was the kindness I had seen days before? He moved his hand up and down, stroking my thigh beneath the blanket, trying to comfort me—but there was nothing comforting about this.

"I know you're mad, and you have every right to be. I'm sorry. I don't care about any of them, Charlotte, Joe, Betty. I only care about you, and I want to make this work," he said.

Calvin studied my face, waiting for me to say something, almost willing me to speak. Sometimes saying nothing was more powerful than speaking at all.

"I love you, Grace Evans. These aren't the best circumstances to tell you this, but I do. I've fallen in love with you." Parts of his face twitched. My silence was infuriating him, but he was trying his best to hide the anger. His best wasn't good enough.

When I didn't speak, he cleared his throat.

"And I don't want you to say it back. I just wanted you to know how I felt." He stood from the bed and walked to the door.

Before he flicked the light off, he smiled and said, "Good night,

Grace." Calvin leaned against the doorframe, waiting for me to respond. After a few moments of silence, he closed the door. But I knew he was standing on the other side. Completely still, like a statue. It was minutes before his shadow finally disappeared, his steps loud and steady, clomping down the hall. I sank deep into my pillows and pulled the covers up to my chin.

"Goodbye, Calvin," I whispered to the dark, quiet room.

My eyes shot open when I felt part of the mattress sink in. I didn't know what time it was. The room was pitch-black so I assumed late. An arm fell across me as I lay on my side. His body spooned me and pulled me closer to him. I considered pushing Calvin out of my bed, but I was in too vulnerable of a position. What if it brought out that anger he was having trouble hiding? I breathed in through my nose, but stopped when I noticed something was amiss. Calvin didn't smell like Jack Daniel's.

I flew out of bed, shouting and screaming. The lights flicked on. Calvin stood in the doorframe wearing only a pair of boxers. In bed laid Albert. He sat up, disheveled and drunk. His eyes were barely open.

"What's going on?" Albert's speech was slurred.

"You're in my fucking bed," I yelled.

Calvin ran to my side and pointed at Albert. "Get out of her bed!"

The old man looked puzzled. He shuffled out of the bed, falling into the wall just as he got to his feet. "Must have got confused."

"Sorry 'bout that, little lady." Albert tipped an imaginary hat and stumbled toward the door, waving his hand as he staggered out of the room. Another door creaked open and then closed with a slam.

I pushed Calvin away from me. "I want a goddamn lock on my door!"

He put his hands up and nodded. "Of course. Whatever you want."

"He needs to leave," I said.

Calvin rubbed his eyes. "I can't kick him out right now. It's the middle of the night. I'm sure it was an accident. He's old and drunk."

"An accident? You didn't see the way he was looking at me." I shuddered. "You promised I'd be safe here."

"I know. I'm sorry." Calvin put his hands on my arms. "I'll install a lock tomorrow and see if I can get him put up somewhere else."

He looked into my eyes, waiting for an answer.

I shrugged his hands off of me and turned away from him, sliding back into the bed. "Close the door when you leave," I said, yanking the covers up past my shoulders.

Calvin hesitated for a moment and sighed. "Okay," he finally said. "Sleep well, Grace." He flicked off the light and closed the door, lingering on the other side of it once again. At some point, I must have fallen asleep but I never heard his footsteps walk away. I think he stood there all night.

Day Eight

36.
Calvin

After tightening the last screw, I dropped the screwdriver in the tool-box and jiggled the door handle, making sure it was securely in place. I should have installed one when I started doing room rentals, but no one else ever complained—so it slipped my mind.

"What are you doing?" Grace jolted up in bed. Her hair went in all directions and dark circles clung to the skin beneath her eyes. She clearly hadn't slept well.

"Sorry, didn't mean to wake you," I said, getting to my feet. "I installed that lock you asked for."

Grace stared at me, not saying a word. Her eyes blinked several times, darting between me and the newly installed lock. I figured after yesterday she had shut me out and was just biding her time here. But I still hoped I could convince her otherwise.

"Just wanted to make sure you feel comfortable." I took a couple steps toward her and held out a silver key. "Here," I said, dangling it in front of her.

If this is what she needed to feel safe, I'd give it to her. That was the thing about safety, you could either have it or feel like you had it, and they were the same thing—until they weren't. Finally, she took it, clutching the key in her hand. I'm sure it felt comforting, like a security blanket does for a young child.

"I hope this makes you feel better."

Grace didn't say anything. She just stared at me with those blue, blue eyes. I couldn't tell if she didn't know what to say or if she was scared to speak. I hoped it was the former, although fear wasn't a permanent feeling. It eventually passed. I studied her expressionless face, from her perfect pout to her soft nose and the arch of her eyebrows, but I couldn't get a good read on her.

"I meant what I said last night." I took a deep breath, waiting for her to say something, anything. She could yell at me for all I cared. I just wanted to talk to her. But it was as though she wasn't here anymore. Physically, yes. But mentally, emotionally—she was gone. Maybe I imagined it, and she was never here to begin with. How could we have gone from lovers to strangers in twenty-four hours?

I looked down at my hands. They weren't steady. I balled them up and relaxed them.

"Well, I've gotta go and run an errand, but I'll be back as soon as I can." I turned and headed toward the door, picking up my toolbox on the way out. I glanced back, hoping she'd say something or even look at me the way she looked at me out in the pasture before everything went to shit. Instead, she laid down and rolled away from me.

I closed the door and let out a heavy sigh. This wasn't how any of this was supposed to go. Somehow it all got screwed up. It always did. Standing on the other side, I pressed my ear against it. I just wanted to be near her. It was silent. I waited a few minutes but heard nothing. Albert's door was still closed, so I assumed he wouldn't be awake until midday, and I'd deal with him when I got back from the grocery store.

In two days, Grace was set to leave, and if she did, I knew I would never see her again. This town had a way of keeping insiders in and outsiders out. But I couldn't let that happen. Grace belonged to me.

37.

Grace

I carried a glass of lemonade and the last book I intended on reading out to the porch. The sun was set high in the sky, its rays scorching the dry grass. Taking a seat in the rocking chair, I placed the lemonade on the table beside me and flipped the book open to page one. After Calvin left, I laid in bed for a while thinking about how I could get through the next two days. I still had a soft spot for him but I was trying to harden that area because I knew something wasn't right with Calvin, and maybe that's why I was captivated by him. Broken people were drawn to broken people.

"Whatcha reading?"

Albert stood just outside the front door, carrying a beer and a crooked smile. I rolled my eyes and refocused my attention on the page.

His heavy steps grew louder as he ambled toward me. Although he was large, he was old and mostly drunk, so I figured I could, at the very least, outrun him if need be. Albert took a seat in the rocking chair beside me, slowly rocking back and forth.

"My memory ain't the best, but I think I owe you an apology," he said.

I simply nodded.

"I'm sorry. I'm not much of a man but my word is pretty solid. It won't happen again, and honestly, it was an accident." He gulped his beer. "I may have a lot of demons, but hurting women isn't one of them." Albert raised his eyebrow over his glass.

"Demons?" I asked.

"We all have them. Even you, I'm sure."

"Yeah," I said, flipping a page.

"Some people are just better at hiding them," he said. The chair creaked with each rock.

I looked at him, my eyes skimming over his weathered skin. A silver medical bracelet hung loosely on his wrist—just a sick, drunk old man, that's what Albert was.

"What's that for?" I motioned to his piece of jewelry.

He glanced down, holding his hand out. "Oh, that." The sunlight reflected off of the metal. "List of things I can't have. Like I said, I got a lot of demons. Things I can't have and things I have too much of." He chuckled while he held up his beer. "I'm what Darwin would call 'not nature's winner.'"

I let on a small smile. "What can't you have?"

"Shellfish, nuts, bees, eggs, strawberries. You name it. I can't have it. That's why my diet is a steady stream of red meat and booze. And that's just fine by me." Albert chuckled again. He set his empty bottle on the table beside him.

"What brought you here?" I closed up my book and gave him my full attention.

"A lot of bad decisions over a lifetime, I suppose. But sometimes after trying to always take the road less traveled, ya just go where it's easiest, ya know?" He glanced over at me.

"I think I know what you're saying."

"What about you? Why you here?" he asked, bringing the beer bottle back to his lips. He clearly forgot it was empty.

"Still taking the road less traveled, I guess."

He sucked on air and then pulled the bottle from his mouth. "Stay on it because it eventually runs out."

"You're not so bad, Albert."

He and I weren't so different after all. He too traveled alone, had his own vices to deal with, and was forever searching for the things that kept life interesting.

"I'm not so good either." He smirked, holding up his beer. "I'ma get me another one of these." Several of his bones creaked and cracked as he got to his feet. "You want one?"

"Yeah." I nodded.

He shuffled down the porch, disappearing inside the house. No more than a moment later, Calvin's truck rolled up with a police vehicle following closely behind. I knew this place was trouble. I felt it as soon as I stepped foot here.

38.
Calvin

Grace rocked back and forth on the porch. I wished every day I came home I could see her. The big blue skies surrounded us like it was our own perfect mini-universe, just for her and me. She was a vision. Her blond hair was tied up in a messy bun. I imagined unraveling it and watching her locks fall around her face. I was happy she'd left her room. A car engine shut off behind me. I didn't even notice anyone following. Wyatt climbed out of his cruiser.

"Hey, man," I said.

His face was beet red, and his fists were clenched by his side. A thick, angry vein in the center of his forehead throbbed, and it looked as though it could burst at any moment. In three large steps, he was right in front of me. Rather than his usual friendly salutation, his fist did the talking. The force pushed me backward, and for me, the sun wasn't the only star in the sky now. My cheek throbbed, but I stood tall.

"What the hell, Wyatt!"

Before he came at me again to deliver another greeting, Grace was between us with her hands on both of our chests. She asked me if I was all right. I knew then she still cared for me. And if she didn't, she would eventually.

He puffed out his chest and raised his chin. "What'd you do to Charlotte?" Wyatt spat.

"What? What did she tell you?"

Grace's hands were still up, separating us from one another. I kept a close eye on the gun that sat on Wyatt's hip. Would he shoot me dead right here? He looked angry enough to do it.

"I saw what you did to her. I saw the gash on the back of her head!"

I blew out my cheeks. My eyes went to Grace then Wyatt. Char wasn't lying. I had done that. I didn't mean to. If I had really intended to hurt her, I would have. It was purely an accident. She told Wyatt because she was using him. That much was obvious.

"Is it true?" he yelled. "Did you do that? If you did, I'm going to make sure she presses charges."

"No!" Grace yelled. She squared up with Wyatt, and he took a quick step back like he was afraid of her.

"Charlotte came here looking for trouble. She was drunk and belligerent. She told me . . ." Grace paused. "She said she slept with Joe. So, if you want to arrest anyone, arrest her for drunk driving and being the town whore."

Wyatt's eyes grew wide in disbelief. They snapped between Grace and me. He let out a heavy sigh and stumbled backward.

Grace left out the part about Charlotte and I sleeping together clearly to protect me.

"She slept with Joe?" he stammered.

Wyatt was in love with Charlotte, but this revelation changed everything. I'm sure he hoped she'd come around—that maybe she was just scared about settling down. But he wasn't the man she wanted to settle down with. I was, and Joe was just a pawn.

I tilted my head, delivering a sympathetic look. "I'm sorry, man."

"Joe's my best friend." Wyatt's lip quivered.

"I know." I closed the distance between us and patted him on the shoulder. In being all caught up with what Char had done, I forgot about what Joe had done. Wyatt and Joe had been best friends since they were boys. He stuck by Joe after the accident, after most others turned their back on him. He never once bought into the rumors that

Joe could have possibly done it on purpose. He even took care of him until he was healed enough to take care of himself.

Wyatt raised his shoulders. "I've gotta go." He hung his head for a moment. "Sorry," he murmured.

"It's fine," I said.

Wyatt got into his cruiser without another word and backed out of the driveway. I had no idea what he was going to do next, but I knew it wasn't good. Once out on the road, his tires squealed, and he flicked on his lights and siren, speeding off in the direction of downtown Dubois.

I shook my head and turned to Grace. "Thank you for standing up for me."

She pointed to my cheek. "You should get some ice on that."

"Everything all right out here?" Albert stood on the porch, holding two beers. "I heard yelling."

Grace nodded and took one of the beers from him. "It's all good." They clinked their bottles together and swigged.

I thought now would be the best time to tell her the truth about everything, but the thought passed quickly. Things were getting better, and I didn't want something silly like the truth ruining it, so I just smiled and joined them.

The carbonation from the beer tingled against my tongue, or maybe it was Grace that made me tingle. She sat beside me, grazing on her ham-and-cheese sandwich. Somehow, after half a dozen beers with Albert on the porch, she had warmed up to me and even let me make her something to eat. The sky looked like a watercolor painting, a mix of blues and yellows and pinks, but the beauty of it paled in comparison to her. Grace rocked back and forth in the creaky, wooden chair. We were back to talking about dating things, learning about one another, likes and dislikes, hopes and dreams, and all that. It was nice, real nice.

"What's your biggest regret?" she asked, pulling the bottle from her lips. The liquid left behind a glimmery sheen that begged to be kissed. But I resisted.

"Leaving here," I said. "But also coming back."

Grace tilted her head. "Why?"

"When I left, I felt like a wild animal being released from captivity. I went out and got a taste of freedom, and realized the world wasn't like I thought it was. Then I was put back in the cage, so to speak." I glanced over at her. I was sure I wasn't making much sense, but she nodded anyway.

She raised an eyebrow. "You don't do Airbnb for the money, do you?" Maybe she did have me all figured out.

I shook my head and drank. "No, I don't."

"Why'd you lie to me?" she asked, setting her empty plate down on the table between us.

"How'd you know I was lying?"

"It doesn't matter how I knew. It matters why you lied." Grace eyed me. She must have been watching me carefully this whole time.

I let out a deep breath and some of the truth came out with it. "I lied because I was embarrassed. My parent's life insurance policies left me a lot of money, but I learned quickly that money ain't everything. So, I started Airbnb simply because I was lonely." My eyes flicked to her.

Grace pulled in her lips and lowered her chin.

I think she felt bad for me.

We sat there for a few moments, rocking back and forth, and staring out at the pond and the green pasture beyond it. I couldn't let that be the end of the conversation.

"What about you? Biggest regret?"

"I don't have any," she said.

"Bullshit."

"No, it's true, I don't have any. If it was good, I enjoyed it. If it was bad, I learned from it. I can't go around regretting the things I've done that made me me." She lifted her chin.

"You are something else," I said, taking a swig.

"Something good?"

"I guess it don't matter whether you're good or bad because I can't regret you. Well, according to your logic." I grinned, shooting her a quick glance before staring at the setting sun. It reflected off the pond making it look like glass.

"You teasing me, Calvin?"

"Of course not. I would never."

She laughed. We were back to day six, like day seven hadn't happened. We were flirting again. We were actually talking. I think she could see it—a future with me. I'd shut out the rest of the world just to be with Grace Evans.

"What's going on with my car?" she asked.

The question was like a punch to the gut. She was always asking about that damn car so she could get away from me.

"It'll be fixed tomorrow." There was no enthusiasm in my voice. I said it like I was reading an instruction manual.

The screen door opened and closed with a *bang*. Albert shuffled out with heavy lopsided steps. His skin was flushed, and his hair was matted in some areas and stuck out in others. I wasn't sure if he had been napping or drinking more.

"Hey, Calvin. I've been drinking." *That solved that mystery.* "I'm out of Jack. Would you mind driving me into town?"

I slightly narrowed my eyes. "I'm kind of in the middle of something."

Grace collected the beer bottles and empty plates. "Oh, just go take him into town. We're out of wine anyway."

Reluctantly, I stood from my chair. I should have never let him stay here.

"Fine. I'll be quick." Before I could chicken out or stop myself from doing it, I planted a quick kiss on her forehead. She didn't pull away.

"Thanks, Grace." Albert threw a smile at her as he walked down the steps of the porch toward the truck.

"Should we really be encouraging his habit?" I whispered to Grace in a last-ditch effort to get out of leaving her.

"He's old. Let him have the small joys he still has left," she said. "Besides, bad habits aren't always all that bad."

"You're a softie, Grace." When I leaned down to kiss her on the cheek, she turned her head and allowed her lips to meet mine. They were warm and soft like my pillow in the summertime. When she pulled away, all I could do was smile. "Be back soon."

"Better get going. Albert's waiting." She gestured toward the vehicle. He was already sitting in the front seat, cranking down the passenger side window.

I nodded and started toward the truck, keeping my eyes on Grace. I never wanted to look away. Some things just have a pull on you, and she was one of them.

39.

Grace

After Calvin left, I found myself standing at the end of the hallway. My eyes went to the door with the padlock, the one that led to the basement, the one that was off-limits. He wouldn't be gone longer than a half hour. I took a couple steps toward it, deciding whether or not it was worth having a look. Did I have the time? He'd been gone ten minutes already. Did it matter what was down there? Would it change anything? Or should I just focus on getting through the next two days? Just two days. Forty-eight hours. Two thousand eight hundred and eighty minutes. Then it would all be over. I hoped Calvin realized this was temporary. Everything was temporary . . . even life itself. But I wasn't sure he knew that or accepted it. He looked at me like I was the beginning and the end. There was no chance in hell I'd stay. But a little hope went a long way. I just needed to make sure my car was fixed by tomorrow so I could hit the road the day after—bright and early.

A knock on the front door startled me. I made my way through the living room and hesitated before opening it. A fist pounded against it, and I jumped. My hand hovered over the handle. Before I could turn it, the door flung open and Joe stumbled in. I backed up quickly, putting distance between us. His clothing was filthy, covered in dirt and dust. His bottom lip was swollen, his nose bloody, and his eye was already blossoming into what would surely be a bruise.

"Joe? What happened to you?"

He touched his lip, bringing a bloodstained finger into his line of sight, and smiled. Staggering farther into the living room, he stopped and stood in front of the framed wooden mirror hung above the couch.

"Damn, he got me good," he said, turning his head side to side. Joe pressed his fingers against his cheekbone and winced.

"Who did that to you?"

He didn't answer. He just started laughing like a madman. I hurried into the kitchen, grabbing a rag and running it under cold water. I took a cold beer from the fridge and popped the top off. Back in the living room, I found Joe collapsed on the couch. He took the rag and beer from me and delivered a grateful nod. He swigged from the bottle and then wiped the blood from his face with the back of his hand.

Charlotte's words swirled around my brain. *I hope Joe keeps you here permanently.*

I took two steps back.

"Where's Calvin?" He clenched his jaw while he spoke.

"He just ran into town. He'll be back soon." I took a seat in the chair kitty-corner to the couch—farthest from Joe.

His bloodshot eyes scanned the living room and landed on me. "Calvin did this."

"What? When?"

When could he have done that to him? He was with Albert and hadn't been gone more than twelve or fourteen minutes now.

"When he told Wyatt that I slept with Charlotte." Joe let out a laugh and took another swig of his beer.

I swallowed hard. I was the one that told Wyatt, not Calvin. I tapped my fingers on my knee and then brought them to my lips, biting on my chipped nails.

Joe shook his head. "I don't even remember it, really. She came down to the tavern, telling me she wanted to talk, and then she came onto me. I don't really recall the rest."

I brought my arms in front of my body, folding them over my stomach. I hoped Calvin would walk through that door because he would do anything for me as long as he thought there was hope for us. Why was he never here when shit was hitting the fan?

"So, anyway. Wyatt came and confronted me earlier today. Told me he knew about Char and me." Joe laughed. "My brother, the golden boy, turning on me again."

He lifted his foot and slammed it against the coffee table. I jumped back in my seat ever so slightly. Predators thrived on fear.

"Did he tell you about our parents?"

I nodded. "I heard about the fire."

Joe laughed again, a forced and terrifying laugh. "There was a fire in this family long before there was one in this house."

I leaned forward in my chair. "What . . . what do you mean?"

"Our father wasn't a good man. He was abusive, a drunk. Calvin got away for a few years. I was happy someone finally got out of this town. I stayed and worked this ranch every day. But I kept my distance from him. That left only one person in this house for my dad to abuse: Mom."

"I'm sorry," I said. I ran my finger over a thick scar on my knee, busying my fingers. I wasn't sure when or where I got it. Sometimes we don't even know where our scars come from.

Joe took his foot off the coffee table and chugged the rest of his beer.

I blinked several times, unsure of what to say. "Why are you telling me all this?"

"Just welcoming you to the family. I want you to know what you're getting into. We may have escaped our father's abuse, but we didn't escape his genetics." Joe smiled.

I stood from my chair and carefully backed toward the kitchen. I needed more distance between us.

"You're scaring me, Joe."

He jumped up from the couch, holding the beer by his side, his fingers gripping the neck of the bottle.

Joe took a step toward me. "Oh, there's nothing to be scared of. I'm the only person that's always been honest with you."

I backed farther into the kitchen, inching my way to where the phone hung on the wall. "I think you should wait outside."

"What are you doing, Grace?"

I didn't answer.

His eyes darkened as he stumbled toward me. I grabbed the phone from the wall and pressed it against my ear. I could barely hear the dial tone.

"What are you doing, Grace?" he taunted.

I backed as far away from him as the cord would give. The coiled cord was already stretched out, and I wondered if this same situation had happened with someone else in this house.

"Nine one one, what's your emergency," a woman's voice on the other end said.

"Please send an officer to the Wells' ranch out on highway 26."

"Calvin's taken everything from me. I think it's time I take something from him." His lips curved into a sinister smile. He hurled the beer bottle. As it shattered against the wall behind me, Joe wrapped his hand around the telephone cord and yanked the phone. It fell to the floor with a *thud*, breaking into several pieces.

"I never remembered driving the night Lisa died." He gazed up at the ceiling like he was trying to conjure up a memory.

I furrowed my brow. "What are you saying?"

"I remember going out with Calvin and Lisa. I really didn't want to because I'd worked twenty-four hours straight between the ranch and the auto shop. I just wanted to sleep, but it was his birthday. We took my truck to Pine Tavern. That's the last thing I remember."

"So, you must have fallen asleep on the drive home," I said, inching away.

He stared into my eyes, moving his jaw side to side. My back pressed against the wall. It was as far away as I could get from him in the small kitchen. Charlotte's words sprung to the front of my mind again. *I hope Joe keeps you here permanently.*

"Maybe. But Char told me something that makes me think otherwise. She said she saw us leave that night." Joe coughed and blood trickled out of his mouth. He spit it onto the floor and wiped his lips with the back of his hand.

"What did she tell you?"

He took a couple of steps and stopped when he was just a foot from me. Joe leaned in and inhaled, sniffing my hair. I'm not sure how I smelled to him, but his scent was a combination of desperation and regret, like dark rum mixed with cigarette smoke and sweat. Pulling away, he smiled. His hand reached toward me, and I flinched (mistake), thinking he was going to put it on me. Instead, he ripped the phone base clean off the wall. It crashed to the floor. Sweat gathered at my hairline. My breath quickened, and my eyes bounced all over the kitchen in search of something to protect myself. The knife block on the counter . . . too far away. My eyes went back to his.

"Don't matter. Doesn't change anything." He shook his head and backed away from me.

"This place should have burned down the first time."

"Maybe it changes everything," I said.

He eyed me cautiously, and I thought he was going to reveal what Charlotte had told him, but his face twisted up.

"You shouldn't have come here, Grace."

I swallowed hard.

From his back pocket, he pulled out a small plastic bottle. Joe stumbled into the living room and looked around for a moment—almost as if he were taking it all in, one last time. He staggered to the large bay window adorned with thick, floral drapes. His head lolled to one side and then the other before he started dousing the curtains with the bottle's cloudy-colored liquid.

Turning back toward me, he chuckled. "This Airbnb is out of business."

I pulled myself from the wall and took a couple of apprehensive steps toward Joe, trying to see what he was doing. He slid his hand into his pocket and faced the window again. *Click. Click. Click.* The drapes burst into flames. He clicked the lighter again and the other curtain caught on fire.

"What the hell are you doing?" I yelled.

Joe ignored my question and burst into a manic laugh. He tried to light the couch on fire, but it wouldn't take.

I bolted to the kitchen, tearing through the cupboards in search of a fire extinguisher. When I couldn't find one, I grabbed a bowl and filled it with water. Back in the living room, I felt arms wrap around me just as I was about to toss the water onto the burning curtains. The bowl slipped from my hands and fell to the floor, soaking my feet.

"Let it burn, Grace," Joe whispered into my ear as he held me tight against his body. His hot breath irritated my skin. I stomped on his foot and tried to wiggle loose, but he was too strong. He held me firmly, laughing as the curtains burned.

"You're hurting me."

Joe ignored my words but loosened his grip enough so I could squirm out of it. I raised my arm, moved my hip to the side, and swung my fist into his groin. He groaned and crumpled to the floor. When I tried to run away, he caught my ankle, sending me crashing to the floor with him. I kicked with my other leg, struggling to free myself from his grip again. A cloud of smoke blanketed the ceiling. My breaths were quick and uncontrolled, and I was inhaling too much of it as a result. The smoke stung my eyes and burned as it entered my lungs, sending me into a coughing fit.

"I'm saving you, Grace," he said. "From Calvin."

My mouth dropped open, and he finally let go of my ankle, allowing me to scramble away.

40.

Calvin

I saw the fire as soon I pulled into the driveway. A flame danced in the living room window. I sped up, pressing my foot firmly against the gas pedal.

"Whoa, what's the rush?" Albert asked as he sipped on his bottle of Jack, completely clueless. Some of the liquid dribbled down his chin and spilled onto his shirt.

"I told you not to drink that in here."

He gathered the liquid from his chin and pushed it back up to his lips with his pointer finger.

I slammed on the brakes. "Grace," I yelled as I jumped out of the truck and ran toward the house.

Inside, I found Grace crawling away from the burning drapes. The fire spread to the wall and ceiling, and the room was cloaked in smoke. Immediately, I sprinted to the kitchen, leaping over her. From beneath the sink, I snatched the fire extinguisher.

Just as I stood and turned, something whacked me in the face. Blood pooled from my nose, and it took me a moment to realize Joe was standing right in front of me, seething with balled-up fists. He was dirty and bloody and didn't look anything like my brother. Thick, angry veins covered his neck and arms. His eyes were black like two pieces of coal had been shoved into his face.

"What did you do?!"

"What I should have done a long time ago," he said, winding his arm back.

When he swung, I blocked it with the fire extinguisher. His knuckles cracked against the metal. He cried out in pain and tried to shake out his hand. His fingers wouldn't straighten, and I knew right away, several had broken. I thrust the fire extinguisher into his jaw, reeling him backward. Joe collapsed to the ground, and the back of his head slammed against the floor. He was out cold. I stepped over him and ran toward the living room. Grace was gone. Albert coughed on smoke while swatting the curtains with pillows.

"Stand back," I yelled.

He looked over at me, dropped the pillows to the floor, and moved out of the way. I swept the fire extinguisher back and forth over the curtains and the wall, not stopping until the fire was completely out. I wouldn't let this place go up in flames again.

Dropping the fire extinguisher on the couch, I heard the floor creak behind me. Joe leaned against the kitchen table, barely able to stand on his own. His eyes were so narrow, a piece of paper wouldn't fit between his lids. I wasn't sure he could even see me.

"Calvin the golden boy always saving the day." Joe shook his head and let out a huff.

I threw my hands up. "What the fuck are you doing?" I took a few steps toward him, squaring up, ready to beat his ass again.

"It should have burned down the first time," he said.

I tried to look him in the eyes, but it was like he was looking right through me. "How could you say something like that, Joe?"

He opened them a little more, making it clear he could see me. "The fire didn't kill Mom and Dad. Mom killed Dad and then killed herself."

"No, they died in the fire." I shook my head. "You're lying."

I heard the screen door close behind me and quickly glanced back. Albert scurried out of the house.

"No, I'm not Calvin. Looks like you and Mom have something in common."

I didn't fully register what he was saying. I took a step back—actually, it was more like I fell back. My vision blurred. It was like I was looking at my surroundings through a dirty windowpane. All this time and no one, not one damn person told me the truth about my own parents—about what happened to them. Who knew? Obviously, the sheriff's department and Dr. Reed. Did Betty know? Did Wyatt? Charlotte? Did this whole fucking town know?

"You're lying," I said in disbelief.

"You know I'm not the liar in the family." He shifted his stance, trying to stand upright on his own. But his body slumped to one side. "You are. There's a darkness here. Can't you feel it?" Joe stagged past me, through the living room and toward the front door. "I know you can feel it, Calvin, because it's in you too."

The screen door slammed behind him. Sirens roared in the distance. I was about to chase after him when I remembered Grace. My eyes went wide, and I bolted down the hallway. Her room was pitch-black and still. A draft of wind came whooshing in from the window, blowing up the curtains. I flicked on the lights.

"Grace," I called out.

The screen had been removed, and the window was pushed all the way open.

"Grace!" I yelled, sticking my head out the window.

I couldn't see anything outside, just darkness and the red-and-blue lights in the distance. I put one foot up on the windowsill but paused when I heard a rustle in the closet. Placing my foot back on the floor, I pulled open the closet door. The end of a closed umbrella hit me right in the chest and I wheezed, falling backward.

Grace held the umbrella in her shaky hands.

I gasped for air and pressed my fist against my sternum right where she drilled me. "Grace," I gasped. "Are you okay?"

She nodded several times; the umbrella shook in her hands as she held it like a bat ready to swing again. I got to my feet and wrapped my arms around her.

"I'm sorry."

The umbrella slipped from her hands but she didn't hug me back. Grace was stiff like a board and quiet like a mouse. She was just there, a warm body pressed up against me. I rubbed her back, hoping she'd soften, but she didn't. I released her and stared into her eyes. The blueness was darker now. Trying to get a better look at her, I pushed a piece of hair from her face, tucking it behind her ear. She was like stone.

"Did Joe hurt you?" I asked. I needed to know. If he did, I'd kill him.

She didn't blink. Her face didn't move. But her head shook. I pressed my lips together and nodded. "Okay. Okay."

Kissing her forehead, I pulled her into my chest again, reassuring her that everything was all right and that she was safe now.

"I want to lie down," Grace mumbled.

I helped her into bed. She sat down, swung her legs over, and laid back, staring up at the ceiling. It was all very robotic, like she was just going through the motions. Her eyes were spellbound by the off-white popcorn ceiling. The sirens shut off but I could see the yard lit up with flashing lights.

"The police are here. I've got to go talk to them."

I wanted to ask her what happened, what Joe had said to her, what he had done, but it was like she was in a trance. I'm not sure if she was in shock or something else.

"Are you okay alone for a bit?"

She didn't speak. She just rolled onto her side, facing away from me.

I stood there for a moment not wanting to leave her. But I knew I had to.

Outside, a deputy was talking to Joe. He had to have been new because I had never seen him around before. Joe was seated on the steps of the porch with his head in his hands. Albert was nowhere to be seen. Must have wandered off when he saw the sirens coming.

"What the hell happened here?" the deputy asked, glancing in my direction as I let the screen door close behind me. "We got a 911 call from a woman. Where is she?"

The deputy put a hand on his hip and let out a deep breath. Another cruiser rolled up the driveway. Sheriff Almond stepped out of it, straightening his belt buckle.

"What's going on, Deputy?" the sheriff asked.

"Just arrived, sir. We got a call from a woman asking for police assistance."

Sheriff Almond took in the scene, eyeing up Joe and then me. He cleared his throat. "This is my third time out here in a week."

"I know, sir. I just got here." I shuffled my feet. "Grace, the woman you met the other day, called."

"Well, I'm going to need to talk to her then. Where is she?" Sheriff Almond cocked his head.

"Lying down in her room."

"Is she okay?" the deputy asked.

I glared at the back of Joe's head. "Yeah, I think so."

"I need to see her now." His tone matched the serious look on his face.

He took a step toward me and his hand went to his pistol. I'm not sure if it was instinctual or he genuinely thought Joe or I were a threat—that we had done something to Grace.

Joe huffed, throwing his hands up. "Just take me down to the station. I'm drunk, and I started a fire."

"I'll deal with you later." The sheriff scowled at Joe but then returned his gaze to me. "First, I need to check on Grace."

Joe got to his feet, wobbly. It took him a moment to get his balance, and when he did, he put his hands in front of his stomach. "Just leave her out of this. Go ahead and arrest me. I know you want to."

"Sit back down," the deputy commanded, pointing to the stairs. He clenched his jaw and retrieved the pistol from his belt.

"Jesus," Joe said, putting his hands up and falling back into a sitting position.

I took a step back.

"Deputy, you stay out here with this goon," Sheriff Almond gestured to Joe. "I'll go and talk to her."

The deputy nodded but kept his gun in his hand, carefully watching my dumbass brother.

I opened the screen door and led the way.

Sheriff Almond followed behind. His hand hovered over his pistol. He took a quick look around the living room, surveying the damage from the fire. His eyes were intense. They scanned back and forth between my hands and my head as if he was anticipating a move on my part.

"Keep going," he said.

I walked down the hallway deliberately, keeping my hands at my sides, so I'd give him no reason to put one of those bullets in me. But sometimes you didn't need a reason.

In front of Grace's door, I turned back slowly toward the sheriff. "She's in there."

He tapped my shoulder, gesturing me to move aside. He knocked on the door three times.

"Grace, it's Sheriff Almond with the Dubois Sheriff's Department." He kept an eye on me while waiting for Grace to open the door. It was dead quiet and nothing stirred on the other side.

Growing impatient, the sheriff turned the doorknob and pushed open the door. He flicked on the light, revealing Grace lying on the bed with her back facing him.

"Grace," he said again. There was concern in his voice. He looked at me and then took a couple steps toward the bed so he was standing over her. I waited just outside the room, peering inside.

"Grace."

She didn't stir. She lay completely still. He bent down and placed his hand on her shoulder, shaking it. Grace jolted up into a sitting position. Her quick movement startled him, and he nearly leapt back.

She rubbed at her eyes. "What?"

"You called the police, Grace. I'm here to check on you. To make sure you're all right."

She pulled the blanket up higher and brought her knees to her chest, hesitating with her response. Her eyes swung back and forth between the sheriff and me like she had something she wanted to say. I was scared, scared she was going to ask for a ride out of town.

"I'm fine," she finally landed on.

I let out a sigh of relief.

Sheriff Almond tilted his head and then turned back toward me. "Give us a moment."

I nodded. "I'll be in the kitchen."

"Close the door," he said.

I didn't want to but I did as he asked. I hoped it wouldn't be a mistake.

41.

Grace

Sheriff Almond was seated on the end of the bed, taking notes on a small pad of paper. His eyes were shifty like he didn't believe anyone, and he was right not to. We were all lying.

"And you're sure he didn't hurt you?"

"No, he just scared me." I grabbed the glass of water from the nightstand and sipped. It went down like I was swallowing a potato.

He nodded and scribbled in his notepad. "When do you leave, Grace?"

My hands shook as I placed the glass back on the coaster. "The day after tomorrow."

"Good."

"Good?" I questioned.

"It's just better you leave. I've got a sixth sense for trouble, and this ranch reeks of it." He squinted his eyes, punctuating his warning to me.

"Am I safe here?"

The sheriff sucked on his front teeth, trying to decide on what to say, what the right answer was, if there was a right answer. He couldn't go around throwing accusations he had no proof of.

"You'll be all right," he finally landed on. Sheriff Almond closed up his little notepad and slid it into the front pocket of his shirt. He stood, pulling a card from his belt. "If you need anything, and I mean anything, call me," he said, handing over his business card.

I flipped it over several times in my hand, deciding if I should tell him anything more. Was what Joe said true? Was Calvin driving the night Lisa was killed? Had he framed his own brother? Joe said he didn't remember anything, so how would he know? And what had Charlotte told him? Whatever she said could have been a lie. She was so hurt by Calvin rejecting her, she'd probably do just about anything to hurt him back. Then, there was the missing woman. I looked up at the sheriff.

"What about that woman? Have you found her?" I asked.

He furrowed his brow. It was clear he hadn't, and I could tell it pained him. He looked haunted by the unsolved case.

"Not yet, but we will." Sheriff Almond twisted a thick strand from his mustache. "Have you noticed anything unusual around here?"

I considered his question. The words sat at the tip of my tongue—the clothes in the dresser, the woman's scream, the locked basement door—but I swallowed them. "I'm from New York. Most everything here is strange to me," I landed on.

He folded in his lips and nodded. "If you do notice anything, you have my number." The sheriff turned on his foot and walked to the door. "Want this open or closed?"

"Closed," I said.

He tilted his head and left the room, shutting it behind him.

I turned the card over and over in my hands. He didn't say I was safe here. He said I'd be fine. Fine. I plucked my book from the nightstand and slid the business card inside of it.

I'll be fine. I'll be fine. I repeated it over and over until I started to believe it.

Outside, the roar of engines startled me. Peeking out the window, I saw Joe seated in the back of a police cruiser. The vehicle pulled out, then Sheriff Almond's, and then Calvin's truck.

Without thinking, I swung my legs out of bed, tiptoed toward the door, and listened for a moment. When I heard nothing, I slowly opened it and stuck my head out, peering down the long hallway. The house was quiet. The floorboards creaked beneath me as I crept across them.

"Calvin," I called out. "Are you here?"

Silence.

I'll be fine.

"Albert," I said.

There was silence save for the creaking the house made on its own, like little warnings to those inside of it.

I stopped in front of the door leading to the basement. The one area of the ranch that was off-limits. But why? I placed my hand against it—willing it to tell me what was on the other side. What did Calvin not want me to see? What was he hiding? I slid a hand into the pocket of my jeans and pulled out a bobby pin. After twisting and bending it, I slid the pin into the keyhole of the door. I took a deep breath and got to work. I needed to know what was down there. I needed to know what he was hiding.

After a few minutes, the lock popped. The open door revealed a set of decrepit wooden stairs jutting out. Moisture and the smell of mildew hung heavy in the air. A metallic tinge wafted into my nostrils, permeating every breath I took. I flipped the light switch on the wall at the top of the stairs, but nothing illuminated the dark cavern below. Pulling out my phone, I turned on the flashlight (the only thing it was good for in this house) and slowly descended the steps. The damp old wood absorbed my weight. As my line of sight dropped below the walls, I began to make out large mounds scattered across the space before me; stacks of boxes mixed with various unknowns formed a jagged and misshaped mountain range, a miniature remake of the mountains just aboveground, beyond the river. The place was the creation of a hoarder who collected various treasures with no intention of relinquishing them. I weaved my way along the path cut through the junk, trying to find anything of importance. I waved my phone, and then I noticed something very odd for a basement in someone's home: pairs of eyes, yellow and dead, following me. My body froze to listen for movement or breathing. Nothing. I wanted to turn back and run but curiosity got the better of me, and I charged forward. As I moved around another stack of boxes, a massive cobweb planted itself across my face.

"Ahh, gross, gross, gross," I squealed and jumped back, knocking into a tower of junk.

I turned to see what I had bumped into, but there were those eyes again, no more than a foot in front of me, paired with razor-sharp teeth, bearing down at me. I put my hands up to block my face and shrieked but . . . nothing happened. I reopened my eyes, and there it was, still in the same spot. Looking at it closer, I realized what it was. A stuffed raccoon. How the hell were there more of these down here? Did he switch them out for each season?

There were other pairs of eyes across the room, and I quickly went to inspect each of them. A weasel, a badger, a coyote, all stuffed and dead, staring me down from somewhere beyond.

I reached out to touch one of them. It was stiff and its coat was coarse. Backing away from the dead creatures, I bumped into another stack of boxes. Inside the top one was a hodgepodge of junk: old books, a belt, a small fishing tackle box, and a stack of photos. I collected the pictures, flipping through them. The first was a picture of Joe and Calvin out by the river with fishing poles in their hands. They had to have been teenagers in it. The next one was Calvin, Joe, and an older man and woman. The older man was unusually large with a stern face full of frown lines. The older woman was petite and beautiful with long brown hair. She wore way too much makeup—more than she clearly needed unless she was trying to cover something up. A forced smile was plastered across her face. These were their parents.

The next photo made my mouth drop open and my hands relax. All the pictures fell to the ground. I stared down at the collage of photos, my eyes glued to the one on top. The one that revealed a lie. I bent down slowly and picked it up, bringing it closer to my line of sight. Calvin and Joe were seated on a bench. Calvin had to have been around eighteen. Sitting in a chair beside them was a much younger Albert without the rosacea. He was all smiles. I turned the photo over and discovered the handwritten message on the back. *Summer of '04. Calvin, Joe, and Uncle Albert.*

I slid the photo into the back pocket of my jeans. Albert was Calvin's uncle. He lied to me. He wasn't his Airbnb guest, not some guy passing through. He was family. Why would he lie about a thing like that?

I picked up the rest of the photos and tossed them in the box, closing it back up.

Making my way through the path, I had every intention of going back upstairs, but something else stopped me. A large notebook sat on top of a tote. The words Calvin's Guest Book were written in thick black letters on the cover. My fingers grazed over them.

Each page was filled with names and dates. I quickly gathered that the dates were check-in and checkout times, beginning one year ago. I found the last page and ran my finger down it, reading the names. Cristina Colton stuck out because the rest before it were all male names. Then Kayla Whitehead. I remembered Calvin's words: *I don't really get any female guests.* Kayla had been a guest just nine weeks before me. My eyes moved down the page and when I got to the last row I gasped. The words were written neatly with a heart over the letter *i*. The check-in column had a date. The checkout column didn't. The final name on the page was Bri Becker. Calvin lied about her. She was here, and according to this guest book . . . she never left.

A car door slammed outside. I jolted and quickly closed the guest book, putting it back where I found it. I ran to the stairs but before I ascended them, I stopped. Something behind the open staircase caught my eye. A folding table sat behind it. Several guns, knives, and bullets were laid out, an arsenal for mayhem. I picked up the small handgun and turned it over and over again. I set it back down, and my fingertips slid over a large hunting knife. The blade was curved, and the handle was wooden. It appeared homemade. I held it, studying it closely. There was a red tint to the edge of the blade as if it weren't cleaned properly the last time it was used. I backed away from the table with the knife in hand and quickly ran up the stairs, closing and locking the basement door behind me.

I slid the knife and photo under the mattress and crawled into bed. I could feel my heartbeat everywhere in my body—from my feet to the back of my head. I'm not sure how long I laid there. Maybe ten minutes. Maybe twenty. When I didn't hear footsteps, I sat up and pushed the curtains aside. I nearly screamed when I saw the ghostly figure standing in front of the house, dressed in a long white nightgown. It was dark out, and it took a few seconds to realize it was Betty. She swayed side to side, staring at the house. I considered staying in bed, but I needed to see what she was doing here.

A few moments later, I was standing in front of her. She hadn't even noticed me. Her eyes were laser-focused on the ranch like she was seeing something that no one else was privy to. I was about to speak when she started to mumble. I stepped closer, trying to hear what it was she was saying.

"The house is evil. It infects everyone," she said just above a whisper. "Nothing good happens here."

"Betty, are you okay?"

She didn't react. She just continued whispering. "You shouldn't have come here because now I'm not sure you'll be able to leave."

"Betty," I said again, but this time I grabbed her hand.

She flinched and let out a gulp, like all the air had been sucked out of her body. She blinked several times. I must have come into focus for her because she turned her head toward me almost robotically.

"Grace, I'm sorry. I don't know what I said." Betty shook her head and took a step back, bringing her hands to her face. She rubbed at it violently like she was trying to wake herself from a bad dream. I was going to tell her to stop but my voice got stuck in my throat. Betty turned and scrambled toward her vehicle.

"Please don't tell Calvin I was here."

Before I could clear my throat and ask her what she meant, she was backing her car down the driveway. I stared up at the ranch. It looked different now.

A truck rumbled in the distance. I sprinted back into the house and closed the bedroom door behind me just as the engine shut off outside. When I reached for the lock, it was then that I noticed what Calvin had done. The handle had been installed the wrong way. Instead of locking others out, it would lock me in. It was no longer a bedroom. It was a cage.

Day Nine

42.

Calvin

It was noon and Grace still hadn't come out of her room. I stood in front of her door three times already, pressing my ear against the wood and listening. It was quiet. I knew she hadn't left yet because her car was still parked in the driveway with the hood popped up. Joe said he ordered the parts and that one of the guys from the auto shop would be here this evening to fix it. I hoped he wouldn't show. Albert wasn't here either. His bedroom door was open, and the bed was made like he hadn't slept in it last night. Grabbing a glass from the cupboard, I filled it with water and chugged the whole thing. I still felt parched, and it seemed like nothing could quench my thirst. Refilling it again, I took a seat at the kitchen table and waited for Grace. My goal was to look nonchalant—like I wasn't waiting for her—but I'm sure it was plastered all over my face, written in Sharpie: *I NEED YOU HERE WITH ME NOW.*

Finally, I heard her creaky bedroom door open. Her footsteps were light and then another door closed—the bathroom, I presumed. I considered getting up and waiting outside of it for her but figured that would be too much, so I stayed put. She was already scared and skittish. I unfolded the local newspaper and pretended to read it. The toilet flushed. The faucet ran. You could hear everything in this house. The door opened. Her footsteps were light again but grew louder. Then they stopped suddenly. She was just standing in the hallway, listening. When she appeared in the kitchen, I let out the breath I didn't realize I was hold-ing in. Cliché, I know. But it's true. Grace always took my breath away.

She was dressed in a white T-shirt and black leggings. Her hair was pulled up in a high ponytail. Her makeup didn't cover the dark circles under her eyes.

"Good afternoon," I said with a smile.

She gave a tight smile back. "Hey."

Grace walked to the coffee pot, not making eye contact with me. I turned around and watched her pour herself a cup.

"Are you okay?" I asked.

She nodded and took a sip. Grace slid a piece of bread into the toaster and collected everything she needed to make peanut butter toast. Her back was to me while she waited for her toast to be done.

"Are you sure?" I asked.

Grace didn't turn around. She just nodded again. The bread shot out of the toaster like a jack-in-the-box. She jumped a little. Her muscles tensed, and she took a moment to compose herself. Grace pulled the toast out and slathered it with butter and peanut butter. She was acting strange, but could I blame her? Joe really shook her up, and I wondered what he had said. She opted to stand at the counter to eat her toast and drink her coffee, rather than sit with me.

"Betty's coming over today to replace the drapes," I said, trying to get her to talk to me.

Grace just stood there, chewing on her toast—not saying a word.

"Joe spent the night in county jail. They're charging him with arson. He just can't stay outta trouble. I told him not to come around here no more." I sipped my water and set the glass back down on the table.

Grace drank the rest of her coffee and then topped it off. She re-turned to her half-eaten piece of toast.

"Have you seen Albert?" I asked.

She shook her head and crossed one leg in front of the other.

"Ummmph. I haven't seen him since last night when the police showed up. Must have spooked him."

Grace said nothing.

I gestured to a chair. "You know you can sit at the table and eat."

She shoved the rest of the toast into her mouth and rinsed off her plate. Grace was a feisty one. Picking up her coffee mug, she started toward her bedroom but stopped before venturing down the hallway. Slowly, she turned around.

"The lock you put on my door."

"Yeah," I said.

Her eyes narrowed in an accusatory way. "You installed it the wrong way." She raised her chin and put her free hand on her hip. "Was that intentional? Are you trying to keep me here?" Her voice had a tinge of frustration in it—mixed with something else. It was fear. Grace was afraid of me.

"No, of course not." I stood too quickly. The chair reeled backward and hit the floor with a *thud*.

Grace took a step back. Her eyes went to the porch door and then back to me.

I bent down slowly and picked up the chair. Shaking my head, I looked over at her. The whites of her eyes were on full display.

"It was an honest mistake. I'll fix it, okay?"

She pursed her lips together. "An honest mistake? Honest? You sure about that?" she asked, cocking her head.

Grace was hiding something, but what was it? What did Joe tell her? What did she find? She was treating me like a stranger—no, worse than that, like I was a danger to her.

"Yes, honest. Like I said, I'll fix it."

"You do whatever you want. I'm going for a run." She stomped toward her bedroom. "One of the guys from the auto shop is swinging by to fix your car tonight," I called out.

"Good," Grace yelled over her shoulder.

I let out a deep breath. How had things gotten so bad so quickly? The more time I spent with Grace, the less I seemed to know about her. She was a peculiar woman, and she was clearly hiding something. I suppose we all were. But living alone on a ranch with only animals to talk to, you learn what the animal will do before it does it. And at the core, we're all animals.

43.

Grace

I stomped across the porch, past my broken car, and down the driveway. I had to get away and clear my head. How far could I get from this place on foot? Could I make it back into town? My head was a foggy mess thanks to a night of no sleep. It felt like someone was in my room watching me. There was a presence. The house creaked all night long, and I could hear someone on the other side of my bedroom door most of the evening. I wasn't sure if it was Albert or Calvin standing outside my room, listening to me sleep. At one point, I even grabbed the knife, clutching it all night. I shook out my left hand, trying to expel the achiness. This wasn't how any of this was supposed to go.

I kicked at the gravel while I walked. My brain swirled with thoughts. I didn't buy that installing the lock the wrong way was an honest mistake. Calvin's a fricking handyman. How could he screw something that simple up? Unless he did it on purpose. And Albert, his fake Airbnb guest. Why was he lying about that? Then, the most damning of it all. The guest book with Briana Becker's name. Calvin lied to Sheriff Almond. She was here. Had he done something to her? Heck, maybe Charlotte did. She was clearly obsessed with Calvin. She hadn't been around in two days, but I still felt like she was around—just waiting for me to leave. Then there was Joe. Was he the only one telling the truth, or was he lying too?

I wanted to scream, and I wanted to be as far away from this place as possible. Halfway down the driveway, I quickened my pace from a fast walk to a full-on sprint. As soon as my stride hit, I stepped onto a large uneven rock and came crashing to the ground at the end of the driveway. My ankle nearly folded under itself. The gravel scraped my knees and the palms of my hands. I screamed out in pain.

"No, no, no, no, no, no," I cried as I held my ankle. "This can't be fucking happening."

"Grace," Calvin called out.

I turned back, watching him sprint toward me. *My lying knight in fake armor. Oh no, no, no.* I flexed my ankle and then wiggled it side to side. It wasn't as bad as I thought. A little pain on the ball of it.

Calvin knelt beside me. "Grace, are you okay?" His brows knitted together as caught his breath.

"Yeah, I just tripped." I looked at my bloody palms and knees.

"Let's get you inside and cleaned up," he said. "Can you walk?"

"I think so." He grabbed my arm and pulled me to a standing position. I took a step. The pain was nothing compared to the fear I felt with Calvin's hands on me. He led me back up the driveway, back toward the goddamn house I so desperately wanted to get away from.

"Are you sure you're okay?" he asked, helping me up the steps of the porch.

I nodded but didn't say a word.

Inside, Calvin set me on the couch. Within a matter of minutes, he had my ankle propped up with a pillow and an ice pack on it. He cleaned and bandaged my scrapes and cuts. It was like he was happy to be doing this. Every touch from him felt like a needle piercing my skin.

"I'm tired of the lies." The words tumbled out of my mouth. I wanted to suck them back in. I was in too vulnerable a position to accuse him of anything. But I knew Calvin liked to be challenged.

"What lies?" He leaned back and stared into my eyes. "I'm not lying to you."

I chose my next words carefully. "Do you keep photos of all your

Airbnb guests?" I slid the picture of Albert, Calvin, and Joe from my pocket and held it in front of him.

"Where did you get that?" His skin flushed, and I wasn't sure if it was due to anger or embarrassment of being caught in his little lie.

I tossed the photo at him. "It doesn't matter."

He picked it up and looked at it fondly. "I told you not to go into the basement." Calvin raised his head, refocusing his attention back on me.

I sat up taller, trying to make myself look bigger like prey would do with a predator. I raised my chin, trying to make myself look unafraid. I widened my eyes, trying to show him that I was not about to back down. Calvin stood and started to pace the living room.

He let out a heavy sigh. "I'm sorry, Grace. I lied about Albert. He's my uncle, my degenerate uncle. And I'm just embarrassed of him. He shows up every few months and crashes with me, picks up some of his stuff from the basement, and then he's gone after a few days. I just didn't want you to associate him with me."

Calvin folded up the photo and slid it into his back pocket. "I'm such an idiot. I'm not good at this type of stuff. I like you, and I didn't want to give you any reason not to like me. It's why I've told some dumb lies." He shook his head. "I don't get many chances with girls like you, and I didn't want anything screwing it up."

Calvin just kept talking in circles, playing the I'm-a-dumb-country-boy routine. I wasn't buying it, not this time. He was cunning and meticulous.

"You can trust me, Grace." His eyes were intense.

Trust. I nearly laughed out loud, but I was walking a thin line between safety and whatever the hell Calvin would do to me.

"Did Bri Becker trust you?" I narrowed mine and pressed my lips firmly together.

He raised his brows. "Bri Becker?"

"The missing woman. The one the sheriff came here asking about."

"I already told you and the sheriff. She never showed up. I didn't lie about that."

I chewed on my words, thinking of whether I should bring up the guest book or not. I saw it. I saw her name. I saw the check-in date and the blank checkout date. How would he explain that away? I took a deep breath and eyed him in a challenging way.

My jaw was so tight I thought I might grind my teeth into dust. "I saw your guest book."

"What?" He cocked his head. His face was unreadable. I didn't know if it was fear, anger, sadness, regret, or a mix of all.

"In the basement. Her name was in it."

"That's not true!" he nearly yelled. I couldn't tell if he was being defensive because he was telling the truth or because he was lying.

Without another word, he stomped out of the living room. I heard the basement door creak open; his footsteps descended the stairs. Things shuffled around, and then there were footsteps again. This time they were coming up the stairs. He held the notebook out. The words Calvin's Guest Book were on the cover.

"Here," he said.

I flipped quickly to the last page that had writing on it. Dragging my finger down the list of names, I found the last one. The paper read, Kayla Whitehead. I remembered seeing her name, but Bri's was last. I flipped several more pages. They were all blank. No, her name was here. Bri Becker with a heart over the letter *i*. It was here. I saw it with my own eyes. Check-in date. Checkout . . . never.

"She was here. Bri Becker was here."

"I don't know what you're talking about, Grace. I told you the truth about her. She was never here." He rubbed his brow.

"But . . . but . . . I saw." My words fell off. I saw it. Didn't I? I scanned the page again. Her name was gone.

"I lied about Albert and liking brussels sprouts and even lied about enjoying reading." He walked to the bookshelf and slid several books out, holding them up. "I've never read a damn one of these. I just bought them to make me look smart." Calvin tossed the books onto a chair. "But I didn't lie about Bri Becker." He let out a pained breath and ran his hands down his face.

My mouth parted but no words came out. I didn't know what to say.

Calvin walked toward the front door, stopped, and turn back to me. "I'm going to get your vehicle working and fix the lock on your door. And then I'm going to make sure you have a great last night on my ranch." He sealed his promise with a heavy nod.

My stomach was in knots. I took a few small breaths, trying to keep my composure. I saw her name, didn't I? It was dark in the basement, and I was on edge, had been since I arrived. Maybe I had imagined it. Maybe he wasn't the one lying.

"Okay," I said.

I didn't know what else to say.

He let out a sigh and smiled. I forced the corners of my lips up. They quivered, but he didn't notice. He smiled a little wider and then headed outside. I closed my eyes and tried to picture the guest book the way I had seen it the day before. It was clear as day. I had seen it. There were few things I trusted, but my eyes were one of them.

Calvin may have been telling the truth about Albert—or Uncle Albert, for that matter. But he wasn't telling the truth about Bri. I saw her name. Checkout . . . never. She was still here. I could feel it.

44.
Calvin

I pulled off my sweat-soaked wifebeater and tossed it in the grass. It splatted against the ground. Wiping my brow, I bent over the hood of the car. The mechanic fixed most of the things wrong with Grace's vehicle, but left me to finish the job. He'd given me pretty clear instructions on how to finish, but I wasn't sure I was doing it right. However, I was determined, and determination could sometimes offset skills or talent. I had less than twenty-four hours with her and it terrified me. I wanted her to stay. No, I needed her to stay. Maybe not forever but just for a while—so she could see what we had. What Grace and I had most people wouldn't experience in a lifetime. It was electric . . . no, it was magic. We had what everyone dreamed of.

"Hey, Calvin," Betty called from behind me.

I was so deep in thought that I didn't hear her drive up or get out of her vehicle. I turned around to find her standing there with a pile of new drapes slung over her shoulder.

"Let me grab some of those," I said, taking them from her.

Betty raised her brows and surveyed my face. "How ya holding up?" She was always so concerned with how I was doing, almost too concerned at times.

I shrugged and blew out my cheeks. "I've been better."

"Where's your guest?" She looked toward the barn, then the pond, then the ranch.

"I think she's showering. She's still shaken up," I said, looking over at the house, imagining Grace in there.

"I bet." Betty gave a slight nod. "Must have been scary."

I led her inside and dropped the drapes on the couch. Betty surveyed the damage. The curtains were nearly disintegrated. The walls around the window and the ceiling were scorched black from the smoke.

"Joe sure did a number on these," Betty said, twisting her lips. "I don't understand what made him act like this." She pursed her lips and looked over at me, waiting for an explanation.

"I think it had to do with our parents." I raised an eyebrow, and my lips formed a straight line. "Did you know what really happened?"

I knew Joe was mad about more than that, but the rest wasn't Betty's concern.

Before she could answer, I already knew she knew. Her eyes glistened. Her lip trembled, and she let out a sigh. She lied to me.

"How could you not tell me?"

Betty lowered her chin. "I was trying to protect you."

"They were my parents. I had a right to know. And Joe knew all along. He had to deal with that on his own. That's why he's so messed up."

"I've tried to help him, but you know how he is. Once I saw how much it affected him, I knew I couldn't tell you too. Someone needed a clear head to take care of this ranch."

"This ranch? That's what you're worried about?" I walked to the wall and forced my fist through the weakest part of it, where the flames had licked and eaten it.

"Calv, don't do that." She put her hand on my shoulder and tried to pull me away. "I'm so sorry. I really am." Her voice shook.

I shrugged her hand off and pulled my fist from the wall. My knuckles were bloody but I didn't feel any pain. I didn't feel much of anything since I returned to this godforsaken ranch.

"Okay. Okay." She sniffled. "Please don't be mad at me."

Betty stood there for a moment.

"I'll give you some space and go check on my bees."

When I didn't say anything back, she left the house. I watched through the window as she walked across the porch, down the stairs, and out toward the woods. What gave her the right to decide what I needed to know and what I didn't? How could she hide what really happened to my parents from me? They say the truth will set you free but they never tell you it'll enrage you first. I pulled what was left of the burned curtains down and started removing the drapery hardware. Part of the drywall would need to be replaced and the whole damn thing would need to be repainted. More work for me to do, when I already had enough on my plate.

A piercing scream echoed outside. It was so loud it felt like the person was standing right beside me. I knew immediately that it was Betty. I bolted out the front door and ran toward the screams. I found her standing near her apiary. She shrieked into her hands over and over again. Turkey vultures scattered from the trees above, flying in all directions. The beehive receptacles were knocked over.

Albert laid on his back, his mouth gaping open. Vomit dripped down the side of his face which was swollen like a balloon blown up past its capacity. His eyes, although open, were barely visible due to the inflammation. His skin was red, blotchy, and covered in hives. Chunks of flesh were missing; most likely the turkey vultures had got to him first. His clothes were damp, and the bees were still buzzing around him, crawling over his flesh, in and out of his mouth, over his glazed eyeballs.

I pulled Betty into me. Her screams turned to uncontrollable sobs. Her body shook violently, and I thought she'd fall apart in my arms.

"What was he doing here?" she cried.

45.

Grace

The roar of police sirens woke me. My eyes shot open, and the cold bathwater slopped onto the floor. The bathroom was the only room I had privacy, so I had opted to spend as much time as I could in there. How long had I dozed off? I climbed out, dried myself off, and redressed.

What the hell happened now?

I slipped on a pair of sandals before heading outside. Betty was seated on the porch, sobbing with a blanket wrapped around her. Calvin stood next to her talking with Wyatt and Sheriff Almond. Parked in the driveway were two police vehicles and an ambulance. Calvin glanced in my direction. His eyes seemed to light up. I walked toward him, slowly and cautiously.

"What's going on?" I asked.

"It's Albert," Calvin said.

Betty sobbed harder.

"Where is he?" I asked.

"He's dead."

My hand went to my mouth.

A squeaking sound grabbed our attention. Two paramedics rolled a gurney carrying a large black body bag. Albert was clearly inside as it was cumbersome, and they were having a hard time moving it over gravel. They pushed and pulled, but the wheels kept getting stuck on every rock.

One of the paramedics wiped the back of his hand across his sweaty forehead. "Can we get a little help over here?"

Both Sheriff Almond and Wyatt nodded. Calvin followed behind. Between the five of them, they were able to get Albert's body into the ambulance. The paramedics shut the doors, got in, and drove off while Sheriff Almond, Wyatt, and Calvin made their way back to Betty.

The sheriff looked to her. "So, you just found him down there?"

She threw her hands up. "Yes, I already told you that." Betty glared at Calvin. "Why didn't you tell me Albert was back in town?"

"It slipped my mind."

"What was he doing here?" she asked.

Wyatt and Sheriff Almond exchanged a look while I stood there silently, trying to stay out of it.

"He was just passing through. You know how he is." Calvin scraped one boot against the other, flicking off a clump of dirt.

Betty's lip quivered. "But why was he down there?"

Calvin rubbed the back of his neck. "He must have wandered off. He's been drinking a lot, even more than usual."

She narrowed her eyes. "You should have been watching him."

"You're the one with the bees on the property. You're the one keeping secrets. Got the goddamn secret life of bees over here. Maybe if you were taking your pills, you'd know what was going on around you," Calvin spat.

Betty stood quicker than I thought an old woman like herself could. "Don't you dare talk to me like that, Calvin." She thrust a finger into his chest. "Your mother didn't raise you to speak like that."

Calvin's face reddened and his eyes tightened. "My mother is a murderer. You don't know what she raised me to be."

Betty let out a gasp.

I didn't react. I had heard Joe tell Calvin about their parents the night before while I was hiding in my room. You can hear everything in that house. I didn't know it was true then. I thought Joe was saying anything he could to infuriate his brother. But I knew it was true now. Knowing that made me believe that Joe was also telling the truth about the night Lisa died. He wasn't driving. Calvin was. But the question now was, did Calvin lie to cover his own ass after the accident, or was it not an accident?

Sheriff Almond's eyes went wide and his brows drew together. "Did you say murderer?"

"All right, that's enough," Wyatt said, stepping in between them.

"Ignore him, Sheriff. He don't know what he's talking about," Betty huffed.

Calvin pressed his lips firmly together but didn't say another word.

Everyone was silent. Sheriff Almond jotted a note down and pocketed the pad of paper. He rocked back on his heels, his eyes swinging from Betty to Calvin. He clearly wasn't in the know about the Wells' family history.

"As of now, it appears to be an accidental death, but we'll know more after the autopsy," he said to Betty. "I'm going have Deputy Miller take you home. Okay?"

She nodded several times and stepped away from Calvin.

If my car was working, I would have packed up and got a police escort out of this town. But instead, I just stood there silently, trying to go as unnoticed as possible. Wyatt walked Betty to his vehicle and helped her into the passenger seat. Sheriff Almond lingered, standing between Calvin and myself.

"When was the last time either of you saw Albert?"

"Last night when he went into town with Calvin," I said.

Calvin's eyes swung to me, unhappy.

"And I saw him just before you arrived last night," Calvin said. "He was helping me put out the fire Joe started but walked off before y'all pulled up."

Sheriff Almond twisted up his lips. "This is the fourth time I've been here this week."

"I know," Calvin said. "It won't happen again."

The sheriff let out a heavy sigh and sucked on his front teeth. Before turning to leave, he threw Calvin an accusatory look. It was like he knew something would happen again, and he would, in fact, be back.

"If it does, I'll find something to arrest you for," he warned.

The sheriff's footsteps were heavy across the porch and down the steps. He glanced back once more, narrowing his eyes as he climbed into his vehicle. The sheriff backed his SUV down the driveway, and I felt a pang in my stomach—like it was telling me that was my last opportunity out of here.

"Are you hungry?" Calvin asked.

How could he think about food at a time like this? His uncle was dead. I was about to call him out, to question him, to throw a fit, when my stomach rumbled. I glanced at my watch. It was just after five. Only sixteen hours left. I looked over at Calvin and simply nodded. He smiled and beckoned to follow him . . . back into the house.

46.
Calvin

Grace sat at the kitchen table, nursing a beer, while I busied myself in the kitchen, preparing a meal fit only for my girl. I considered making my specialty—brown beans, bacon, and hot dogs—but decided she deserved better than that since it was her last night. That meal held a special place in my heart. It was the dinner I fell in love with Grace over, and it was the meal that earned her trust. She didn't believe that combo of ingredients could taste good, but it did. I proved her wrong once, and I'd do it again. I glanced over my shoulder at her. She was watching me. Her gaze started at my feet and went all the way up to my head. I smiled and refocused my attention on sautéing the fresh green beans from my garden and checking on the boiling pot of noodles. It felt like she was looking at me for the last time, but I hoped it was the last of many, and I know that didn't make any sense. I was used to things not making much sense.

"Are you doing all right?" she asked, breaking the silence. I grabbed my open beer from the countertop and swigged.

The question caught me by surprise. I wasn't sure she cared about me anymore but it appeared she did. Why else would she ask about my well-being? Why would she be concerned with my grief? I leaned against the counter, crossing one foot over the other.

"I will be eventually," I said, wiping at my eyes.

Time healed all wounds and those it didn't scabbed over nicely enough.

Grace raised her chin and then lowered it, about to say something but then deciding not to. I sniffled and rubbed at my eyes, wondering what she was going to say. Her words were so careful now, like she was playing a game of chess.

"You looking forward to heading home?"

I knew she was but I hoped she would lie to me. Sometimes lying was the best thing you could do for another person. A lie provided comfort honesty never could. That's why I lied to her. My muscles tensed, waiting for her answer.

She shrugged. "Don't think I'll be able to since my car's not working."

"It's working now."

I thought I saw the smallest smile on her face, but I hoped my eyes were playing tricks on me.

"I'm sorry about Albert," she said.

"Me too." For more reasons than she would ever know.

Turning back to the stove, I stirred the beans a couple more times. The key to cooking green beans is butter, lots and lots of butter. The meatballs sizzled in the lard, and the noodles were nearly done. I was going to make something fancier like steak or shrimp for Miss Grace, but I didn't want to have to run into town and leave her alone. Plus, I was scared she'd find a way to leave while I was gone, and I couldn't have that.

I turned and smiled at her again. "Almost done."

Her lips made a tight smile, and she quickly brought the beer to her mouth and tipped it back. What was going on behind those blue, blue eyes? Was Grace thinking about leaving me?

47.
Grace

I dabbed at my mouth with a napkin and placed it on the table, signaling I was done. I did everything I could to appease Calvin tonight: returned all his smiles, stayed by his side, and ate his food. I hoped he hadn't done something to it. I watched him closely while he prepared the meal, just in case. It was obvious who he was, and I knew I had to be careful.

"Dinner was delicious," I said.

Calvin sat across from me, winding his spaghetti noodles around his fork. He ate slower than I did—purposefully, I assumed. He was trying to savor every moment he had left with me. I was just trying to get through dinner so all of this could be behind me come morning. I wasn't interested in getting any closer to Calvin. I'd gotten close enough, maybe almost too close.

"Thank you. I'm glad you liked it." His smile was beaming. He twisted up another fork of tangled noodles and stabbed a meatball with force.

"I'm sorry to bring this up again." I eyed Calvin cautiously. "What do the police think happened to Albert?"

He set his fork down and scratched the back of his head. "They think he was drunk, stumbled down there, and well, it was an accident."

I raised my brow. "But he was allergic to bees. Why would he go back there?"

Calvin leaned back in his chair and folded his arms across his chest. "How'd you know that?"

"I saw his medical bracelet and asked him about it. He told me he was basically allergic to everything." I leaned back in my chair, matching his posture.

"He was." Calvin shook his head. "Something like this was bound to eventually happen."

I swallowed hard. It was a strange thing for Calvin to say.

"Don't you think it's odd he went back by the bees?"

He wiped at his eyes. I didn't understand why he kept wiping them; they were dry. Had been all day.

"It was dark out. He was drinking. Probably got turned around."

Turned around? On a ranch he was clearly very familiar with? That picture of him, Calvin, and Joe was more than a decade old. I considered prying more but decided to play it safe and just agree with him.

"You're probably right. It's just such a shame," I said, delivering a sympathetic glance.

Calvin nodded. "It really is." He didn't break eye contact. But he wasn't really looking at me anymore. He was studying me.

"Do you need help cleaning up?" I knew it was time to put an end to this night.

He brushed my offer away with a double flick of his wrist. "Oh no. I got it."

I gave a small smile and tried to make my eyes appear big and puppy-like. "Mind if I head to bed? I've got a big day of traveling tomorrow."

Calvin coughed. There was a sadness in his eyes along with tinges of anger, frustration, and fear—all mixed into a perfect recipe of what, I presumed would be, a disaster. I nearly flinched waiting for his reply. Instead, I raised my shoulders and my chin. I had learned confidence was the best armor.

"Yeah, of course," he finally said.

I stood from my chair and inched away from the table. "Thanks for everything. I'll see you in the morning."

He gave a slight nod. "Good night, Grace."

"Good night, Calvin."

I smiled and headed toward my bedroom. Right as I reached the long, dark hallway, I felt a hand on my shoulder. It whipped me around with so much force that I didn't realize what was happening until it was too late. Calvin's lips were on mine, and they were hungry, as if he hadn't eaten enough at dinner. His hands ran up and down my back. His tongue pried open my mouth and forced its way in. His lips and tongue were wet and sloppy, not like I had experienced before.

I put my hands on his shoulders and shoved him. He stumbled backward, immediately lowering his head. I closed my eyes for a brief second and inhaled. The breath got caught in my lungs, and I held it there. Maybe it would never escape. Maybe that breath of air would always be there, like a pain just beneath my ribs that I couldn't get rid of—one that would always remind me of this moment with Calvin.

"I'm sorry. I can't," I said.

He scratched at his forehead.

"I'm leaving tomorrow."

Calvin took a deep breath that sounded more like a grunt.

"I know you think you are, Grace," he said, narrowing his eyes.

I blinked a few times and stepped back. "What did you say?"

"I said I know you are, Grace."

I took another step back. Is that what he said? I wasn't sure. I wasn't sure about anything anymore.

"I'm sorry. I just misread things." He slapped the palm of his hand against his forehead. "Sleep well," he said and then he slunk back toward the kitchen.

I retreated down the hallway, not turning around until I felt the door handle in my hand. I opened the door and closed it behind me. When I reached for the lock, I realized he hadn't fixed it like he said he would. Before getting into bed, I leaned the desk chair against the door, securing the back underneath the handle. I hoped he'd leave it unlocked for me in the morning.

In the middle of the night, my eyes shot open. The room was pitch-black, silent. I wasn't sure what it was that had roused me but something must have. My body was soaked with sweat. My heart raced, and my breathing was quick and uncontrolled like I had just run a marathon. I listened for any sound, any movement, but nothing. Perhaps it *was* nothing, a freak anomaly of the mind jarring me back to consciousness. But no— the brain doesn't just do that, not for nothing. Then a hand, cupped to fit the curvature of my face, rested over my mouth, gently at first, but then the pressure began to force my head deeper into the pillow, sending pain up the sides of my jaw.

"Shhhhh, time to be quiet, Grace Evans."

I still couldn't see well enough to make everything out, but that was Calvin's voice. I'd know it anywhere. I went to grab for his hand, but a tight burn dug into both of my wrists. I had been tied to the bed in my sleep, legs as well, a bound victim afloat on a padded mattress. I tried to scream but it was nothing more than a muffled wail through the hard-pressed skin and bones.

"Now, now, now, Grace. I said it was time to be quiet. Haven't we caused enough trouble already?"

Just as quickly as it came, his hand lifted away—but then something rough and coarse was shoved deep into my mouth, almost gagging me. No sound could escape now. Tears rolled down my cheeks in fear of what would come.

"I'm sorry, Grace. Truly, I am. I can't promise you will enjoy any of what is about to happen to you. In fact, I can promise quite the opposite. But just know that it wasn't your fault. You merely, well . . . made it worse."

Goose bumps covered my body as something cold and lifeless pressed into my center. And then a heat like I have never felt before, followed by immense wetness. It was as though I had pissed the bed. Then it came. The worst pain I had ever felt in my life. My muffled screams were drowned out by Calvin's deep laughter. The steel moved up toward my navel, meeting resistance as it passed every sinew and fiber of muscle, bone, and tendon. I was being treated like a freshly caught fish, laid out on a newspaper.

"Remember what I said about fishing? The trick is to get the hook all the way through it from end to end, so it can't get off. You're the worm, Grace. You could have been the fish, but you wanted to get away from me so badly." He laughed maniacally.

I felt the steel press farther inside of me, scraping and tearing my insides. A hand squeezed my throat, crushing it further like a vice grip. My last breath was mere moments away. My mind closed off as the steel and barb began to push up through my esophagus and then . . .

"UGGGHHH." Panting breaths and cold sweat consumed me as I jarred awake, sitting up in the bed. I ran my hands all over my body, my throat, my wrists, my stomach—all unscathed. Oh my fucking God! What was that? I looked around the dark room. There was nothing— just blackness and silence. When I was convinced no one else was in the room, I laid back down and closed my eyes, repeating over and over to myself, "One more sleep."

Day Ten

48.
Calvin

"Shit," I muttered. The time on the clock read 9:07 a.m. I hadn't slept in this late since I lived back in Colorado, when animals weren't depending on me to be fed and watered. The evening before was all a blur. After Grace went to sleep, I went deep into a bottle of whiskey, trying to forget her as I knew she'd leave me in the morning. I realized it after she pushed me away and looked at me like I was someone to be avoided and feared. Running my hands over my face to wake myself up, I noticed how quiet the house was. My eyes went wide. Had Grace left? She couldn't have. I hopped out of bed; my heels thudded as they hit the hardwood floor. Tossing on a pair of jeans and a T-shirt, I came barreling out of my room. Grace's bedroom door was open. I peeked my head in to find that all of her stuff was gone and the bed was made. It was like no one had ever stayed here.

"Shit," I yelled.

Then I heard the trunk of a car close and all my worries melted away. Glancing outside the living room window, I watched Grace toss a bag in the back of her vehicle. She was ready to go. She looked back at the house and started walking toward it. I breathed a sigh of relief and ran to the kitchen.

I poured myself a cup of joe, waiting for her to come say her good-byes. She'd clearly been up a while because the coffee was lukewarm. I guzzled the whole thing and refilled it again. The tepid acid coated the sides of my stomach as it made its way down, not much different than the whiskey that played the same role just several hours prior. The screen door creaked open and then closed, the wood slapping against the frame, a punctuation mark for the person entering the room. But unlike the free-swinging door, her footsteps were light and quiet, traveling through the living room as if she were gliding a few inches above the floor.

"Hey," she said, standing at the opening of the kitchen, her arms crossed and guarded.

"Hay is for horses," I joked and sipped the coffee.

Grace gave a tight smile and glanced around the house like she was taking it in one last time.

"You heading out?" I already knew the answer, but I wanted to hear her say it.

She nodded. "Yeah, I've got a long drive ahead of me." Grace jingled the keys in her hand. "I really appreciate all you've done. Thanks for showing me the Wyoming way."

"It was my pleasure." I took another sip. "You got everything?"

She nodded again.

I finished the second cup of coffee and set the mug down on the counter. It being lukewarm made it taste funny. Not hot enough to punch with bright acidity and warm the body, but not cold enough to thicken into a sweeter, smooth experience—the worst of both worlds, something undesirable. My eyes returned to Grace. She was dressed in the same outfit she arrived in: a black knee-length skirt, heels, and a black top with that bunched-up fabric on the front of it. It was like she had come full circle. The big city once again making itself known out here in the untamed wild. I took her all in like a glass of lemonade on a hot summer day, from the heel of her stiletto up to her golden hair that fell perfectly below her shoulders.

When I stepped toward her, she stepped back, a scared animal ready to dash. "Let me walk you out," I said.

"Yeah, sure."

Grace walked backward a few steps before turning around. She glanced over her shoulder at me, not letting me out of her sight for too long. I slid on my pair of work boots at the door and followed her out onto the porch. She looked back again. Perhaps she discovered something that gave her pause, or maybe it was intuition.

The sun was a blaze of glory set halfway up that big blue Wyoming sky. The animals were agitated, making all sorts of noises—probably because they hadn't been fed at the proper time. My boots clomped down the steps of the porch. Grace was already to her car, opening the driver's side door. She paused and turned to me.

"I really enjoyed our time together," she said, and for the first time, I saw the dimples her smile created. I wasn't sure if they were there before. I assumed I would have noticed something as cute as Grace's dimples, but maybe I wasn't seeing things clearly—enamored by the entirety of her and not the details.

"I did too," I said. My smile was as wide as a six-lane highway as I slowly strolled toward her. "Will I ever see you again?"

Her hand gripped the top of the door as she glanced at her driver's seat and then back at me. Her fingers repositioned the keys. They jingled slightly.

"I don't think so," she finally said.

I was only six feet from her now. I slid a thumb into the loop of my jeans and rocked back on my feet. I liked that she thought she was leaving. It was cute.

"Goodbye, Calvin." She got into her vehicle and closed the door.

Grace slid the key into the ignition and delivered a small smile before turning it. The engine went *click, click, click*. She struggled, turning the key again. *Click, click, click.* The engine wouldn't turn over. Her face became panicked, and she tried a third time. *Click, click, click.* Music to my ears. Her arm flailed like a windmill as she cranked the window handle on her dated vehicle.

Grace gritted her teeth, clearly displeased. "I thought you said you fixed it?"

"I thought I did too," I lied. "Go ahead and pop the hood." I moseyed over to the front of the car and lifted the hood, toying around with some wires, pretending to examine and make adjustments to random parts.

The car door squeaked open. Her heels munched on the gravel. From my peripheral vision, I saw her come into view. She huffed, folded her arms in front of her chest, and pushed out her hip. Quite the attitude for a woman without a working car or cell phone.

"What's wrong with it?" Her voice had an edge of annoyance to it.

"I'm not so sure. I'm not a mechanic, Grace."

"You promised it'd be fixed by today."

I turned my head toward her and a sinister smile slowly crept its way across my face. The mask beginning to slip. "I promised a lot of things."

"What the hell does that mean?" she nearly yelled.

I couldn't help but laugh and, in an instant, I was lunging toward her. She had no time to react. Grace tried to swat me away, but her pretty blond hair was already wrapped around my hand. She screamed so loud her voice cracked.

"I promised I'd let you leave, and we both know that's not happening," I said, dragging her back toward the house. Her legs gave out, and she kicked at the ground. One of her heels slipped off. A Cinderella in the making. Grace's hands shot up to my arms. She pinched and slapped and clawed. Her nails dug into my skin, drawing blood.

"Fucking bitch," I yelled. Stopping just before the steps, I struck her in the side of the head with my other hand. It was a warning. She cried out.

"Let me go," she screamed, kicking and flailing.

"It's too late for that," I said, caressing her face with my hand. "You shouldn't have come here, Grace, but I'm glad you did." I smiled.

She craned her head and opened her mouth, snapping at my hand. I didn't pull away fast enough and her teeth clenched down on my pinky finger. A pained scream escaped my mouth, and I released my grip on her. Grace hit the ground and bit down harder. I tried to pull away, but her bite was like a vice. My steel-toed boot struck her ribs and she coughed, forcing her pretty little mouth open. My finger was a mangled bloody mess with bone exposed. Grace rolled to her side, coughing and gurgling on my blood.

"That wasn't smart, Grace."

She was on all fours, trying to stand, while I ripped the sleeve of my T-shirt off and wrapped it around my hand. The pain was nearly unbearable, and I hoped Dr. Reed would be able to fix it. I thought she'd try to run. I enjoyed the chase. But instead, she completely caught me by surprise. Grace charged at me, hitting me in the stomach like a lineman on a football field. I gasped, falling backward. This wasn't the first time she took my breath away. When I first laid eyes on her, I knew she'd be a fighter. My back cracked against the wooden porch step. I winced and rolled to the side. While I collected myself, she was already running back into the house. Had she ever seen a horror movie? You never run back inside.

"Where are you going, Grace?" I yelled, getting to my feet.

I threw open the screen door. The living room was empty. The kitchen was empty.

"Oh, Graaaace . . . where are you?" I sang out like a child playing hide-and-seek.

No answer, but I heard shuffling down the hallway. I walked toward the noise nonchalantly, running my fingers along the wall, taking my time. The hunt is always much more fun than the catch.

I sang slowly as I strolled down the hallway.

"Amazing Grace, how sweet the sound,
That saved a wretch like me,
I once was lost, but now am found,
Was blind but now I see."

The bathroom door was open. Empty. Albert's room was the same. That left two rooms—the room she had stayed in and my bedroom. Both doors were closed. I went to the guest room first and, rather than opening it, I simply turned the lock. If she was in there, she'd stay in there until I said otherwise. I walked to the end of the hall where my bedroom was, the last one on the left. As I put my hand on the door handle, I felt a wave of dizziness come over me. I rubbed my forehead and patted my cheeks, immediately regretting getting into the bottle of whiskey last night. Turning the handle, I threw the door open. There she was, my amazing Grace, standing in the corner, holding my knife. She must have found it when she was snooping around the basement. *Such a naughty guest.* The sun seeped through the window and hit the blade, making it shimmer. What separated me from her was my king bed and a desk off to the side with my computer. Grace held the blade out steadily. Her blue, blue eyes fixated on me.

"Oh, you want to take this to the bedroom?" I chuckled. "I knew you were an easy lay but this takes the cake, Miss Grace."

I took another step toward her. Her knuckles were white from gripping the handle of the knife so tightly.

"I wouldn't do that if I were you," she said.

That dizzy feeling hit me again, causing me to stumble to the side. I caught myself on the desk and stood upright. Why had I drunk so much last night? I knew I had a big day ahead of me. The room began to spin like I was on a merry-go-round. Grace was at the center of it, still and beautiful and unmoved by what I was going through.

"You're the one that shouldn't have come here, Calvin," she said.

The room spun faster and faster, and no matter how fast it spun, everything was a blur but Grace. I wanted to close my eyes and never open them again, but I forced them though they begged to be closed. I fell to the bed, rolling onto my back. My head spun. And then I felt like I was floating, just above myself, just enough to see nearly everything . . . everything but Grace.

"What's happening to me?" I yelled. I tried to bring my hand to my head but I felt paralyzed. The only thing I could do was blink and look up at that popcorn ceiling. The ceiling fan spun 'round and 'round, much slower than the rest of the room.

Her one heel clicked against the floor, and then she was standing over me. Her eyes stared into mine. I tried to swing my arm at her but I couldn't pick it off of my chest. My other arm laid by my side, stuck, like concrete had been poured around it. Grace pressed the tip of the knife against her finger and twirled it like she was taunting me.

"What did you do to me?" I asked.

"A little of this. A little of that."

My heartbeat pulsated in my feet, my neck, my arms. It was usually steady but now it raced.

"Is this about that goddamn missing bitch?" I spit.

"Is she here?" Grace tilted her head.

My eyelids so badly wanted to close. Tears streamed from the corners of them, slithering down the sides of my face. I struggled again to move my arms and legs. Nothing.

"Yes." Even speaking became a chore, every muscle in my body seizing up, useless.

"Is she alive?"

"I think so."

Grace nodded.

"Did you really think you'd be able to keep me here?" she asked.

"Just . . . stupid bitch."

"That's not very nice, Calvin. You shouldn't call people names." She raised the knife above her head.

"Please . . . no," I begged. "Just call the police. The girl is . . . in . . . a shed . . . the woods. Forty yards . . . behind the apiary."

She tilted her head to the other side. "Did you kill Albert?"

"No." I panted. "That bitch . . . was . . . hollering and . . . Albert's drunk ass . . . must . . . have heard it. He stumbled right . . . into the bees."

Grace brought the knife to her side and glanced out the window, taking in the scenery while she twirled the weapon in her hand. I tried to move again, but I had no control of my body. It was like I had been dipped into a pool of quicksand. I wasn't sure what she would do. She seemed conflicted about calling the police. But why?

Grace's eyes scanned my body.

"Are you going to call them or not?" I forced the words out all at once.

"No cell phone service," she said.

I tried to point at the computer but I couldn't. I sucked in a gulp of air. "The computer. There's a Wi-Fi router beside it. Just plug it in."

She raised an eyebrow. "You lied about the Wi-Fi too?" Grace walked to the desk and pulled out the chair, taking a seat. One movement of the mouse made the screen turn on. I strained to see what she was doing. I knew my Airbnb account was pulled up because it was the last thing I looked at to confirm my next guest's arrival in a few days.

"Review guest. Don't mind if I do," she said with a devious smile. She placed her fingers on the keyboard and typed away, reading aloud the words, "Grace was a terrific guest. She's welcome back anytime."

"What the hell are you doing?" I yelled and then gasped for air.

She dramatically clicked the mouse. "Rating: five stars."

"I have to know," Grace said, standing from her seat. "Because it's been bothering me. What really happened the night Lisa died?"

I sighed. "Will you call the police if I tell you?"

"Sure."

I took several deep breaths.

My eyes closed for a moment and the memory flashed across the back of my lids like a movie in a dark theater.

Lisa sat in the passenger seat beside me while I drove Joe's truck on the black twisting road. It was dark outside, the only light coming from the moon and the vehicle's headlights. I couldn't tell if the rumbling was coming from the truck or Joe asleep in the back seat, snoring away. She glanced over at me and smiled. Her hair was full of blond ringlets and her eyes were green like emeralds. The evening was perfect until it wasn't anymore.

"Calvin, I'm leaving next week," she said shakily.

"What do you mean?" I tried to keep my eyes on the road, but I kept looking over at her.

"My assignment is over."

"I thought you extended it already." I gripped the steering wheel a little tighter.

Lisa tilted her head. "I tried. But they don't need me anymore, so I accepted a temporary nursing position in Alaska. I start next week."

"You didn't even talk to me about this," I yelled.

She reached out and put her hand on my shoulder. "I'm talking to you right now."

"No, you're not. You're just telling me how it's going to be." I flicked her hand off and shoved her back.

"Calvin," she nearly cried. "This doesn't have to be the end for us."

I saw red and pressed down on the gas pedal. The truck sped up from forty to forty-five.

"Yes, it does," I said.

"Slow down, Calvin," Lisa begged.

Up ahead an animal prepared to cross the road. The headlights made its eyes glow.

Lisa swatted me several times, telling me to slow down. I shoved her again, harder this time. Her head cracked against the passenger window. Joe was still dead asleep in the back. Lisa cried and held her head. The truck's speed climbed to sixty.

"Pull over now," she yelled.

I unclicked her seat belt, setting her free from me and this world, and braced myself.

She yelled, "What the hell is wrong with you?" while she tried to re-fasten it.

It was too late. The truck went from sixty to zero in an instant, a collision of metal, flesh, and glass. It all went black. The sound of gur-gling woke me, almost like a babbling brook. But it wasn't. Lisa was pinned against the passenger seat, trying to breathe. The elk's antlers had gored her, and her pierced lungs were quickly filling with blood. She coughed and choked on it, spitting it up, attempting to speak. Her eyes were wide and soaked with tears, pleading to me for help. I just stared. I couldn't bring myself to call 911, until I knew that she would never leave for Alaska.

My eyes reopened, the memory rescinded to the back of my mind, compartmentalized.

Grace narrowed her eyes. "And then you moved your brother to the driver's seat and put it all on him?"

"Yeah," was all I could manage to say.

She shook her head and left the room, reappearing in the doorway not more than thirty seconds later.

"I almost forgot," she said. From behind her back, she revealed the stuffed teddy bear I bought her.

Grace crawled on top of me, straddling my hips. Her eyes stared into mine. I begged her to stop, to leave, to call the police, and to take anything she wanted, at least I think I did. I'm not sure what words were coming out and which were still swirling around my brain.

"Please . . . don't do this . . . Grace."

"For your comfort," she said, placing the teddy bear beneath my arm.

Grace lifted the knife high above her head. The sun hit the blade again, making it shimmer. I let out a labored scream.

"You said you'd call the police if I told you," I panted.

She dragged the tip of the blade lightly down my ribs, feeling the metal rise and fall, up and down the peaks and valleys of the bone. Then between the bottom two ribs, she leaned forward; she and the knife simultaneously moved into me.

"I guess I lied too, Calvin."

My eyes widened so much, it felt like my lids would split at the corners. Grace raised the knife above her and plunged it into the center of my chest. My white tee turned red. She yanked the knife from my chest. Blood sprayed from the wound, splattering onto her.

I gurgled and coughed, choking on a pained scream. Without hesitating, she thrust the knife into my cheek. The tip nearly touched the back of my throat. It slid through my skin like butter. I knew this was the end. Where had it all gone wrong? How did she know? How did she get the upper hand? The weight in my muscles seemed to go away. Finally, I was free of the spell. Free of the dizziness and fear. I finally let my eyes close, allowing them to get the rest they deserved.

49.
Grace

I pulled the knife out and shoved it into him over and over again. His face, his neck, his chest, his arms, his stomach. The human body is an endless soft canvas to enter and draw upon. I raised and lowered it until my arms were tired, finishing long after Calvin stopped breathing. I propped his lifeless eyes open so he could gaze up at me. He enjoyed looking at me when he was alive, so I'm sure he'd enjoy it in death too. His chest looked like a pit of tar. The headboard and walls were splattered with blood. I was soaked in Calvin. I climbed off his body and laid beside him for a few minutes, caressing his shredded face. Mr. Snuggles was a blood-soaked mess.

The drugs had timed out perfectly. He was lucid enough to know what was happening but quickly went into darkness not a moment later, Charon arriving right on time to ferry him across the River Styx. The handle of the knife was sticky and his white T-shirt was a fantastic canvas for the color show on display. Like a paper towel soaking up juice spilled by a child having far too much fun. This part was inevitable. Calvin's own behavior made it so. One of us wasn't going to leave here, and it wasn't going to be me.

I needed to clean up, but the shock of what I had done was finally setting in. I did what I did because I had to. I never had a choice. I brought the knife with me to the kitchen sink, running hot water and bleach over it again and again. It was like cleaning a fillet knife after gutting a fish—the pieces of blood and viscera that had already dried clinging for dear life to the edge of the steel, not wanting to disappear into the black hole at the center of the sink basin.

The process was long and tedious with lots of cleaners and chemicals and even more double- and triple-checking every detail. No fingerprints, no strands of hair, no threads of clothing. Nothing that is or ever was part of Grace Evans could remain in the ranch. But then again, did that really matter?

I tossed the empty hair dye box into a garbage bag beside the bathroom sink. My hair was swooped up into a bun, covered in brunette hair dye, my natural color. I looked at my bloodstained face in the mirror. Leaning closer toward my reflection, I pressed a finger to my eye and pulled out a blue contact from one and then the other—revealing my caramel-colored irises. Just as the timer on my phone went off, I undressed completely. Steam rose from the shower, and I let the water burn my skin. It felt good. The hot liquid turned pink as it removed Calvin from me, swirling down the drain. I rinsed the hair dye, careful to get all of it out.

After drying off and getting dressed, I did a once-over around the house and grabbed a canister of gasoline from the garage. Returning to Calvin's room to finish up, I threw several items on the bed beside him, things I needed to get rid of and things to help him burn. There was so much blood, so I knew more kindling was required. I threw open his closet doors, expecting clothes, but it was nothing like that. Startled, I screamed and nearly fell backward. Three motion lights flicked on, each one lighting up a mounted head. But they weren't animals. Their faces were frozen in the fear they experienced just before their last moments. Small wooden plaques hung below them, each one with a name carved into it—Cristina, Kayla, Amber. I closed my eyes for a moment. *You were sicker than I thought you were, Calvin.* I shook my head, noticing two plaques hung on the wall beside the others. No mounts were above them, just a white wall, a blank canvas for his vile art. The names carved into them were Briana and Grace. I slammed the closet doors closed and turned back toward Calvin's lifeless body.

"Liar, liar, pants on fire," I seethed as I doused him with gasoline, using up the entire canister. I wanted to make sure he burned. One flick of the match, and he was up in flames.

Outside, I repacked my items, putting them in Calvin's truck, and looked out at the woods, deciding whether or not I should check on the missing girl. Was she even alive? Was it worth the risk?

Sliding on a pair of Chanel sunglasses, I headed toward the apiary with my new knife in hand. The horses neighed and the ducks quacked as I passed them. The dry grass crunched under my tennis shoes. As I got closer, I could hear a low hum of buzzing from the bees. I entered the woods, pushing aside branches and stepping over fallen trees. Just as Calvin had said, a small wooden shed sat around forty yards back. In death, he had finally told the truth. The windows were boarded up and a large padlock was on the front door. I pulled a bobby pin from my hair and went to work on the lock.

"Hello," a voice called from inside the shed.

I didn't respond. The lock clicked, and I threw open the door. Light flooded the dark room, revealing the woman I had seen in the police photo. She had lost her vibrancy. Her skin was dull and dry and covered in dirt. Her greasy hair was pulled back into a low ponytail. A rope bound her wrists together. One of her legs was tied to a post, giving her about four feet of room to roam. Tears streamed down her face as she looked up at me.

Her face crumbled, and she seemed to laugh and cry at the same time. "Are you Grace?" Her voice croaked.

I tilted my head. "Yeah. How did you know that?"

She let out a howl of a cry, a mix of relief and sadness. "Calvin told me about you. You were going to replace me just like I replaced the last girl."

I glanced around the shed. A couple of empty cans of Coca-Cola and a bowl of rotten brussels sprouts sat near her. Calvin had been keeping her alive out here like she was one of his ranch animals. Of course, he was feeding her my brussels sprouts.

Her eyes darted all around me. "Where is he?" she panicked.

"He's dead."

A relieved smile spread across her face, revealing the dimples I had noticed in her photo.

"Please help me," she said, holding up her bound wrists.

I hesitated for a moment. Holding out the knife, I nodded and walked toward the bound girl. Her bottom lip trembled, and she cried harder.

"Don't worry, Bri. You're safe now."

50.

Grace

Briana rubbed at her wrists, walking beside me through the pasture. They were covered in rope burns, angry red and raw skin. She was wobbly on her feet—thanks to being bound for at least ten days—and she struggled to keep up. But I wasn't slowing down. I needed to get out of here.

"How did he die?" she asked.

"Slowly," I said as I continued toward the truck.

Her mouth dropped open but she quickly closed it and eyed me cautiously.

"Did you call the police?"

I stopped and turned, facing her suddenly. Her reflexes were slow, and she nearly fell backward. "No, and I'm leaving."

The whites of her eyes shined. "Can I come with you?"

Up close I could see fingerprint-shaped bruises around her neck and popped blood vessels surrounding her eyes. Her lips were dried and cracked, peeling in several places. She was obviously dehydrated. I turned from her and kept marching forward.

"No," I said over my shoulder.

I pulled open the driver's side door and hopped into the truck. Bri sprinted toward me, but it was more like fast stumbling. She was so weak.

"Wait, you're just going to leave me?" she said in disbelief, thrusting her hand in front of the door. "You can't leave me."

I let out a sigh. Where was my thank-you? I rescued her, and she doesn't even have the courtesy to express her gratitude. She would have been dead by nightfall if it weren't for me.

I brought my foot up and kicked her square in the chest. "Yes, I can." She gasped, reeling backward and landing on her ass. Bri let out a painful moan.

"You're welcome." I slammed the door, turned the ignition, and pulled out of the driveway.

Glancing back in the mirror, I watched her slowly get to her feet and dust herself off.

She'd be fine, thanks to me.

51.

Grace

There it was. Gunslinger 66, the same gas station I had stopped at ten days prior. It was still Ope, not Open. I pulled the truck up to the side of the pump and got out of the vehicle. Once again, I was the only customer—nothing in both directions for miles and miles. I already knew it was cash only, so I started across the parking lot. I tied my long brown hair back into a low ponytail and entered the station. The door squeaked as I pulled it open. That same fan buzzed in the corner, oscillating the smell of beef jerky and gasoline throughout. The man with the lazy eye stood at the counter. I could tell he recognized me right away because he raised his brows, deepening the lines across his forehead.

"Back again, I see." The words came out slow.

I nodded. "Can I get eighty on pump one?"

He punched a couple of keys on his register and grabbed the four twenties I held out, placing them in the drawer.

"I like the hair." He smiled.

I was surprised he had even noticed the change. I must have been the only customer he's had in the last ten days.

"Thanks." I nodded, turning toward the door.

"Avery," he called out.

The word made me freeze instantly, stopping me dead in my tracks. I swallowed hard and tightened my jaw. I couldn't have heard that right.

"What was that?" I turned back toward him. Calvin must have knocked something loose in my head because that wasn't possible.

The old man twisted his wiry beard. "Avery Adams."

My shoulders tensed, and I took a deep breath.

He slid out a drawer underneath the register and flipped through a stack of papers. The old man held out his hand, extending a driver's license. "You dropped it when you were in here. Tried to tell ya, but you sped off like a bat out of hell, so I've just been holding it for you. In case you came back." He smiled, revealing cracked yellow teeth.

I closed the distance, retrieving the ID from him. "Thank you." I smiled. "I appreciate it."

"Of course. Safe travels," he said with a wave of his hand.

52.

Avery

In the rearview mirror, I watched the sun go down. A ball of fire engulfed the skyline for a moment as Gunslinger 66 officially went out of business. The explosion was sudden and fiery, sending debris in all directions. Everything that was Grace Evans burned. The blood-soaked clothing, license, credit cards, and anything else that tied me to that identity. Grace Evans was dead. Same with that poor old schmuck. They both didn't exist anymore. I wasn't worried about fingerprints or DNA or anything like that. Avery Adams wasn't in the system. She was a saint, an upstanding citizen. Grace Evans was here, but Avery Adams had never been to a place like Dubois, Wyoming.

I took my eyes off the rearview mirror and focused on the winding road in front of me. My work here was complete. You might be wondering how or why. Who would do a thing like that? Let me reintroduce myself. My name is Avery Adams. I'm your next-door neighbor. The woman at the café. The girl who jogs in the park every day. Says hello to strangers. Holds the door open. Gives up her seat for the elderly. A volunteer for an animal shelter. I'm the girl at a bar on a Friday night and the woman in church on a Sunday morning. I'm every girl you've ever known and every girl you have yet to meet. My name is Avery Adams. I love meeting new people—and I love killing them too.

Day Eleven

53.

Avery

I slid the key across the counter at an Enterprise Rent-A-Car location. "Hi, I'm here to return my rental."

The robust man collected it. He placed his thick fingers on the keyboard in front of him and asked for my name.

I smiled. "Avery Adams."

He pecked at the keys, typing my name. "As long as there's no damage, you'll get your deposit back," he said matter of factly. A piece of paper shot out from a printer. He slid it across the counter and asked me to sign at the bottom.

I nodded and signed. "Perfect. Have a nice day." Turning on my heel, I pulled my luggage behind me. As I exited, I held the door for a middle-aged man with a weak chin. He smiled and thanked me.

"Of course."

The Uber app notified me that my driver, Joseph, was approaching. Calvin's truck was somewhere in Nebraska. I swapped it out for my rental car. The Mazda I had driven to the ranch was purchased privately for five hundred in cash from a shady guy who couldn't say more than a few words. The VIN had been scraped off, so I knew it was stolen. Even better.

My driver pulled up in a Prius and swiftly got out of the vehicle to help me load my bags into the trunk.

"Want that in the back?" He gestured to my messenger bag.

"No, that stays with me." It had my prized possession in it, a token of my travels, the knife I had snagged from Calvin's collection.

He closed the trunk and got into the driver's seat. "Lincoln mall?"

"Yes."

We arrived twenty-five minutes later. Once there, I walked to a parking ramp and got into my Audi A5, setting the navigation to Chicago, Illinois. I would be home in just under eight hours, right in time for dinner.

Everything had gone according to plan—mostly. This wasn't my first rodeo. This was what I needed to do. It kept my life in balance. It kept me in equilibrium. Have you ever had an itch in the middle of your back, just out of reach? I have, and I've learned how to scratch it. From a young age, I knew I was different. I wasn't like the other kids. Nothing bad ever happened to me. My parents didn't abuse or abandon me. I was never sexually assaulted. I was just different. My brain was wired like the handy work of an electrician in the middle of an apprenticeship—not right by normal standards, but it still worked, just a bit different.

Some people kill because they enjoy it. And I know that's frustrating to hear. There is no why. There's no rhyme or reason. I just enjoy it. Call it a hobby if you will. You like to read. I like to watch the life drain from a person. To see the light behind their eyes flicker out. To watch their face go lax. To watch the future they had envisioned for themselves disappear. Like a magic trick. *Poof*, it's all gone. Call me a magician, why don't you? *Serial killer* has a nice ring to it. But I actually prefer just Avery. You can call me Avery.

I pulled into the driveway of my two-story house just outside of Chicago in the suburbs. It was white with red shutters and big bay windows—a normal home where mostly normal people lived. Before exiting the vehicle, I opened up the Airbnb application on my phone and deleted my Grace Evans account. Calvin's body surely must have been discovered by now. Typically, it took a few days because of my isolation process, separating my target from their friends and loved ones. But the missing woman kind of screwed that up. Charlotte was easy to push away because she was obsessed with Calvin, and her presence threatened the "blooming" relationship between us. Joe was even easier. I just acted as though he had said or done something wrong at the bar, going as far as slapping him to solidify how inappropriate he was. I had no idea how screwed up their sibling relationship was though. Honestly, I probably didn't need to do anything at all. It would have gone off the rails regardless. Betty wasn't even an obstacle. She was off her meds, and no one took her seriously. And Albert—well, Calvin took care of him in a way. I considered killing Bri or leaving her tied up, but that wasn't a part of my process. Just the host. No one else. Calvin being a psychopath himself was a nice surprise. I knew it the moment I laid eyes on him. He was like me—well, not exactly. I'm not that sick, and I was born this way. Calvin was molded into it. The whole nature versus nurture argument. I saw it in him, but he didn't see it in me. Survival of the fittest, as they say.

I unlocked the front door of my home and entered the lit-up house. Directly in front of me was a large carpeted staircase jutting up to the second floor. The formal dining room sat off to the right and the living room to the left.

Daniel lifted his head from a book and smiled like he was seeing me for the first time. He always looked at me that way.

"Right on time," he said, closing his book. He embraced me with a hug and a passionate kiss. His five-o'clock shadow scraped at my skin, but I didn't mind it.

"I missed you," Daniel said in between kisses.

"I missed you too."

His large hands ran down my back. "How was your retreat?" He pulled away, looking into my brown eyes.

"It was great."

"Did you *Eat, Pray, Love*?" he teased.

"Yeah, something like that."

He squinted, leaning a little closer. "What happened to your eye?" His finger grazed over my bruised skin.

I turned from him and set my purse on the buffet table. "Took a branch to the face on a hike."

He made a humph sound. "Where was this retreat again?"

"Outside of Seattle."

"I barely got to speak to you. Only a couple of text messages. I was worried." He raised his brows.

I placed my hand on his shoulder. "That's the point of a retreat. It wouldn't be very relaxing to be on my phone the whole time, now would it?" I tilted my head.

He curled a piece of hair around his pointer finger. "Did you do something different to your hair?"

I pushed his hand away gently and kissed him on the cheek. "Just some spa conditioning treatments."

"I like it."

"Mom's home!" Margot yelled.

My two children came bundling down the stairs. Margot, my ten-year-old, and Jacob, my eight-year-old. I knelt extending my arms out. They practically knocked me over when they plowed into me for a hug. I held them tightly, smelling them, taking them all in.

"I missed you two so much." I kissed them on their cheeks and foreheads.

"Not as much as we missed you." Jacob giggled.

"Oh, is that so?" I released them and gave my little lanky boy a poke in his belly. He giggled louder.

"It's true, Mom. We missed you a million times more," Margot said with a smirk.

"I don't know about that. I thought about you two every minute of every day I was gone." I stood, placing a hand on my hip.

"Well, we thought about you every second," Margot quipped, copying my stance.

She was too clever for her own good, and she reminded me of myself. She too was a little different.

I shook my head and smiled. "Who wants pizza?"

"I do. I do. I do." Jacob and Margot said in unison. They danced around one another. Daniel wrapped his arm around my shoulder and pulled me into him.

"I'm so happy to be home. I feel like me again. Complete. Balanced."

He kissed my forehead and hugged me a little tighter.

"Can I come with you next time you go on a retreat?" Margot asked. She clasped her hands together and followed it with a "Please, please, please."

The corner of my lip perked up. "Maybe when you're a little older."

Margot cheered and hopped around on two feet, then one, then two again. Jacob followed suit, always copying his older sister.

"I'm going to call Lou's and order a pizza," Daniel said, and he disappeared into the kitchen.

"I get to go on Mommy's retreat," Margot repeated over and over as she jumped around.

I smiled wide, and all of a sudden—I felt it.

Right in the center of my back.

An itch.

Acknowledgments

First, thank you to my agent, Sandy Lu, for seeing in me what most others didn't. In just two years, you've sold eight of my projects (and counting) but most importantly, you've been beyond supportive on and off the page.

Thank you to the team at Blackstone for continuing to champion my work! Especially: Celia Johnson, Rachel Sanders, Josie Woodbridge, Stephanie Koven, Kathryn Zentgraf, Ananda Finwall, Sarah Riedlinger, Jeffrey Yamaguchi, Naomi Hynes, and Rick Bleiweiss. Special shout-out to Samantha Benson for keeping me sane on my last book tour and for being the best publicist an author could ask for. Sorry, I couldn't get you all VP titles, but you're all MVPs in my book.

There are people I have to thank who take one for the team by reading early drafts of my novels. Thank you and sorry to Kent Willetts, Briana Becker, Andrea Willetts, Cristina Frost, and James Nerge for reading the less polished versions of *You Shouldn't Have Come Here*.

Thank you to my family and friends for supporting and encouraging me throughout this entire journey! To my mom, I wish you could have been here to see my dreams come true, the ones you always knew I'd achieve. It's been bittersweet without you, but you're in my heart and in every word I write.

Thank you to April Goodman (aka @callmestory on Twitter) for being an incredible and invaluable beta reader. You made this book better!

Thank you to Kayla Whitehead for winning the "have a character named after you" contest on my Instagram and for allowing me to borrow your name.

Thank you to the real Avery Adams for letting me borrow your sweet name for the opposite of good and thank you for also not being anything like my fictional Avery Adams (that I know of). Special shout-out to Katie Colton and Yale Viny for your friendship, endless support, and thoughtfulness.

Thank you to the booktokers, bookstagrammers, and book reviewers for taking the time to not only read my work but also shout about it in such creative ways. I absolutely love seeing the videos and photos you create to highlight the books you adore.

Thank you to the booksellers, librarians, and everyone else who has helped put my books in readers' hands. I appreciate your endless support and tireless work. You make the book world a better place!

To my readers, "thank you" seems too small for what you have all done for me.

So, let me make the font bigger and bolder. **THANK YOU!**

Sorry, it's still not big enough, but just know you've changed my life for the better, and I am eternally grateful.

And last but certainly not least, thank you to Drew for being the greatest hype husband of all time! You're the first to read my work, the first to tell me it's great, and the first to celebrate my successes and my failures. Without you, I wouldn't be "Drew's wife."